For Josh, Rhys & Harry

For Emma, for believing in and inspiring me

To Phil for being the friend that everyone should have

Thank you to my two guinea pigs Emma & Jo

Thanks to Michelle Dickson for the artwork

For my OI family, you are all superheroes

Home

The cul de sac was busy; some children had built a makeshift ramp in the road knowing full well no cars would interrupt their fun. It was a warm July afternoon and the sun shone brightly in the blue cloudless sky.

Ben from no 23 looked up just as the sun reflected off the upstairs window of number 19 where the new people lived, he'd seen a boy there but he never played out and he wasn't sure why.

Behind the reflection in the upstairs window sat Jack who was 12, he often sat and watched the kids play but he never ventured out, it wasn't that he couldn't or he wasn't allowed he just knew he couldn't join in, he knew there would be a list of don't dos and be careful so he just stayed in his room.

He'd moved here 6 weeks ago, with his parents and Merlyn his dog, he'd loved where he lived before and his friends there knew all about Jack and his "condition". He'd cried when they pulled away from his home and his friends waving him off but he hadn't let his parents see, he knew he couldn't it would have upset them too.

His dad had lost his job so they were having to "downsize" Jack wasn't exactly sure what that meant but he'd known it couldn't be good. They'd moved to a fixer-upper, so it meant his parents had no time to spend with Jack, they were either painting or sanding or sawing. Jack didn't think it would ever get finished, it was so old and the garden was like a jungle scene from Jumanji.

He looked around his room, he'd gotten his superhero posters up, Jack loved his comics he wished he was a superhero, he knew every kid wanted to be a superhero but he felt like he wanted it just that bit more than everyone else. His mom always called him her superhero but he never felt like one he felt the exact opposite to one. At no point in his life had he took a risk, he'd understood from an early age he was different, his parents had tried to explain to him and he sat there and said" yea ok uh uh" but it didn't make sense and he didn't understand at first. then there were the treatments which at first, he hated, but he now associated with time off school, a treat that varied greatly from chocolate to either a comic or maybe even a new figure, and of course after it had finished on the journey home a choice of food but he wasn't allowed to choose MacDonald's every time.

The worst however where the breaks he'd had 8 so far thankfully he can only really remember the last 4, 2 arms and 2 legs. Nothing major had happened, the last one was in January he'd gone outside to get in the car to go to school and slipped on the ice, he'd known straight away, the sound that seemed to reverberate through his body as if he hadn't heard it with his ears but somehow inside. This time it was his femur, he'd got very good at knowing the names of the bones in the skeleton. He'd spent 6 weeks in traction, this was the second time in under 12 months now and the doctor said if it happened again they'd think about a rod. He wasn't exactly sure what it meant as he wasn't really paying attention but the look on his parents faces said it wasn't going to be good. He knew his condition was rare and he'd never met anyone else with it, it had a really long name osteo something or other he couldn't remember but he knew he had brittle bones.

There was a shout from the kids outside breaking Jack's daydream, he looked out of the window to see the girl from no 20 had fell off her bike going over the ramp, Jack held his breath, but then he noticed she was sat on the ground laughing, he knew he would never be able to do that, every fall was followed by the checklist, 1 slight panic, 2 anything hurting straight away, 3 can I move everything 4 ok stand up if I can, slight inward cheer then carry on. He saw the girl get back on her bike and immediately try the jump again.

He so wanted to go outside and say hi but he knew the questions would start pretty quickly and he didn't want to have to answer them yet, he didn't want them to look at him differently, he knew they thought of him as the weird kid but he preferred that at the minute.

Suddenly his mom shouted him from downstairs " Jack! Jack!" Yes, mom, I'm coming" Jack shouted with as much enthusiasm as he could muster.

Jack slunk downstairs, plodding one step at a time. His footsteps echoed through the house, as yet the stairs were still uncarpeted, halfway down the stairs the sunlight blazed through the arched stain glass window above the door, bathing Jack in blue, red, and green light. The window had been the first thing Jack had noticed as he took his first steps along the path towards his new home.

The window had drawn his attention because it depicted a large tree in the middle with all sorts of weird creatures around it, in the middle of the tree was what looked like a door.

"Jack !!" his mom's shout broke him from his trance and he continued down the stairs.

He reached the bottom of the stairs and turned right down the corridor past the walls with peeling wallpaper, the corridor had a very old smell, he knew it had been empty for a few years before his parents bought it. He reached the door at the end his hand rested on the latch, he could hear his parents voices through the door, a muffled giggle and then a loud burst of laughter, he couldn't help but smile, he loved his parents and he didn't blame them for moving he was just finding it hard to adjust at the minute.

he opened the door, immediately Merlyn bounded over to him, Merlyn was an old English sheepdog and they both were the perfect partners in crime, on more than one occasion Merlyn had taken the wrap for him, as he was being told off Merlyn would just look at Jack as if to say it's your fault, Jack always felt guilty after. Merlyns wet nose nudged his hand Merlyn knew not to jump up, Jack rubbed him behind the ear as his parents turned towards him.

"Jack at last" exclaimed his mom, his mom was Emma, she had piercing blue eyes and dark brown hair cut short, she was tall and slim, her smile always made Jack feel better. Jack thought she was beautiful and so did his old-school friends who often referred to her as a sort.

" What you been up to? You hibernating up there it's gorgeous outside"

"Hey up scamp," said his father. His father Joe was a little bit older than his mom, he had warm brown eyes and brown hair that had flecks of grey showing at the temples. He smiled at Jack his mom always said your dad's smile could light up a room.

They were both wearing white overalls and were covered in specks of paint.

"well we've nearly finished the kitchen," said his dad

"yay," said Jack "It's only taken 6 weeks" and immediately felt guilty as he saw his dad's smile lessen just slightly.

"I know champ, sorry it's taking so long but it will be worth it, I promise" he saw his mom take his dad's hand and squeeze it.

"orange juice!" said his mom a little too loudly, " we all need orange juice it's so hot in these things" she dashed over to the fridge, removed the orange juice and poured 3 glasses. She handed one to his dad and one to Jack.

"Cheers, here's to new beginnings" They all clinked their glasses and drank deeply. The cold felt good, it wasn't until this point Jack realised how hot and thirsty he had been.

He felt like he needed to show some interest "so...... which room next?"

"living room next," said his mom without hesitation. "lot of work to be done there" his dad sighed "you can help if you want?"

"no thanks dad, I've got loads of homework to do"

"Oh, ok yea I bet your swamped buddy"

Again, Jack felt guilty, he knew his Dad had been upset when he lost his job and he knew he blamed himself for them having to move. His dad had worked for a company that had moved to somewhere in another country because it was supposed to be cheaper. He'd heard his dad say they'd sold them all out but he wasn't sure exactly what had happened, the news that they had to move had been the worst news ever, he'd had 3 months to get used to the idea before they moved but it was still a shock having to pack up all his things into boxes.

"do you need me for anything else" Jack looked at both his parents expectantly

"erm nope buddy, just wanted to check in" his dad looked at him as if he wanted Jack to say something specific

"ok I'm going back upstairs then"

Jack turned to leave, as he closed the door behind him he heard his dad sigh and his mom said "Its ok babe, he will be fine, he just needs a bit of time"

Jack pulled the door closed and proceeded back down the corridor, he stopped to look at the living room on the way, it was a large room, with a very high ceiling. There was a big ornamental fireplace in the centre of the back wall, he'd never noticed before but there were 2 very strange animals carved into the wood holding up the wooden shelf across the top. In the middle of the shelf was carved the same tree as the window in the hall, weird thought Jack, he looked around the rest of the room, it was in just as bad a shape as the rest of the house and it smelt. He glanced through the window, he could still see the kids playing outside. They'd changed their bikes for a ball and were taking it in turns to see who could kick it the highest. Jack turned away and proceeded back upstairs, his footfalls echoing around the quiet upstairs.

He went into his room and sat back on his bed, he picked up his comic, it was neutron man, it was his favourite, he'd got his superpowers when an alien ship had landed on earth and selected him to represent humanity in a series of trials, each participant was given a suit, the suit gave each one powers that were somehow inside each of them. Any illness or unfair advantage was taken away by the suit, it was to give a level playing field.

Jack had discovered these comics when he was 8 and the thought of an alien suit that would give him superpowers appealed so much that he had been hooked straight away. On more than one occasion when lying in a hospital bed he'd wished for it to happen to him.

He'd built up quite a collection but this was the latest one and he was about half way through.

There was a very loud "watch out" from outside, he had a quick glance out of the window as all the kids had gone quiet, it seemed like they had all gone in.

BANG, BANG, BANG the knocker on the front door was being used very robustly.

"Can you see who that is Jack" shouted his mom from the kitchen

Jack sighed and got off his bed "OK" he shouted back.

As he got to the top of the stairs he could see 2 shapes through the glass, he made the journey again down the stairs, halfway down the sun shone through the glass window and blinded him, he squinted against it and blinked a few times, he took 2 more cautious steps down as he tried to clear his eyesight. Then he stopped and stared at the window, it looked like the creatures were moving towards the tree, he blinked hard and looked again........the door on the tree was open, he could hear his heart beating and it felt like it was beating out of his chest

BANG, BANG, BANG the knocker shocked him so much he fell backward so he was sitting on the stairs, he grabbed the rail, his gaze had been broken from the window so he looked back, but it was back to a normal closed door, no moving creatures.

"Jack the door" his mom shouted even louder

"Yes, I'm going"

He got to the door paused and opened it, there stood Ben from number 23, he knew his name because he'd popped round with his parents once just to say hi and welcome them to the neighbourhood and the girl from number 20.

"Er hi," said Jack

"we've kicked our ball into your garden, can we get it" said Ben, who was clearly one of the popular kids from school. He had green eyes and Jack was sure he had no shortage of girlfriends.

The girl from number 20 gave Jack a dazzling smile that completely took his breath away

"Ball??" said Ben

Jack knew then he was staring at her, she was still smiling but it looked a little bit more nervous now.

"oh, er yea sure, go around the side I will open the gate"

Jack closed the door and headed off down the corridor towards the kitchen, the door on the left before the kitchen led to the utility room and then the garden.

"who is it?" his mom shouted to Jack from the kitchen

"They've kicked the ball into the garden just going to go and open the gate" yelled Jack back

"Ok be careful, it's a jungle out there" replied his mom, he could also hear his dad sniggering at his moms attempt at a joke.

Jack opened the door to the utility room, it was really hard to open and Jack had to give it a good shove to open, the wooden door scraped across the old tiled floor. The room was full of boxes mostly from the move but some from the old occupants of the house. No one had looked in these boxes yet as they were stacked so high.

Suddenly he heard the gate rattling and it snapped him out of his thoughts. Better go open the gate he thought. He grabbed the key to the gate which hung next to the door into the garden. It was a large old key, he hadn't realised before how ornate it was for a gate key.

He looked more closely and noticed again the familiar tree design from the window and the fireplace. The roots of the tree wrapped around the shaft of the key, it felt really warm which he thought was a little odd, but then he thought well it's a warm day.

He opened the back door and ventured out, it was a very warm day, birds were singing and he could hear voices coming from the other side of the gate.

"Coming" shouted Jack

The gate was to the left of the utility room door, there was a huge brick wall around the garden and the gate was built into it, the gate looked older than the house, it was made from a dark wood of some sort. Jack put the key into the big brass lock and turned the key, there was a few weird whirring and clicking noises as the lock opened.

Suddenly the key got even hotter and Jack snatched his hand away in surprise, he must have let out a little noise because Ben on the other side said: "You Ok?"

"Yea sorry" and Jack opened the gate, he forgot to look back at the key, if he had he'd have seen it glowing a bright green colour.

"Hi," said Ben "this is Grace" finally Jack had a name to the face. Grace smiled a big smile at him. "er hi I'm Jack"

" yea we know" they both replied in unison, Jack felt his cheeks go a little red and hoped they hadn't noticed.

"our balls in your garden," said Grace. Jack stepped away from the gate and turned to look at the garden as Ben and Grace stepped inside.

"Oh crap," said Ben as he saw the garden for the first time "it's like a jungle"

Jack felt a little smile find its way onto his face as he remembered his mom's words and then was annoyed at himself for finding it funny.

This was as much of the garden as Jack had been into the rest was so overgrown you couldn't see more than a couple of metres in front of you.

"How big is your garden," said Grace looking from left to right

"Dunno" replied Jack "I've not been in it at all, it's just a mess"

"We are never going to find it" sighed Ben

"There's a path down the middle could try that" Jack suggested

"ok lead the way" offered Grace

The path was opposite the door to the house, it went in a couple of metres then turned sharply left. Jack stood looking down the path into his garden, either side of the path bushes and weeds and flowers grew so high they had leant over and touched to create an arch over the path as if the two sides of the garden were old friends reaching over for a warm embrace. The path, however, was clear which Jack thought was a bit odd.

"Go on," said Grace making Jack jump a bit.

They walked down the path to the first bend as they turned the corner they were met with 2 stone statues either side of the path. The statues were decidedly weird and seemed to be a cross between a panther and some sort of dragon, the eyes were a deep blue.

"wow that's fancy," said Ben "wonder what else you got in here"

Jack looked up the path continued for a few more meters then bent to the right, he took a step forward, with Ben and Grace right on his heels. As they stepped past the statues there seemed to be a burst of electricity in the air for a few seconds and then it was gone.

"you feel that," said Grace looking at Jack and Ben enquiringly

"yea" they both agreed

Jack, Grace, and Ben carried on along the path, Jack felt like they were walking longer than the path looked but thought it must be all the overgrown plants making it seem that way. They reached the bend and turned right, straight in front of them another 2 statues, similar to the others but tigers instead of panthers and the eyes were orange.

"You have one cool garden," said Ben "don't think I'm gonna find my ball though, we may as well go back"

Jack felt his heart sink a little, he wasn't exactly sure why but he was enjoying not being on his own.

"No way, I'm following this path "exclaimed Grace

Both boys turned and looked at her, she stood there with a very determined look on her face, her eyes challenging them to say no

"Ok" mumbled Ben "Err yea ok" shrugged Jack

Again, as they passed the statues, the electricity hit them again, this time stronger than before, the air seemed to crackle and Jack was sure he saw flecks of orange in the air, he was about to say something but thought they'd think he was stupid so kept quiet.

As the electricity subsided they all came to a sudden halt and looked at each other, the air was silent, no birds, no breeze nothing at all moved. Ben moved his feet and even that sounded muffled as though you were underwater.

"What's going on with this place," Grace asked with a slight quiver

"It's getting creepy" Ben replied his eyes darting about

Strangely Jack felt calm, he was a bit nervous but not scared

"Let's carry on," Jack said this as a statement but it was more of a question

The path once again stretched ahead for a few metres and then disappeared to the right. The difference this time was that the undergrowth was thicker, making it much darker.

"How are all these flowers growing without any sun" enquired Grace

Jack noticed there were a lot of flowers growing up on both sides of the path, he was no expert but they seemed like very exotic flowers to be growing in a garden in England.

"right we gonna do this then?" Ben was taking the lead here and he stepped passed Jack and moved down the path, followed by Grace.

"Anyone think this path is longer than it looks?" said Ben looking back at Jack and Grace

"Yea and it's getting wider" replied Jack

They all stopped and looked around the path was now easily wide enough for them to walk side by side now.

I don't know where your garden goes but it's bigger than it looks from the outside, we've been walking for ages. Of course, they had no way of knowing if the path just went in circles because they couldn't see through the overgrown plants, all they could see was in front and behind.

"It's got to end soon," said Grace with a sigh "C'mon" she ushered them forward

They were now walking side by side down the path Jack in the middle Grace to his right Ben to his left. They reached the bend and stopped, already that could feel the electricity in the air, it seemed to pulse around them and made a low hum in their ears.

Jack took a deep breath and took a step around the corner followed by Grace and Ben.

They all stopped dead in their tracks, the air was alive around them, it whizzed and crackled. They all gasped in disbelief, it wasn't the air that caused it, it was the sight in front of them. There was another brick wall with a gate in it, the gate looked like it should belong in a castle.

Jack noticed the lock was the same as the gate by the house, it had 3 solid brass hinges and it looked like oak or some very old wood. The face of the door had the tree carved into it surrounded by the creatures they had encountered as statues along the path. Panthers at the bottom, then tigers above them, then 2 Large Lions above them either side of the trunk of the tree.

As impressive as this gate was that isn't what created the gasps, either side of the gate were 2 enormous statues dragon-like but crossed with lions, their eyes gleamed red.

"wow" Bens voice broke the silence

"what is going on with the air," said Grace

Jack could see red specks of light darting about in front of him

" can anyone else see that red lightning?"

"yea, sure can" Grace and Ben both agreed

Jack took a step forward, he realized Ben and Grace were staying exactly where they were.as he got closer to the gate he found as if the air was getting thicker, as though it was pushing against him. He reached the gate, the carving on the gate looked so real, the tree looked like it was moving in a gentle breeze. He raised his right hand and placed his palm on the tree.

Suddenly there was a loud crack like lightning, Grace screamed and Ben yelled, underneath Jacks's hand a green glow started to get brighter and brighter.

"Let's go back" shouted Grace

"C'mon Jack time to go," said Ben

Jack stood transfixed staring at the glow, the air was alive around him with red, orange and green mini lightning bolts. Then there was calm, everything stopped, everything was quiet.

Jack slowly took his hand away from the door, his heart was pounding in his ears, his eyes opened wide and he gasped

"What? "both Ben and Grace shouted at the same time

Jack said nothing just turned to look at them but moved away from the door. There below where his hand had been was engraved in the most ornate writing Jack, Grace, Ben.

"How the hell," said Ben

"Jack" a voice whispered from the other side of the gate

Jack jumped back with a yelp and stood with his 2 new friends

"Jack, Ben, Grace" an eerily whispering voice repeated over and over, getting louder and louder and louder, then there was a loud crash against the gate from the other side

"help us" the voice shouted

That was enough for all 3 of them, with varying yells and screams they turned on their heels and ran back along the path.

Jack could manage a run but he was constantly eyes on the floor looking for any tripping hazards, he did not run as fast as he thought he could because he didn't want to push his body that much, it had let him down before.

Luckily Ben and Grace seemed to be matching his pace and not leaving him behind, they passed the tigers and the panthers and they soon found themselves back at the gate, all breathing heavily. No one spoke that just looked from one to another with total disbelief on their faces

"Obviously, you can keep the ball," said Ben raising a chuckle from Jack and Grace.

Then Grace stopped still she was staring past both Jack and ben towards the gate, Jack and Ben both turned slowly and they all stared at the key in the gate as it was blazing a bright green.

"Right I'm off," said Ben, "wait" exclaimed Jack "what do we do about the thing?"

"the thing" laughed Ben "the THING!!" he seemed a bit hysterical "what do you expect us to do about the damn THING!"

"Ben," said Grace softly "don't"

"you two can do what you want I'm outta here" Ben shot through the gate, you could hear his footsteps get faster as he ran down the drive and away from the house "sorry" whispered Grace and she turned to leave

"erm don't go yet" blurted out Jack

"I've got to, I need to be away from here" she too disappeared through the gate

For a few seconds Jack stood there staring at the open gate, he looked at the key, it was now just a normal key. He cautiously reached out his hand and took hold of the key it was now cold, he pushed the gate closed and turned the key in the lock.

He went back inside and hung the key on the hook next to the door, he wondered if the key would open the gate at the other end of the garden, then he shuddered as he remembered the voice. Well, I'm certainly not going back on my own.

He turned and went back through the utility room door, once again it scraped across the floor echoing through the house. Just then the kitchen door burst open, Jack yelped, his mom screamed

"what the hell Jack you'll give me a heart attack," said his mom now laughing

Merlyn was trying to push passed to see what the commotion was, he soon realised it was nothing and went back into the kitchen to lie on his bed.

"Sorry mom, I've just come in from the garden," said Jack rather nervously

"you find the ball?"

"no mom, its er.... its er too overgrown to see anything"

"They seem like nice kids, you should make more of an effort with them"

"Yes, mom" replied Jack as he retreated down the corridor towards his room.

Back in his bedroom, he just sat on his bed thinking about what had just happened, he looked out of the window, there was no sign of Ben or Grace, he presumed they were probably doing the same as him right now.

The rest of the day flew by, he went up to bed not knowing how he would sleep, but he got into bed and lay his head on the pillow, straight away he found his eyes flickering as sleep encompassed him like that old familiar blanket.

His eyes shot open wide, he was stood at the start of the path once again.

Dreams

Am I dreaming? Surely this is a dream? He could smell the flowers, he reached out and touched one, its blue petals shone in the sunlight, it felt so real.

Then he started to walk forward slowly one step at a time. I don't want to be doing this he thought, but he couldn't stop his legs from moving, slowly along the path to where the panther statues stood. Well should have stood, but they were no longer there, he felt his heart racing, his head went from left to right looking for anything strange, he was sure he heard Grace gasp but she was certainly not there with him now.

SNAP a twig snapped to his left Jack spun round, then a rustle of leaves as if something was approaching him. He couldn't move, he was petrified, then out of the overgrown bushes the large panther statue appeared, but it wasn't a statue anymore.

It looked like a panther, its fur shimmered in the light as it moved around, its neck was a band of scales, a multitude of colours shone on these scales as though they were made from a million precious gems. It had the same scales on its legs rising nearly all the way up, its claws looked like they were made of solid gold. On its back sat 2 huge wings that shimmered and were almost translucent as if they kept disappearing and then reappearing. Its tail was like you would imagine a dragons tail with the arrowhead point at the end.

Jack couldn't move, he wanted to but he couldn't, his eyes were locked with the deep blue eyes of the panther creature, it began to open its mouth.

Jack had a realisation it was a dream, but then a million thoughts came crashing down and he stumbled backwards away from the creature.

"I can't outrun this thing," he thought "I'm gonna die"

It was then the unexpected happened, the creature spoke

"Do not be afraid little one?" said the creature in a softly toned voice

"I am a guardian and I am here to help you"

A piercing scream filled the air, Jack sat bolt upright in bed, he looked around wildly, blinking his eyes, scanning the room for what he had just seen. His heart was pounding, he was breathing rapidly and was covered in beads of sweat.

A dream, could it have just been a dream Jack thought. He sat there thinking about what he'd just seen, it seemed so real, he was sure he could still smell the flowers from the garden.

His heart started to calm down and the reality of it being a dream, a vivid one but still, a dream sank in. He lay back down on his pillow and eventually drifted off to sleep.

He was awoken next morning by his alarm, it was a school day so the usual routine of getting ready ensued. He could get ready in his sleep and most of the time he was at least partly asleep as he got ready.

He was still getting a few aches and pains in his left leg from his last fracture, six weeks in a full-length plaster had meant the muscles needed time to get back to strength. He'd broken his leg when his foot slipped off the kerb trying to cross the road. It had been painful but he was more embarrassed than anything as it was so close to school.

He went downstairs still half asleep, to the kitchen for breakfast.

"Hey champ, what you want for breakfast" his dad smiled broadly at him.

"Just some toast please "Jack yawned a reply

Merlyn ambled over and began to weirdly sniff him just like he does when you've been near another dog. "weird" thought Jack

27

His dad placed the toast in front of him, "lunchbox is packed and it's in your bag" said his dad placing Jacks schoolbag down by his side.

Jack glanced at his watch "I'd better get to school" He grabbed his bag "see ya later dad"

"see ya champ"

Jack opened the kitchen door to leave just as his mom was coming through from the other way, she grabbed him and kissed him all over his face.

"MOM!!", "aw don't be like that baby, mommy's gonna miss you," she said laughingly

Jack wriggled free of his mom's clutches and briskly walked down the corridor to the front door.

"Bye Honey" shouted his mom

Jack opened the front door and stepped outside, he turned and closed the door behind him. He walked down the path away from his house. The front of their house had a tall wall down one side, the other side had a hedge that was at least seven feet tall. The hedge continued along the front of the garden and was just split by an opening with a small gate.

jack opened the gate, stepped through it, and was greeted by Ben and Grace staring at him, Grace looked like she hadn't slept and Ben looked wide-eyed and a little pale.

"Er Hi," said Jack

"You dream last night?" whispered Ben

"About your garden?" said Grace with a slight quaver.

Jack stared from one to another and gulped "about the statue?"

They both nodded in unison "you mean we had the same dream?" once again nodded heads greeted his question.

"We gotta get to school," said Grace, who looked in no fit state to go to school

"We can talk on the way"

They set off to school, the walk was only about ten minutes and they realised as they approached the gates that they had walked there in silence, each one lost in their thoughts.

"We will meet at break by the tennis courts" suggested Ben

"Ok" they all agreed.

As the bell sounded for break Jack couldn't even tell you what lesson he'd been in let alone what the lesson was about. He was the first one to arrive at the tennis courts, Grace arrived next, then Ben.

"What are we going to do," said Grace

"Do?" said Ben questioningly

"Yes do, about the dream, about the garden"

"what can we do" asked Jack

"We need to go back with the key" replied Grace

"No way, no chance, why would you want to do that are you nuts!" exclaimed Ben

"what do you think?" Grace turned to Jack

"Er I don't know, maybe we should..."

"you pair are nuts" Ben cut Jack off mid-sentence

"how about after school?" Grace looked at them both

"Ok" agreed Jack

"no way, not a chance," said Ben and walked off

"Just us then," said Grace

"Yea," said Jack, feeling the heat rise in his cheeks as Grace smiled at him

"I will meet you at the gates after school," said Grace as she picked up her bag and began to walk away

"Ok," said Jack and went even hotter as she turned and flashed him a smile

The rest of the day went without a hitch, until the last period. The whole year were gathered in the hall to watch a film about Remembrance Day. He saw Ben and Grace seated in the Hall as his class made their way in and sat down.

All the curtains were pulled so it was dark in the room, the film started projected onto the large screen at the front of the hall. Images of world war1 and 2 flickered across the screen. Then images of wounded soldiers and rows and rows of gravestones. the film panned out from the stones to reveal a huge field with row upon row of headstones. It then zoomed back into a large monument to fallen soldiers.

Jack gasped and blinked, as the camera zoomed onto the memorial the image flickered to the gate in his garden. He looked around, no one else seemed bothered, had they not seen it, he couldn't see Ben or Grace.

Perhaps I imagined it he thought as the film seemed to return to normal. The voiceover was reciting a poem about the war, a wind whistled in the background, then he heard it "Jaaaacccckkkk, Jaaaacccckkkk, Jaaaacccckkkk" as though it was carried on the wind. Again Jack looked around, no one was taking any notice, Jack realised that only he could hear it.

Well, that's, that he thought I've got to go back, cause it's not going to leave me alone.

The film finished, the headteacher said about the importance of remembering the sacrifices made and they were dismissed.

Jack grabbed his bag and rushed to the gates, Grace was waiting for him.

"Did you see it; did you hear it say my name" Jack almost shouted at her

"Yes, I saw it, but it said my name," Grace said with a shocked look

Someone tapped jack on his shoulder, he spun around a little too quickly because he winced slightly. There stood Ben, a concerned look flashed across his face before he said "It said my name, I'm in"

They looked at each other, "ok let's go" said Jack

They set off together, Jack fought the urge to run, he knew he couldn't run all the way, he knew his leg would hurt and he would have to stop so he decided on a brisk walk.

He wanted to say something but he didn't know what to say. Grace and Ben seemed happy to walk in silence, he glanced at both of them, they were both lost in their own thoughts.

They entered the gates to the park, sunrise park was the go to for all the kids from school, it had a playground a skate park and tennis courts. Jack usually cut through on his way to and from school.

As they entered the park the path split into two, they took the right path which led down through an avenue of trees, the trees had arched over the path and grown together, it reminded him a bit of the path in the garden. the right side of the trees had dense undergrowth and bushes, a great place to hide for anyone.

He looked down the path and could see the gate the other side. The sun was blocked by the trees which meant the bushes on the right grew even darker. Jack felt his eyes drifting over to the bushes.

Suddenly he froze, "What," said Ben, they both looked in the direction Jack was staring.

"What is it? I can't see anything" said Grace shakily.

Jack knew he'd seen something two eyes, a dark shape he wasn't sure what, he just knew they were all in danger.

There was a rustle of leaves, everything went silent, no birds, no people shouting, no cars, the air was deathly still.

Then they saw it, two red eyes appeared from the bushes followed by a large black shape, as it got closer it was as though the light around it was getting sucked away, everything was getting darker.

"We need to move," Ben said in a voice just slightly louder than a whisper, they couldn't, they were all frozen to the spot as the thing got closer and closer. Then it growled a noise like no other animal, so deep you could feel it inside your head.

Grace screamed a loud piercing scream that shook them all free of their trance.

"GO!!" yelled Jack. He knew he had no choice but to run now. They set off down the path, the first few strides Jack kept pace but Ben and Grace soon pulled away from him. He could feel the pain in his leg but he knew he couldn't stop, his eyes were now glued to the path looking for any trip hazards, he knew if he went down he would go down hard and the likely hood of him breaking something would be huge.

He could hear the thing crashing through the undergrowth as it pursued them, for some reason he knew if he could get into the sun he would be ok. he looked up to see Ben and Grace emerge into the sun, he hadn't realised how far ahead they had gotten.

"C'mon move!!" shouted Ben at Jack

Jacks leg was really painful now, he could feel himself slowing, feel himself starting to limp more and more with every stride.

"JAAACCKKK HURRY UP!!" screamed Grace

He knew the thing was almost level with him but he pushed himself on, he could feel the darkness closing around him, he looked up again, he was nearly there, just a few more strides.

There was a deafening roar and Jack felt like he was pushed and almost lifted from behind as he burst into the sunlight. He immediately looked behind him, whatever it was had disappeared.

They all stood there breathing heavily

"What the hell was that," Ben asked them both

"How should I know" Graces face flashed with anger

Jack shrugged, he couldn't speak, the pain in his leg was dying down but he needed a rest.

It wasn't far now to his house so he said "come on let's go"

They arrived at the gate to Jacks front garden shortly after, they went through and up to the front door.

"My mom will be in so let me do the talking" Jack opened the door and stepped inside.

He heard his mom moving about in the living room so he gestured for Ben and Grace to follow him.

They all bundled into the living room so closely together that Jacks mom looked up and her face turned from a smile to a puzzled look.

"you ok Honey bear"

Jack groaned on the inside as he heard Ben snigger.

"Yes mom"

"Who's your new friends?"

"This is Ben and this is Grace" Jack introduced both of his new friends

"Hi Mrs. Knight," said Grace, "hello Mrs. Knight," said Ben

"Emma please, no formalities here not to my fluffy bear's friends"

Ben sniggered again

"MOM," Jack said desperately

His mom smiled back a very mischievous smile and Jack couldn't help but smile back.

"We are gonna go in the garden have another look for that ball," Jack said to his mom

"Ok sweet pea, be careful its..."

"I know a jungle out there"

His mom laughed a little too loudly as Jack turned to go outside.

Ben and Grace followed him through to the utility room, as they entered Grace said "wow you've still got some unpacking to do"

"most of these were here when we moved in" Jack replied

"And you've not looked inside?" said Ben flipping open a box lid

The box was full of old books, old may be an understatement, these books looked ancient.

"These look old," said Ben "bet you could sell these"

Jack turned and grabbed the key from the hook by the door, then he opened the back door and went outside.

The sun was still burning brightly and it was really warm, he sat on the old bench by the door, he had to give his leg a rest.

"The keys got the same markings on as the gate," he said as he offered it to Grace.

Grace took the key and it started to glow, she immediately dropped it with a squeal. It fell by Bens feet; the glowing had stopped so he reached down gingerly. As soon as his fingers touched the key it started to glow. Ben picked it up and turned it over and over in his hand.

"I can feel it," he said

"I know what you mean" Jack replied

"What are we going to do?" Grace asked

"We've got to go back to the gate," Jack said with a determination he didn't exactly feel.

Ben passed Jack the key and it continued to glow as he stood up from the bench and made his way to the garden path.

They moved down the path, a lot more cautiously than last time towards the corner. The feeling in the air wasn't there anymore.

"I can't feel the buzz this time," Ben said

This was as good a way of putting it as any he thought as both Grace and he nodded. They reached the corner and stopped the statues were gone. They all looked around, backwards and forwards, you could see where they had been but they were no longer there.

"How's that possible" Grace asked frantically

"Have your parents moved them?" Ben asked

"Uh Uh they've not been in the garden yet"

"What do we do?" asked Grace

"Keep going," Jack said forcefully

They could see where the path disappeared again and Jack set off cautiously towards it, the path began to widen and he felt Grace by his side.

There was a noise in front of them, a rustling to the left of the path, they all froze staring at the spot. Suddenly a huge paw with solid gold claws emerged from the undergrowth followed by the head and body of the panther from his dreams. It turned and stood on the path in front, staring at them.

Jack didn't feel threatened at all but they all began to take steps backwards, then there was another rustle behind them and another one emerged from the bushes. They were trapped.

Jack stared at the creature in front of him, as powerful and scary as it looked, it was also divinely beautiful. Colours cascaded around its neck and on its legs, its wings seemed to appear and disappear.

He felt Grace grab his arm and Ben bump into him from behind

"Do not be afraid"

Everyone's head snapped forward as the panther spoke

"We mean you no harm, we are guardians and we are here to protect the gate" its voice wasn't threatening it was so gentle for such a powerful looking creature

"Jack, Grace, Ben, you have been chosen and now you must come with us"

Guardians

"How does he know our names" whispered Ben

"What, why?" stammered Jack

Jack felt someone grab his arm, he couldn't help but jump, he looked down to see Graces hand gripping tightly onto his arm. She was just staring saying nothing at all, just staring straight forward at the creature before them.

"My name is Joken and that is Kraal" the creature in front of them spoke nodding towards the other creature behind them "you must come NOW!" The slightly raised tone on the last word shocked the three out of their frozen state and somehow, they all began to walk forward.

The one called Joken turned and began to walk down the path towards the gate.

Jacks mind was racing, why was he following the creature in front when he wanted to shout and run to the house, but somewhere deep down he felt safe with the creatures.

They were approaching the next bend in the path, the stone Tiger statues still remained either side of the path, Joken and Kraal both nodded as if in greeting as they passed.

"Everything will be explained soon" said Kraal from behind. At these words, Jack felt Graces grip tighten on his arm, he had almost forgotten it was there.

Jacks leg still hurt from the run and he noticed he was limping a bit more noticeably now, he was hoping Ben and Grace had other things on their mind than ask about it. This was not the time for the talk about his condition.

They continued down the path, the air became more alive as they drew closer to the gate, again the path had widened enough for them to walk side by side. The air was once again silent as the stopped before the gate, the enormous lions looked on with a proud, commanding stare.

Joken stopped by the gate and bowed down, Kraal came around from the side so that he stood next to him and they both bowed together.

"This is a portal children" Joken whispered, "A portal to a realm that needs your help, you have been chosen, you are the Katari, the chosen ones"

"Do you have the key" Kraal asked turning to look at Jack

Jack placed his hand in his pocket and pulled out the glowing, vibrating key. It shone so brightly it was almost too bright to look at, small green lightning bolts cracked and spun around it as he held it out.

Joken sighed "the portal has not been opened for thousands of years"

"You've not been through it?" Stuttered Grace

"No, not since we came through with the other guardians to protect it" sighed Kraal

All of a sudden, a huge roar echoed down the path from behind them, followed by a crack of lightning and the earth trembled beneath their feet.

Ben, Jack and Grace all span round

"What was that?" shouted Ben

"The second seal has been broken" shouted Joken as he leapt passed the three of them with Kraal following him. They both stood in front of them staring down the path, their front paws pressed so hard into the path that their golden claws had pierced the ground.

There was another loud roar, followed by a piercing scream that cut right through the three of them.

"open the gate" Grace yanked on Jacks arm "open the gate NOW!" Grace almost screamed at Jack

"Do it" agreed Ben

Jack saw Joken nod to Kraal and Kraal leaped forward down the path.

"It is time" Joken turned to look at Jack, "It is time for you to go, you must hurry, the second seal has gone, there is only one more"

Jack turned to face the gate, he really didn't want to do this but he wanted even less to see what was happening behind him. He moved to the gate and raised his hand with the key towards the lock, he could feel it being pulled towards the gate. He let his hand hover with the key a centimetre from the lock.

"Do it" he felt Grace right by his side, "go on?" said Ben as he moved to his other side

More roaring from behind and another piercing scream

"GO!!!" roared Joken

Jack plunged the key into the lock, electricity roared around them, the light was so bright he had to close his eyes, he heard a roar right behind him and knew it was Joken, he started to turn his head and caught a glimpse of the massive lion statue starting to move.

The gate opened, Jack, Ben and Grace tumbled through the gate, there was a roar of electricity and a thousand colours flashed before their eyes.

They fell, Jack shouted along with Ben and Grace as they fell, somehow, they had grabbed onto each other as they fell. The noise was deafening, the light so bright, Jack felt himself losing consciousness, "Got to hold on" he told himself, he was keeping the panic in as he thought about the fall, well more the landing than the fall. He knew if he passed out the fall was probably going to result in a break and then what.

But the darkness was starting to draw in on his mind, just a little fuzzy around the edges at first then it grew and grew as he slowly passed out.

Meeting

The sound of bird song slowly filtered through Jacks ears, he could feel the warm sun on his face, a gentle breeze whispered through some trees overhead. He slowly opened his eyes, a shock of colour and light streamed in so he quickly closed them again. he could smell grass and flowers on the breeze as it blew past his nose.

He slowly opened his eyes again, cautiously and with the intent of letting a bit in at a time. This worked and slowly into focus the world appeared again.

He was lying under a tree, staring up at its swaying branches, the leaves whistled in the wind like the most perfect wind chime. He felt grass in his hands, then the panic rushed back in.

"I fell," he thought, he was frightened to move, slowly one by one he moved first his arms, then his legs. So far so good, he turned his head from side to side catching a glimpse of Ben and Grace both lying near him, both unconscious.

"I'm ok," he thought "I am actually ok" he screamed in his head as he slowly sat up and looked around.

They were in a small clearing surrounded by trees, the trees stood tall, almost as if they were proud to be there. Their trunks covered in bark that shone bright silver, the undergrowth was thick, so thick you couldn't see past the edge. He could hear birds but he couldn't see any as he scanned the trees around him.

The edge of the clearing was covered in flowers, a cacophony of colours of all hues and shades. The smell was almost overpowering, it was like a symphony of smells and he couldn't help but breathe in deeply.

He turned his head as he was sure he could hear water but with the rustling of the leaves, it was hard to tell.

The grass beneath him was like the finest velvet, so soft to touch he kept letting it run through his fingers, this allowed the sweetest grass smell to escape from beneath him.

A large stone arch stood at one end of the clearing, the stones were carved with all sorts of creatures and at the top the familiar tree. He suddenly grabbed his pocket and felt the familiar shape of the key to the gate.

He remembered Ben and Grace. He moved over to Grace still quite cautiously even though he was fairly sure he hadn't injured himself.

"Grace" he spoke her name softly and she slowly began to stir.

He couldn't say it any louder as it felt disrespectful to the clearing "don't be stupid" he admonished himself with a little chuckle.

Graces eyes slowly opened. "You ok?" asked Jack

"Yea I think so" Grace replied blinking.

As she slowly sat up Jack moved over to Ben, "You ok? Ben, you ok?" he gently shook his shoulder as he heard Grace say "wow it's beautiful"

Jack looked round to see Grace taking in their surroundings

"What the hell was that," Ben said sitting bolt upright

Grace and Jack both smiled at each other

"Everyone ok? No one's hurt? Jack asked them both

"Yes, I'm fine," said Grace

"Yea I'm ok" agreed Ben

Jack stood up wincing slightly and rubbed his leg

"You ok Jack" Grace asked with a worried look on her face

"Er yea I'm good thanks"

he looked at Ben, Ben was looking at him as if to say I don't believe you.

Quickly Jack said "I can't see a way out of this clearing"

"There's a path there," Jack said pointing off to the left

"What?" Jack turned to look as he hadn't seen any path, but there it was plain as day.

A tree stood either side off the path their branches entwined as if they'd just opened their arms to invite them in.

"Well, what are we waiting for" Ben jumped up and set off towards the path

"Any idea what happened," Grace asked, "where did the creatures go?"

"no idea" Jack replied remembering the glimpse of the lion moving.

The three of them got to the start of the path, it looked exactly like the one in Jacks garden.

An avenue of trees stretched before them, flowers continued down both sides with glimpses of sunlight breaking through the canopy.

"How do these flowers grow with so little light" queried Grace.

Ben shrugged as he stepped onto the path, Grace followed him and with a look over his shoulder, Jack followed too.

As they walked down the path it looked as though the flowers followed them, as if they flowed alongside them like a stream. Every colour you could imagine was represented either side of this path as if someone had set out to design the most beautiful, cascading flower show ever.

Then a sound seemed to arrive from further down the path, carried on the leaves and flowing with the flowers "welcome Katari, we have been waiting". It was a voice on the breeze, a whisper in their ears.

Ben slowed down and Jack found himself out in front. They were nearing the end of the avenue, you couldn't see any further as the sunlight seemed to shine right at the entrance.

Jack emerged first then Ben, then Grace all of them blinking as though they had just woken from a dream.

Rolling meadows filled with flowers greeted them. Trees were scattered about of all shapes and sizes, in the distance snowcapped mountains stood like wise old men waiting in judgement. The colours were so vivid, the air was so clean and fresh.

The meadow they were in gently rolled away from them, and there before their eyes stood a massive tent. The tent was as large as a circus tent, from the two points flew two flags, on one the tree from the gate the flag was emerald green with a silver tree emblazoned on it. The other flag was a crimson red with a golden lion on it.

The tent itself was deep forest green with silver edging around the roof and along the bottom. The door to the tent was pulled open and either side stood two huge men, fully clad in silver and green armour. They held shields with the silver tree embossed into them, they both held golden spears.

"Wow," Ben said

"I don't think they've seen us," Grace said

They all stood there staring at the sight before them.

"What do we do," Jack said

Just then a horn sounded a deep rich sound that emanated from behind them. They all spun around expecting to see someone but there was no one there.

They looked back to the tent, more people had emerged now and were looking up the hill towards where they stood.

Another horn sounded from the camp below as three figures began to make their way towards them.

Jack watched them approach slowly, he felt a bit anxious as he waited for the three mysterious figures, "could this day get any stranger" he thought.

He felt Grace and Ben slowly shuffling behind him so he was clearly out in front, he gulped and returned his gaze to the three figures.

The one in the front was a female, she had long flowing golden hair with streaks of silver, she wore a dark green tunic which had gold trim around the edges. On her chest was emblazoned a golden stag. She wore a brown belt around her waist with what clearly was a sword hanging from the right-hand side. Jacks gaze locked onto the sword and worried what exactly that was for.

He raised his gaze up again to her face and realised how beautiful she was, her eyes were a piercing blue and slightly pointed in the corners. They locked eyes and she gave him a warm smile that made him feel warm all over.

To her left strode a man with a staff, the staff looked like it was made from the trees they had seen in the clearing, it almost shone with a silver glow, on the end was carved an eagle. The shaft was covered in silver markings of some description, Jack couldn't really make them out.

He was wearing a dark blue tunic with no sleeves and underneath he wore a silver shirt, he wore what looked like blue leather trousers and boots.

The man looked slightly older than the woman, his brown hair interspersed with shocks of grey. He had green eyes that almost seemed to have light dancing about in them. He had a brown short beard with a streak of grey in the front.

Jack noticed that he also wore a sword, smaller than the woman's but nonetheless it was another sword.

"Who are they?" whispered Ben

"I want to go home now" sighed Grace

"I think it will be ok" Jack turned and glanced at them

"How do you know?" Grace chided

"I've just got a feeling," Jack said as he turned to look at the third figure.

This man was huge, he must be seven or eight feet tall, as tall as he was, he was no less big across. His arms were bare and showed huge muscles, he wore a golden breastplate across his enormous chest, emblazoned with a lion. His legs were armoured also on the thigh and the shins. He also had a sword at his waist, but it was the huge axe he held in his enormous right hand that made Jack gulp. Jack was sure the axe was bigger than him.

He had a golden helm on his head with a white plume on top, he could see parts of his face, his eyes were a steel grey, determined and steadfast. His mouth was a tight line and showed no emotion.

They were close now and Jack braced himself for what came next.

"Welcome Katari" the woman spoke first with a soft voice

The other two just nodded at the three of them

"I'm sure you have many questions, my name is Silari" she turned to the man holding the staff "this is Straven" he nodded a greeting to the three. She turned to the giant "and this is Kron". He nodded again to the three children.

"Will you accompany us to our tent and we will explain everything"

Jack turned and looked at Ben and Grace. Ben was staring open mouthed so Jack gave him a nudge

"He's huuugggeee" Ben stammered looking towards Kron. Jack followed his gaze and was sure he saw a smile flicker across Kron's face before the steely gaze returned.

He felt Grace grab his arm and pull him towards her. "We need to go" she whispered

"Do not be afraid Katari, no harm will come to you here," Silari said as she turned and gestured towards the tent. As she turned her hair moved away from her ear to reveal it was pointed.

"A giant and now an elf" Ben exclaimed, followed by another nudge from Jack

"Yes, I am an elf as you say" Silari spoke as she made her way back down to the tent "please, come"

Her companions turned and followed her back down towards the tent. Jack started to follow.

"Where the hell are, you going" Grace grabbed Jacks arm

"Down there to find out what's going on," Jack said

"What about you?" She turned and dared Ben to agree with Jack

"Er yea, what he said"

Grace sighed, "I'm surrounded by idiots, come on then let's go"

They watched as the three companions entered the tent and disappeared. Jack, Grace and Ben were not far behind them. They got to the entrance and stopped, staring at the two huge guards either side of the opening. Clearly, they were the same as Kron. Neither of them looked down at them, they had the same determined, steely gaze as Kron.

"Why can't we see inside," asked Ben

Jack and Grace both looked, clearly the door was open but you could see nothing inside, just shadow.

"guess we are going to find out," said Jack as he stepped forward

The three of them all entered the tent at the same time.

As they walked through the entrance there was that now familiar crackle of electricity, but not as strong as before. Then they were inside the tent, they were clearly in just a section of it because the tent was huge. On the floor was an elaborate rug, woven into the middle was the familiar tree and around it, the guardians were fighting what looked like shadows with burning red eyes.

Set in the middle of the room was a large round table with six chairs, the table was made of a silvery wood that shimmered and glistened. On the table was a selection of food, fruit, bread and some sort of different meats. Golden plates and goblets were set in front of each chair.

The chairs themselves were of dark wood, almost black, on the backrest of each was carved the tree in silver. A luxurious silver cushion lay on each seat.

On the back wall stood three banners each depicting the sigils the three companions had on their chest.

"Please take a seat" gestured Silari

They had already taken their seats around the table

Jack, Ben and Grace stayed put as if they were still taking it all in

"Please eat, have a drink you must all be hungry and thirsty" She again gestured towards the table.

Ben moved first and sat down, picking up his goblet and drinking

Jack heard Grace sigh as she moved to sit next to Ben.

Jack sat down last and immediately felt better for it, just to get off his leg for a bit was heaven.

He noticed Grace was also drinking, so picked up his goblet and took a gulp.

The liquid exploded a taste sensation in his mouth, he swallowed deeply and took another mouthful. With each mouthful, he felt more and more refreshed, the pain in his leg was fading rapidly.

"That was amazing," said Ben setting down his goblet with a clunk

"Where are we?" Grace asked suddenly

"There is a very long answer to that question, my dear," said Straven for the first time

"Please eat and I will try to explain," said Silari

Ben didn't need asking again and was already tucking into the food. Grace was picking at the fruit, some of which Jack recognised others he had never seen before in his life.

Jack was starving so picked up a chunk of bread and began to nibble on it.

"You are the Katari" she began

"The what?" asked Ben through a mouthful of grapes

"The Katari are the chosen ones"

"Chosen for what?" asked Grace quizzically

"Millennia ago Gaia our world was a peaceful place full of wonder. Magic was an everyday tool used by everyone"

"Magic? You mean like tricks?" Jack asked

"No young one, real magic," Straven said. He raised his hands and blue lightning crackled between his fingers, he rolled it round and round in his hands creating a ball that fizzed and crackled. Then he threw it up into the air above the table and it exploded and gave off a shower of multicoloured lights that slowly disappeared.

"WOW," said Grace with her mouth open

Silari continued "Magic was everywhere, in the earth, the trees, the water even the breeze. It was a life force for the planet. The centre of all magic was the great tree" she waved her hand across the table and an image of the tree they had seen so often appeared before them.

The tree was huge it looked like it almost touched the sky, its trunk was bright silver and energy could be seen running up and down like electricity through a cable. Its branches seemed to stretch for miles and were adorned with leaves that shimmered a thousand different colours.

"This was the heart of Gaia, it was called Selendrial. On Gaia there were seven races, my people the Elhuri, Straven's kin were the Hanori, Kron's were the Kandar. There were also the Seraphs who were a beautiful race so elegant and were born with the ability to fly. They had wings on their backs and could soar through the skies"

Jack noticed her eyes were filling with tears as she spoke, a single tear ran down her cheek

"Did something happen to them?" Jack asked softly

"We will come to that soon enough," said Silari "Also there was the Dwafen who lived in the mountains, they were a robust people, small in stature but large in heart and their bravery saw no bounds. Finally, there were the Hellions and they have the largest part to play in this story"

Jack, Ben, and Grace all waited with bated breath for her to continue the story but she seemed lost in her own thoughts. Straven placed his hand on her arm and said "Silari" softly and clearly with so much love

"Oh yes, I'm sorry it is still difficult to talk about"

Silari continued "All the races lived together in peace, sharing everything, there was no conflict, no disease or illness just peace and love."

"Then one being destroyed everything"

The Gathering

"Apuch was the Queen of the Hellions, she was like a sister to me, but eventually she decided she had become tired of this life and wanted to rejoin Selendrial and become one with everything. So, a great celebration was held and representatives from all the races gathered at the tree to bid Apuch farewell on her final journey. Her son Thrall was to become the new king of the Hellions.

At first, he was a good King, but slowly stories started to emerge from his realm that he had built a huge fortress to reside in and had created an army. Until this point, we had never had a conflict on Gaia. I sent an emissary to his realm to seek an audience, this was declined on several occasions.

Then one year at the gathering"

"The gathering?" asked Grace staring intently

Straven spoke "The gathering was when all the realms gathered at the Tree to give thanks and rejoice, it happened every year"

Silari sighed "All the realms had their contingent at the tree except Thrall and the Hellions. Halfway through the ceremony, a dark cloud appeared in the East, rolling towards the tree. The ground began to shake like thunder and on the horizon Thrall appeared with a huge host, an army so huge it spread further than the eye could see. But something was wrong, the host wasn't Hellions they were twisted distorted beings so corrupt they were unrecognisable"

Silari let out a little sob "I'm sorry" she wiped a tear from her eye

jack looked around the table, he could see the sadness in Straven's eyes, yet in Kron's there burned fierce anger. Jack noticed he was gripping the side of the table so hard his knuckles and fingers were turning white.

"none of us were prepared for the sight of that host, none of us were prepared for war," Silari said looking down at her hands "how things have changed" she sighed

"There was panic amongst the ones gathered at the tree, we had nowhere to go, no weapons to defend us only magic, but we had never used it against another living thing. You see magic was a pure energy incorruptible or so we thought.

It was the Hanori that stepped forward, you see they studied magic, we all used it but they were the ones who kept expanding its horizons, they were the masters of magic." Silari looked down at the table. Jack, Ben and Grace followed her gaze.

The table came alive with an image of the tree, hundreds of people milled around its base. There was a rumble of thunder in the distance and the ground shook. The three were transported to the events of that day. Jack could feel he was still seated at the table but he was also there. He could hear the screams and cries of anguish, he could smell the panic in the air.

He reached out and gripped Ben and Grace's arm as the events unfolded before them.

The Hanori in their blue tunics formed a semi-circle around the panicked mob, Jack gasped as he saw Straven stood in the middle, his staff glowing brightly.

Jack heard a roar and there off in the distance was the host of the Hellions, writhing twisted creatures of different kinds screaming and crying uncontrollably as if in perpetual torment. They were all armed with weapons and armour of the blackest night. Their flags and banners were a jet black with just two red eyes menacingly staring at them.

Then from the middle of the group a huge creature appeared, it looked like an elephant in characteristics but that was where the similarity ended, its tusks and eyes were a crimson red, its body longer than a normal elephant, more like a crocodile but not quite. Its legs were powerful looking with crimson red claws and its tail was thin and pointed and curled and writhed like a snake. Jack then realised what the body was, it was like a dinosaur, a carnivore built for hunting. It opened its mouth and let out a scream that turned your blood cold.

Jack felt Ben and Grace go tense and he knew they were seeing the same as him.

Atop this huge beast sat what Jack could only describe as a demon and knew this was Thrall. He wore blood red armour all over, covering his whole body, the helm on his head had two horns protruding from the top, it reminded him of Loki's helmet the horns were that big. In his hand, he held a three-pronged weapon.

He turned his head and looked straight at Jack their eyes locked, it was like looking into the deepest darkest pit but it was illuminated by a red flame. Jack began to panic as he couldn't break his gaze, he heard Ben let out a little whimper and Grace screamed.

"It is but a memory children" Silari's voice cut through and broke the gaze and Thrall looked away.

Thrall raised his arm in the air and there was a loud whoosh as the sky turned black, followed by a whistling scream as thousands of arrows launched from within their ranks swept towards the tree.

Jacks head snapped around to where Straven and the Hanori stood, they all raised their staffs and it was as though the arrows just stopped dead in the air and fell harmlessly to the floor. This happened over and over again, slowly the odd arrow started to get through.

Jack saw a couple of Hanori fall with arrows in them. Jack noticed that while this had been going on the rest of the people by the tree were being ushered through a portal at the rear. Grace gasped as two figures arose from the crowd on beautiful white wings, they had on simple pale silver tunics and golden flowing hair. They looked so out of place amid the chaos.

More whistling, shrieking and more Hanori fell, they were half the number that previously stood there.

Jack could see Straven was sweating and breathing heavily he knew he was exhausted.

Suddenly the arrows stopped, Jack could see Thrall sitting atop his huge beast, he could guess what was coming next. Out of the corner of his eye, Jack noticed Kron with his people lining up behind Straven, they had branches of wood in their hands for makeshift weapons. They were joined by some people half their size "these must be the Dwafen" Jack thought. They carried hammers and picks and other digging implements.

"They haven't got a chance," Ben said

A horn blast sounded from the vast host, then another, then another and a black wave of screaming creatures erupted towards the tree.

It was like an earthquake as they rushed forward, the Hanori all stepped back behind the ranks of the Kandar and Dwafen. It was a hopeless fight within minutes three quarters of the defenders were lying dead or wounded on the floor. The cries of pain and anguish were just as loud as the blood lustful screams from the hellions.

Jack saw most of the others had now disappeared through the portal, a group of Seraphs stood by the portal looking back at the carnage by the tree. Jack caught a glimpse of a Seraph arguing with someone when she turned and pointed to the battle he could see it was Silari. They were arguing heavily, suddenly the Seraph gestured to his people and as one they took off towards the battle.

What remained of the defenders were all huddled into what looked like a magic bubble that the Hanori were trying to hold onto. There were probably twenty left inside this pocket of magic.

The Seraphs arrived and swooped down one by one into the magic bubble picking up a person and carrying them to the portal. They had rescued about five when a horn blast again echoed around the battlefield. As three Seraphs emerged from the bubble carrying three Dwafen they were all mercilessly shot down by arrows, they along with their rescued brothers fell to the floor dead.

The Seraphs who had escaped the first time foolishly flew back into the battle and were shot down before they even reached their trapped comrades.

Jack squinted, the sun must have changed position as the light was blinding, no it was coming from the tree. The trunk of the tree was emanating a silver light, as it spread from the tree and touched the hellions they screamed in pain as if burnt.

It spread out further and further, encompassing all the black creatures of hate. then there was a flash so blindingly bright it could be seen through closed eyes. A surge of power and electricity that washed over you with a feeling of calmness.

Jack blinked several times trying to clear his vision when it cleared he surveyed the battlefield. Thrall and the Hellions had disappeared all that was left were the dead and dying of the other races. The cries of anguish as loved ones held their fallen family.

The scene started to mist over as if the world had decided no one should see the atrocity that had happened that day and Jack found himself back in the tent sitting at the table. He looked at Grace who was now pale with tears running down her face. Ben had a stunned look on his face, his eyes glistened with tears.

"That was the first battle with Thrall" Straven said with an ashen look on his face "That day I lost my son and my father"

"Were they not destroyed by the tree?" Ben asked

"No, the tree does not destroy, it gives life, it is pure energy, uncorrupted. Thrall and his host were just sent back to their realm" Silari sighed

"How did they become like that?" Grace asked

"We aren't sure, Thrall was always hungry for power but he had a kind heart, his people were compassionate, hard working. We don't know what corrupted them all so quickly" Straven replied

"No one saw them again for many many years, during this time we prepared ourselves, we prepared ourselves for war. The Dwafen forged us armour and weapons. We trained our people to fight. For the first time, we built huge citadels to hide our people in. We sent spies into Kralls realm to try and find out what was happening, but they never returned"

"Our only option was to place an outpost on each border. Hella was bordered by the Dwafen realm and the Seraph one. The Dwafen King Grath built Stonehaven in the mountain range between their two realms. A great city carved into the mountains, its walls as thick as they were high. Grath said that Thralls forces would break on the walls like the ocean on the rocks. It was occupied by what became the Dwafens elite troops. You see as much as we had heard nothing or seen nothing there were still the odd skirmishes across the borders which we dealt with easily" Straven spoke proudly

"They were testing us, our strengths, finding our weaknesses" Kron spoke for the first time his voice as powerful as his stature

"Yes, yes they were" Silari was looking so pale clearly this was taking its toll.

"What about the Seraphs" Ben enquired

Silari smiled "A people so pure of spirit, they found the wars more difficult than all of us. Fighting went against everything they stood for. But eventually, they became some of the fiercest, bravest warriors, and The Hellions despised them above all others."

"On their border, they built the gleaming silver city of Arcandru, it was constructed with the help of so much magic that it was like a beacon of hope and love. Its walls were hundreds of feet high, the towers and spires stretched up into the sky. There were no doors in any of the walls, the only way in was to be flown in. Their queen Gabrella made this her home"

"They also had the odd meeting with the Hellions but they were very few as they seemed more scared of the Seraphs than any other people"

"The peace lasted for hundreds of years, we did not grow complacent but we did relax more than we should have. During these years, we found that magic was becoming harder and harder to use as if it were running out. Then one day all the leaders were called to the great tree by the keepers."

"We all arrived at the start of spring when the new flowers were starting to bloom, we were all shocked when we arrived, the great tree looked duller than ever before, as if, as if it were dying"

"We all stayed for a week trying to figure out what to do, what we could do. Then one morning there was an enormous crack, like thunder, we all rushed outside to see a crack had appeared down the trunk of the tree. As soon as this appeared the tree began to die"

"A few days passed before we learnt of the fall of Stonehaven and the death of Grath and most of the Dwafen people. We figured it must have been why the great tree cracked. The only survivors were the messengers Grath had sent to warn us all.

It seemed Thrall had spent his time growing in strength waiting to strike back at the other realms. We thought we were prepared, how wrong we were.

The Fall of Stonehaven

Grath stood on the balcony of his room surveying his city before him. His people had worked hard to create this fortress and they felt safe behind these walls of granite and stone. Rock was something they knew, something they could rely on, no need for all the magic just strength and sweat went into its creation.

The outer walls were two hundred feet high and a hundred feet thick, there were passageways cut into the walls that allowed moving about the wall unseen and in safety. Also, there were windows in the wall not visible from the outside that could be used to rain arrows onto any attackers.

The city was a horseshoe shape at the rear was the mountain of Krom, the Dwafens home, the place they had lived for thousands of years. The mountain swept down from its sides to create the horseshoe shape, it was across this space the Dwafen had constructed the wall. The other side of the wall was a chasm with four bridges that crossed to a secondary wall half the size of the first. Each gate protecting the bridges was of solid oak reinforced with the strongest Dwafen steel.

There was just one gate in the main outer wall, two towers stood either side of it, a gate stood one end of the wall, and a second gate a hundred feet passed this one on the inside of the wall. Through the second gate and the nearest bridges were off to the left or right a deliberate ploy to slow any attackers who got this far.

Passed the secondary wall were the barracks, there were ten placed along the wall each housing five hundred men, beyond this was the hustle and bustle of everyday life. Markets selling food, shops of all sorts, blacksmiths making the finest weapons and alehouses. Grath smiled as he remembered his

71

previous night's exploits in one such establishment "the twisted knee" the best ale in all of Terra.

Passed the city was another wall this was cut from the mountain itself and was more like the outer wall for size, beyond this was the citadel whose spires were nearly as tall as the mountain itself. This was where the royal family lived Grath, his wife Hemoen, and their sons Gars, Hagen and Vanga. His sons were officers in the elite royal guard who numbered two thousand and lived at the base of the citadel.

Krom itself was interspersed with tunnels and escape routes that led through its heart to the sea the other side. Here they had created docks and had ships anchored at all times.

"Sire" a voice from behind shook Grath from his contemplation. He turned to see his trusted friend and advisor Glima stood at the door.

"Today's order of business sire, we have scouts returned this morning with news" Gilma said looking slightly pale

"What is it?" Grath demanded

"They are waiting in the throne room sire"

It was a short walk to the throne room and as he entered his eyes were always drawn to the stone dragons that seemed to be holding up the high vaulted ceiling. Fires burned in their open mouths, it was an imposing place for any visitors. He walked to his throne which had been carved from a huge piece of granite and ordained with gold, silver and precious gems. Another stone dragon stood menacingly looking over the rear of the throne.

Dragons were considered the keepers of the mountain but it had been hundreds of years since they had all disappeared, some say they had returned to the mountains from where they came.

Grath took his place on the throne, he nodded to his sons who were stood to the side in their armour.

Two Dwafen stood before the throne, clearly, they had had an arduous journey, they looked exhausted.

"Speak," said Grath kindly

They both bowed "Sire we have news from Thrall's kingdom, we are sure he has another army, maybe bigger than before and it seems to be coming this way"

Grath felt his heart sink "How sure are you?"

"it is difficult to say sire as a black cloud seems to be moving with it obscuring the view" the scout replied

" We must know for certain" Hagen said with a gruff voice

The scouts looked terrified as if they would be sent out again

Grath looked at them and said "Thank you, go and get food, ale some clean clothes and some sleep. We are indebted to you"

The scouts left the throne room and Grath beckoned his council forward.

He looked at Hagen "You are correct we must find out what is happening, but we must also warn the other realms. Glima send messengers to the other realms tell them Thrall has returned and we are investigating"

Gilma bowed and left the throne room

"Sire" Gars spoke "Let me take some men and scout the land see what I can find out"

Grath wasn't sure about this but he knew it was the only way. "Ok take five hundred elite guards and see what you can find out"

Gars bowed and turned "Gars!" Grath shouted, gars turned back and saw not his king but his father "Be careful do not go too near"

"I won't father" and he turned and left

"Vanga go down to the outer wall, make sure everyone is on high alert and double the sentries"

Vanga bowed and left

"Hagen get the garrison ready just in case, get all the women and children into the citadel"

"Sire are you sure we need to do that, we don't know for sure there's anything to panic, everyone, about," Hagen asked

"I'd rather be prepared," Grath said with a sigh

"Yes sire" and he left

Grath made his way to the balcony overlooking the city, the hum of noise and the occasional laughter, he hoped it would stay like that and he was panicking over nothing.

He watched as Gars led his troops out of the citadel all marching in formation, their armour gleaming in the bright sunlight. These were his best troops, the finest warriors in all of Terra, Gars would be fine with them.

He stood there and watched as they made their way through the busy streets across the bridges to the main wall. He watched them enter the wall section by section until the marching feet echoed hollowly in the tunnel and they were gone. Grath felt a sense of dread as they left and had to stop himself from sending a runner to fetch them back.

he could see people streaming into the citadel and new they would be panicking now but it was for the best. He sent a runner to call a war council meeting in one hour, and another to find Gilma. He sat back on his throne lost in his thoughts, thinking about how to prepare his people for what he knew deep down was coming.

The war room was a long rectangular room with a large stone table down the middle, the king sat at one end, his sons and various other city officials and army personnel sat around the other sides.

"I think war is upon us again," Grath said breaking the silence "We must prepare for the struggles ahead"

"The garrison is on full alert and all sentries have been doubled," said Hagen

"The women and children are being moved into the citadel along with all the food stores, I have also taken the liberty of preparing the ships in the docks," Vanga said

"The ships" Gilma exclaimed, "Why?"

"Just in case" Vanga replied

A horn blast resonated through the walls of the room, a low guttural sound that you felt as much as heard. The door crashed open and a guard appeared "Sire Gars has returned and he's being pursued"

The whole council jumped to their feet and looked to their King.

"Open the outer gate, get archers to the wall and load the ballista" Grath bellowed. he grabbed his helm from the table and placed it on his head as the room cleared. leaning against the wall was his war hammer, he picked it up and strode purposely from the room.

There was a unit of ten royal guards waiting to escort him. He knew he had to get to the wall and fast.

Making his way to the wall took longer than usual people crammed the streets making for the citadel, children cried and many faces he passed were pale and scared. The smell of burning oil filled the air as the defences were readied.

He reached the inner wall and was greeted by Hagen. "Sire the bridges are prepared, all troops are in full armour and ready. The wall garrisons are in position" Hagen said as he barked orders to those around him.

Grath nodded and proceeded across the bridge to the first lift to take him to the top of the wall. Before he entered he turned to Hagen "Get a unit of your best men ready at the gate, gars may have company when he comes in"

Hagen nodded and turned away.

Grath entered the lift with his ten guards and proceeded to the top of the wall. As he rose he surveyed his city before him, saw his panicked people, his city already looked like it was under siege. The cries of children and women, the acrid smoke in the air, the sounds of clanging metal as armour brushed against armour or the smiths hammered out new weapons. He was glad Gilda was not here to see this, his son's mother died during childbirth of his last son, a part of him had died that day but now he was almost glad she was not here to see this unfold.

They reached the top and he strode to the battlements and looked out. There in the distance, he could see Gars banner flying, he could make out several figures around it, nowhere near enough to represent all the men who had left with him.

Then the blackness caught his eye, a rolling cloud of dense black fog following behind his son and his men. he gripped the handle of his war hammer and wrung his hands around it, he knew he could do nothing but watch.

Dwafen were not particularly fast but they could run forever, he was hoping that now they would be fast enough.

As they got nearer he could see Gars out in front, he was covered in blood and had about twenty men with him, they all looked exhausted and as frightened as he had ever seen anyone look.

"C'mon run, run" Grath muttered under his breath. He looked around to see the shocked, worried looks on his means faces.

Then things started to appear in the blackness, writhing, screaming wraiths with blood-red eyes, he felt his eyes widen and saw a couple of his men take a step backward.

"STEADY" he bellowed "Sergeant," he said turning to the nearest guard, "get down the wall and warn Hagen what's coming. The soldier nodded and left.

He turned back to the wall, Gars and his men were just a few hundred metres away now.

"ARCHERS READY" Grath shouted the order was continued down the wall.

Grath saw some of the creatures reach a small group of men who had drifted away from the main group, they were engulfed in seconds, their cries for help silenced as soon as they had started.

"FIRE" Grath gave the order

Thousands of arrows swept from the walls and into the black mist. Satisfying screams greeted their arrival and Grath smiled knowing they could hurt them.

"PREPARE TO OPEN THE GATE" he paused as another volley of arrows left the walls

"NOW" he heard the great gate opening slowly below him, he looked down to see Hagen and his men form up outside the gate, Gars and his remaining men flew through the gap in the shield wall just as the black mist obscured his view, the mist hit the wall and rolled back like the ocean on the beach. He could hear the sounds of a fierce battle below, the clash of weapons, the cries of his men and the screams of the unholy creatures.

He heard the gate begin to close, he turned and strode to the lift. he needed to see what was going on. "General !! protect these walls" He said to the head of the royal guard

"Yes sir" he replied and began shouting orders

The lift seemed to take forever as it reached the bottom he couldn't believe what he was seeing. There were dead and dying soldiers everywhere, he looked for his sons and caught a glimpse of Gars standing with a group of men all huddled around something.

Grath marched over and grabbed Gars meaning to hug him, but then he noticed he was staring at something on the floor behind him, he turned.

There lying on the ground was Hagen, his face ashen and his chest rose and fell with quick sharp rasping breaths. A doctor knelt by his side, he turned and looked at Grath "I'm sorry sire"

Grath fell to his knees, grasping his son's hand, he brushed a stray lock of hair from his forehead like he had so many times before as a child. A tear rolled down his cheek

"My son, my beautiful son" Gars knelt down beside him, he put his arm around his father's broad shoulders. His father looked suddenly older, there was so much pain etched onto his face. Grath turned to see tears streaming down his face. Gars reached out and took his brother's hand "Do not worry little brother, you are not alone, we are here with you now and always" At that point Hagen took his last breath and so the first death inside the mighty walls of Stonehaven occurred. There would be many more before the siege was over.

Battle

Hagen's body was taken to the family crypt and laid to rest, there would be no time for mourning yet, they had to win this fight.

After the first encounter at the gate, the enemy had fallen back and the black mist sat across the valley just out of range of the archers.

Gars had filled the council in about what had befallen his men, the enemy seemed to have guessed they would come and had ambushed them in a valley, it was a miracle any had gotten out alive.

Gars looked at his father's pain still etched into his face but he had now taken the role of the king and was laying down plans for the defence of the city. All the woman and children were now in the tunnels beneath the citadel, all able-bodied men and those women wishing to fight were mobilised at the walls.

All the ships were ready in case the unthinkable happened. Luckily messengers had been sent to the other realms so hopefully help would arrive but it would not be soon.

Gars looked at Vanga, he had broken down when they told him about Hagen and screamed a cry so full of pain and anguish it had chilled everyone who heard it. Now he sat there with a face of stone, vengeance filled his eyes.

"Gars I want you to take two hundred men and wait in the courtyard by the entrance to the citadel," Grath said looking towards his son

"BUT sire" Gars began then stopped as his eyes met his fathers "Yes sire"

"Vanga you are in charge of the bridges and secondary wall, IF they get through let three go and keep the last as long as possible so we can get everyone from the walls"

Vanga nodded. Grath stood up "Good luck everyone"

Grath made his way to the wall to organise the defence, he hadn't been there long when the horn sounded. "THE MIST IS CLEARING" a lookout shouted. A few cheers erupted from the wall thinking they had retreated but they soon tailed off when they began to see what it revealed.

Thousands of creatures filled the plain before them, rank after rank of the most hideous creatures all dressed in jet black armour. The creatures varied in size and shape but they all had one thing in common, blood-red eyes.

A drumbeat started at the rear of the horde, thump, thump, thump the horde began to bang their weapons against their shields in time with the beat. Thump, thump, thump, it echoed around the valley, through the corridors and chambers of Stonehaven.

A huge black shape was coming forward, Grath recognised Thrall immediately.

Thrall stopped his huge beast he rode and looked straight at Grath

"Grath my brother, will you not except an old friend inside" screams and shouts followed this from the horde

Grath shouted it back "You are not welcome Thrall" his voice seemed to emanate from the mountain itself.

"My dear brother, there is no need for more blood to be spilt"

"Go back to your pit and take your vile creatures with you" Grath shouted

Thrall laughed a sound that turned your blood to ice "So be it" he raised his trident and as one the horde rushed forward, screaming and slathering towards the wall.

"FIRE" Grath shouted as arrows once again poured down like the deadliest rain. Hundreds fell in the first volley but still, they came.

Grath noticed some creatures with eight legs and huge claws charging to the wall in packs. Grath frowned as he watched one jump against the wall, its huge claws dug into the rock and there it stayed. The next one did the same using the one below to get a little higher, they were creating ladders.

"The ones with the claws, get the ones with the claws" Grath shouted

They moved so fast, within minutes they were three quarters up the wall and the others climbed up with little trouble. This was going to get up close and personnel very quickly.

Grath turned to a runner "Go find Vanga tell him to be prepared, they are nearly on the wall"

The runner departed just as the first of the horde reached the top of the wall. How quickly they had breached this first defence, for the first time Grath felt a chill run down his entire body.

The fighting on the wall was fierce, but they were losing ground steadily. Large pockets of the wall were now occupied by the horde and they spread out like a cancerous growth consuming anything in its way. His men were fighting hard but falling fast.

The first of the horde reached his position, he swung his great war hammer with a bellowing cry killing two with one blow. His royal guard joined him in the fight. The crash of metal on metal, the screams and cries as they fought for their lives.

Grath was grabbed from behind and pulled backwards, his sergeant stood looking him in the face "Sire it's time to go the wall is lost". Grath had been so consumed in his own personal battle he had lost touch with everything around him. He blinked and looked along the wall, there were still small pockets of his men fighting but the top of the wall was mainly black. He turned and looked out over the wall, the horde still stretched as far as the eye could see.

Grath felt his knees weaken slightly but caught himself "Sound the retreat"

His sergeant nodded "Sire lets go, sound the retreat" the sergeant shouted as horns echoed along the wall.

Grath made his way down the wall to the bottom, for a while the battle sounded distant but slowly it got closer and closer. He reached the base and emerged into the sunlight, he looked up and saw the pale blue sky, felt the warm sun on his face and smiled.

He noticed one bridge remained, he could see Vanga on the other side and raised his hand to his son. His son waved back and beckoned him across.

86

Grath could see the horde streaming out of the base of the wall either side of the bridge, he knew there was no one left alive now on the wall. About eight hundred men were starting to file across the bridge.

Grath knew this was not going to be a retreat. "TO ME MY BROTHERS" Grath shouted, his voice echoed through the city as if a great stone giant had awoken. He raised his war hammer and the sunlight gleamed from its head.

With a shout, he charged into the advancing horde his men following behind.

"NOOOOOOO" shouted Vanga from the other side of the bridge as all the soldiers crossing the bridge turned to follow their King into battle one last time.

Vanga watched as his father disappeared beneath the horde, and so died King Grath King of the Dwafen lord of Stonehaven.

"Sir the bridge" Vanga's vision snapped back to the bridge, the horde was upon it already

"Take it down," Vanga said as he turned and retreated to the second wall.

The bridge fell taking some of the evil creatures down into the chasm.

"FIRE" shouted Vanga as he exited the wall on the other side.

All across the wall arrows and rocks rained down onto the horde, hundreds fell but soon they retreated back into the wall and a stillness erupted through the city

"Captain," Vanga said, "How many made it from the wall?"

"About six hundred Sir" the Captain replied

Six hundred, Vanga knew there had been six thousand men on that wall. He couldn't hide the shock from his face

"Send for my brother"

When Vanga told Gars of their father's death he just nodded

Vanga was the eldest so he now assumed leadership, he felt no fear or trepidation, he had been in the military all of his life so had commanded men daily.

"Gars take two hundred of your reserve force and get everyone you can onto the ships," Vanga said looking deep into Gars eyes. Gars knew exactly what his brother was saying, he expected Stonehaven to fall.

Gars stepped forward and embraced his brother, this took Vanga a little by surprise but he smiled as he hugged him back.

"May the mountain watch over you and I will see you soon brother in this life or the next" Gars said to his brother with a voice full of emotion.

Vanga could see his eyes filling up and felt a lump in his throat as he tried to keep his emotions in check.

"Farewell, little brother," Vanga said and turned towards the wall. He looked back once to see Gars disappear around a corner "Be safe, live for us all"

Vanga climbed the stairs to the top of the wall "anything to report Captain"

"No sir, it's quiet, too quiet"

Vanga stared across the chasm looking for what was coming next, what did happen next took them all by surprise.

The black mist began to roll out from the wall and poured into the chasm

"READY" Vanga called to his men

Black ropes came shooting across the chasm, hundreds of them straight to the top of the wall, one landed near where Vanga stood, he looked down the rope had hit the wall and the end had spread out like roots from a tree and stuck there.

"CUT THEM" he shouted as he drew his sword and hacked at the rope.

The Dwafen weapons were second to none but the blades were having no impact on these ropes, then the ropes started to bounce slightly.

"Here they come, ARCHERS FIRE!!" Vanga shouted as black shapes emerged from the mist scurrying along the ropes towards the wall.

"Burn the ropes" Vanga heard his captain shout as oil was poured onto them and set alight

This seemed to work at first but for everyone, they burnt down three more appeared from the mist. He saw they had reached the wall in two places and fierce fighting had broken out. It was all happening so fast, there was so many of them.

Two creatures leapt over the wall where he stood, he swung his sword and severed the head of one before it landed, he brought his blade down and pierced the second through the stomach.

He heard fighting behind him and turned to see they had breached the wall in several places now. he knew his men were losing.

"Sound the retreat" he shouted.

Horns cried out above the screams and mayhem as his men tried valiantly to fight a retreat away from the wall.

Vanga made it to the base of the wall and exited into the courtyard beyond. The main street to the citadel lay in front of him. He heard footsteps approaching as Gars reserve force came into view. He was relieved to see Gars was not at the head of it.

"TO ME!" he shouted to his men. The numbers who had made it from the wall were very few. He reached the reserve force just as the black horde rushed from the wall. This was the only way to the citadel, he had to give Gars time to get them into the boats.

He formed his men into a shield wall and they braced for the onslaught. The fighting was fierce, close hand combat. They were so tightly packed together it was hard to swing a sword.

Left and right he hacked with his sword, cutting down creature after creature, still, they came on and on and on. More and more of his men were falling, the ground was slippery with spilt blood.

But they held, they held for longer than should have been possible, they held until Vanga had just ten men around him, surrounded by a screaming horde of creatures. The horde flew at the remaining troops and ripped them to shreds screaming with bloodlust as they did it.

Gars watched with tear-filled eyes as his brother fell, he had gotten all the ships full and they were leaving the harbour. There were about two hundred men women and children they couldn't get onto the boats so Gars remained with them. He was going to lead them into the mountain.

The tunnel they had left by they had collapsed behind them, no one knew where these tunnels went just that they went deep into the mountain. There was a small cove they passed through before they entered the deep tunnels, this would also be collapsed as soon as everyone was through, this would be the last daylight they would see for a long time.

Gars stood there and watched the ships leave the harbour, he had no idea where would be safe for them but anywhere was better than here.

He heard the shrieks of the horde as they appeared from the citadel into the harbour, he knew there was now no Dwafen left alive in Stonehaven. Then these huge spiders appeared.

Gars and the others watched in horror as they shot a black thread to the nearest boats and swarmed on board, one by one the boats were consumed by the horde.

Gars could not take the screams of pain and anguish anymore and sobbing he turned away walking into the tunnel. The others followed either open mouthed or also sobbing.

As they vanished into the tunnel the rocks crashed closed behind them.

Tent

A young girl entered the tent and walked over to Silari. She wore a light green tunic, she had brown hair tied back in a ponytail, which revealed her pointy ears. She had a silver bow slung over her back and a quiver of arrows at her belt. She looked extremely serious as she handed over a scroll and bowed.

"Thank you, Phoebe, please wait for a moment"

Jack, Ben and Grace looked on as Silari read the scroll.

"Thank you, my child, that is all"

Phoebe bowed, turned and left the tent.

"News?" asked Straven

"We shall discuss the matter soon enough" Silari responded

"What happened to the tree," Grace asked

"The tree had split" Straven replied "We all heard about Stonehaven and sent word back to our peoples to prepare for war. We all mobilised our armies and the plan was to march to Arcandru as we thought that was where they would strike next"

"We all marched North to Seraphina, it was only a few days before each army was mobilised and on its way"

"It was at this time we noticed how magic seemed to be leaving us, it had been the very essence of each of us for so long we all felt the emptiness it left behind. We all felt despair and dread that this was a war we couldn't win."

Straven sat back in his chair and pushed a hand through his hair. "I need a drink, Kron?"

"Always," Kron said with a wry smile.

Straven got up out of his chair and entered one of the rooms off the main one.

"Straven doesn't like the next part of the story," Silari said

"We all came to a decision that we may need something more than arms to defeat Thrall, so we tasked Straven and his most powerful practitioners of magic to create something if all else failed"

"What did they come up with?" Ben asked

"They came up with your world"

Jack, Ben and Grace all gasped as one

"They what?" asked Jack

"The Hanori created your world and the plan was to send him and his horde through a portal and trap him there for all time"

"I take it something went wrong," Said Grace questioningly

"Unfortunately, yes" Silari looked down at the table "this was powerful magic and as we mentioned magic was vanishing from our world"

"It took our armies three weeks to merge on the plains of Allinon, situated in the North of Hanoria. Our combined force stretched as far as the eye could see. Kron and the Kandarians occupied the middle as they were our fiercest fighters. On the left flank, the cavalry of the Elhuri, On the right the Hanori archers and magic users.

We sent scouts forward to Arcandru to get word of where the horde was. Two days later they returned to say Arcandru had fallen and the horde was three days away"

"We never thought Arcandru could fall, it was a beacon of light against all darkness"

Arcandru

Arcandru, the city of clouds as it was known by the other realms. The city of white. Gleaming white walls surrounded the city and stretched as far as the eye could see in both directions. They rose from the grasslands like huge teeth erupting from below. The walls were famous for having no gates anywhere, which meant any attackers had no focal point to launch an assault.

The tops of the walls were tipped with silver which reflected the sunlight for miles around, a shining beacon for all to see. At regular intervals along the walls were huge spires, the spires themselves stretched into the sky, so high that on a cloudy day the tops disappeared from view. The tops draped in silver gleaming in the sunlight. At the top of each spire flew the banners of the Seraphs, a dark blue background with silver wings.

Beyond the walls, the sight was breathtaking. As any visitors were flown in by the city guard and taken to the arrival area for checks this was your first view of the city.

All the streets and buildings gleamed white, scattered about were parks and gardens giving brilliant flashes of colour against the gleaming white. The parks were huge in their own right, some almost like forests, trees of all colours resided inside. The smell from the plants and flowers filled the city with a beautifully rich aroma of honeysuckle, lavender, Jasmine and eucalyptus amongst a myriad of others.

Animals roamed the parks and streets of the city, the Seraphs were the closest to nature and could converse with animals of all kinds.

Markets were scattered about the courtyards that were always situated next to a park, people from all over the realm came to sell their goods. During the day, these were the busiest points of the city. Their crude wooden stalls standing in contrast to the immaculately constructed buildings around them.

Beyond the homes and parks there stood a second wall, this wall had a north and south gate that was normally never closed. There was never any trouble in Arcandru as soon as you entered a feeling of calmness and happiness came over you.

This wall also gleamed white but the four towers that stood at the corners of the wall had silver running down them from the spires. As though some giant had picked them up, dipped them in silver and placed them back whilst it was still wet, the silver then running down the wall to the ground below.

Beyond this wall was the heart of the city. Around the walls stood the barracks and training grounds for the army of the Seraphs. The blacksmiths and weapon makers also resided here. The blacksmiths were different from the rest of the realm as they didn't use burning fires and hammers to manufacture weapons and armour. They used magic, magic and tools created with magic. They had the best trained army in the land, they couldn't outdo the Kandar in strength and skill but their training of fighting together made them the best.

In the centre sat the palace of Queen Gabrella and King Hanie. Surrounding the palace was a crystal-clear lake, the water was an azure colour and was said to be the sweetest tasting water in the land. Swans were regularly seen swimming around on this vast lake.

The palace had one entrance, the only way in was across the crystal bridge. The bridge was ornately carved from millions of crystals fused with magic. Across the length of the bridge were carved animals of all descriptions. At the entrance to the bridge were two panthers, watching all who entered. In the middle of the bridge, a pedestal sat either side, on each pedestal a large tiger was carved almost jumping to meet the other across the expanse of the bridge. At the end of the bridge before you entered the palace sat two huge lions, regally watching all who entered.

The huge gates that marked the entrance to the palace were made from pearls and glistened with a million iridescent colours.

The palace itself was decorated in gold and silver, an ornate staircase swept from the entrance hall up to the other floors, carpeted with a dark blue carpet. The banner of the Seraphs hung from the high vaulted ceiling of the entrance hall.

At the top of the stairs two huge wooden doors, each carved with a picture of the tree, beyond these doors was the throne room.

Inside the gleaming throne room, with its arched ceiling sat two thrones either side of the thrones two trees grew up and through the ceiling as if they were fused into the fabric of the building itself. On the back wall, a crystal waterfall cascaded down through the floor joining the lake below.

On each throne sat Gabrella and Hanie with concerned looks on their faces. Before them stood the messenger from Stonehaven.

"It took less than a day for it to fall, no one survived," the messenger said through tear-filled eyes.

"I watched from a mile away on a hill" he paused "I watched until the fighting stopped and, and until the screaming stopped" he hung his head as though telling this message was all that had kept him going, now exhaustion set in.

There was a stunned silence in the throne room.

"Should we send troops?" Gabrella said softly knowing the answer.

"There is no point my lady" at these words he sank to his knees and sobbed.

Hanie raised his hand and ushered two stewards forward, "Take care of our guest, see that he gets everything he needs"

They moved forward and helped the messenger onto his feet, they then helped him out of the throne room.

Hanie looked at his wife "They will come here next, we must be ready"

"Can we stop them on our own?" She asked

"I don't think we have much of a choice" he replied

Gabrella turned to her servant "Go call the council, we meet immediately"

Council

The council meeting place was situated on a roof terrace overlooking the city.

To one side the sheer white wall of a tower disappeared into the clouds above, there were a few clouds about today wispy and thin being blown in the gentle breeze. Mainly there was blue sky and today Gabrella thought it was the bluest she had ever seen. The city seemed alive with colours from the sun reflecting off the various surfaces around the city.

The rest of the terrace had a crystal wall around it, intricately carved with a variety of animals and plants, the floor was made from pearl and changed colour with every glance.

In the middle was a round solid oak table with six chairs. Two of the chairs were bigger than the others and had carved wings escaping from the top.

Gabrella stretched out her wings and felt the sun on them, the gentle breeze ruffling through the feathers. She closed her eyes and got lost in the sounds of the city and the breeze.

"Gabrella" Hanie said, "Its time"

She turned to see all the chairs occupied, there sat her two generals, the city warden and the master of arms.

"Gentlemen welcome, we have grave tidings to discuss"

She took her seat at the table alongside Hanie and they told the council the messengers story. As in the throne room after she had finished no one spoke.

Altor the city watch commander spoke first "I will ready my troops, your highness, I am sure our walls will hold"

Anor the army commander replied "We cannot rely on the walls we must prepare and evacuation, if Stonehaven fell so quickly we must be prepared"

"I agree" replied Faria the city warden "I will make preparation's immediately" he looked straight at Hanie who nodded, Faria, got up and left.

"Our weapon houses are full your highness, we have enough for every fighting man and woman," said Stello the master of arms.

Gabrella looked from face to face while she decided what the best course of action would be.

"Altor prepare every available person to fight in the city, Stello equip everyone with weapons and armour" they both nodded

She turned and looked at Hanie with a look of trepidation.

Hanie spoke "Anor prepare the troops, as we have decided we will go out of the city and meet Thrall before he gets to us"

There was a gasp from Stello "Yes sir" replied Anor straight away

"Your highness are we not weakening ourselves by dividing our forces" Altor spoke with concern

"We have discussed this and feel this is our best chance" Gabrella replied

Altor nodded "Now go and prepare Gabrella said

All three got up bowed and left.

"Are you sure Hanie?" Gabrella asked

"I am my dear sweet Gabrella," Hanie said looking into her eyes.

Leaving

Hanie stood in the courtyard behind the wall, regaled in his silver armour and helm, a white plume cascading from it down his back between his pure white wings.

Around him were three thousand troops all in silver armour and helms, carrying a variety of weapons, bows, spears, swords and shields. The shields were like an arrowhead that they wore on their left arms, the point projecting out past their hands, the other two points of the shield went passed the shoulder. Each shield bore the winged sigil of Arcandru, on the breastplate of every soldier was the tree of life.

Their weapons were forged with magic which made them unrealistically light so as not to hinder their flight.

Hanie turned to Gabrella and took her in his arms, he pulled her close and kissed her "Do not worry my darling, I will fly straight and deadly, if I do not return I will await you in the afterlife"

Gabrella tried to speak back but could not as the tears rolled down her cheeks, all she could mutter was "come back to me"

He smiled and turned, as he did he withdrew his sword, the sun caught the golden blade and illuminated the courtyard about him "Brothers, sisters, the darkness will not take us this day, the darkness will not avail this day, we fight with light on our side, we will be triumphant this day" he unfurled his wings, with a cheer the whole arm unfurled their wings and began to take off. The wind blew up dust from the floor obscuring their vision as the rose up and up until they cleared the wall and vanished from sight.

A guard flew down from the wall, "Your highness, they are here, the horde is here"

Already she thought, how is that possible. "How goes the evacuation"

"We haven't even begun yet your highness"

"What, why?" exclaimed Gabrella

"There wasn't enough time"

"Get everyone who we can get out, out now"

"Of course" and he flew away

Gabrella flew up onto the wall and stood next to Altor on the wall. She looked at him and saw he was just staring out over the wall. Gabrella followed his gaze across the vast plain that stretched out before the wall, there in the distance was the horde, a black mist rolling along behind it so that just the first few front ranks were visible.

This wasn't the frenzied unleashed horde from before they looked organised like a well drilled military force. However, as she looked along the line of vile creatures approaching her city she realised they were greatly outnumbered.

She then looked down to see Hanie leading his troops across the plain, four rows of troops flew low to the ground in perfect formation, their silver armour shining bright in the sunlight, their pure white wings like an avalanche of snow rolling across the ground. Their battle horns sounded as they drew closer.

Gabrella turned to Altor, "Call them back now!!"

A beating began, like a giant heart pulsing across the plain, thump, thump, thump.

Gabrella's head snapped back around, she could see the horde banging weapons on shields.

"Call them back now!!" she almost screamed

"Sound the recall" Altor shouted and a horn pierced the heartbeat rolling across the plain

"Its no use your highness" Altor took his Queens arm as they both stared out at Hanie leading his troops into battle.

"There" a guard was pointing to the distance as breaks along the lines of the horde appeared, huge creatures akin to spiders shuffled back into the lines every fifty feet.

Hanie's force was closing fast, a blast from a horn, and the rear line slowed and reared up, the archers at the rear fired into the horde. The horde raised their shields as a silver rainbow of arrows arced over into their ranks, a few got through but most hit raised shields. The Horde responded with a volley of their own, a black stain covered the sky as the arrows swept towards the onrushing troops.

A horn sounded and the troops as one tucked in their wings using their momentum to still carry them forward, they raised their shields, but some arrows got through, a few soldiers fell and rolled along the floor to lay lifeless in the dirt.

Then it happened, the spiders shot something from their abdomen, as it shot forward it split into five.

Hanie's troops were too close to react the thread pierced soldier after soldier, in the first volley over half the troops lay dead or dying, some were pinned to the ground by these gruesome threads of destruction. Screams and shouts echoed across the plain.

"Call them back" Gabrella whispered open-mouthed, the colour had drained from her face as she watched the horror before her.

The spiders fired again, even more, troops fell or were pinned.

Gabrella heard Altor gasp as she watched Anor fall pierced through the chest.

Hanie's archers were trying to give as much cover as they could but their numbers were dwindling fast. Within minutes about a quarter of Hanie's troops remained, he raised a hand to signal the retreat when a cord pierced his leg and he fell to the floor pinned.

Gabrella cried out as she saw him fall knowing she could do nothing to help any of them.

About twenty troops flew towards their King and landed around him shielding him from arrows, they hacked at the spider's cord to free him but even with their magic infused weapons, it was taking time.

All the while the thump. thump, thump continued as the last few troops died, any surviving troops now surrounded their fallen King. A bright gleaming beacon in a mass of blood and blackness. There were about fifty men now trying to protect and free the King.

Suddenly the thumping stopped, the lines parted and Thrall appeared atop his great beast. The elephant-like creature stared with its blood-red eyes at the small force a few feet in front and let out a piercing cry, then it charged, bravely the men tried to stand in its way, tried to bring it down, tried to protect their King but within moments it stood towering over Hanie who was still pinned by the spider thread.

Thrall looked down at him "And so shall all fall before me" he shouted with a voice like thunder. The creature raised a mighty leg and crushed Hanie beneath it.

Gabrella screamed and Thrall turned his head to look, a low guttural laugh rolled across the plain. He turned and disappeared back into the ranks of the horde and the horde began to advance, killing any troops still alive.

"My Queen, what shall we do," Altor asked worryingly

"My Queen!!" he exclaimed snapping Gabrella back to reality

"Your orders?"

"I……. I er" she paused appearing to try to regain some composure "Get Stello and Faria here now, prepare the troops to defend the walls"

Stello and Faria joined them in the courtyard below the wall.

"How goes the evacuation?"

"Currently no one has left the city, everyone wishes to fight for their homes, the children are being housed in the palace" Stello replied

"We need them out of the city as soon as we can" Gabrella responded

"Do you think the city will fall?" Faria asked

"I do not know, but I don't want these decisions to be made in the final moments, we can still fly them out safely"

"My Queen, my Queen" a messenger ran towards them

"The spiders surround the city my Queen"

Altor pulled him to one side to get all the information

"It would seem they do not want us to leave," Faria said

"Surely they cannot fire that high" Stello said

"I cannot risk the lives of our children, we must find another way," Gabrella said

Gabrella turned to Altor and asked "Do you have a plan to defend this city"

"Your highness, my suggestion is to leave three quarters of the troops on the walls, the rest we will hold at the bridge to the palace, Stello you take charge of those at the bridge the captain there is expecting you"

Stello turned and started to leave, then he turned back and uttered "Good luck to you all" then he turned and left.

"My Queen I hope you will go to the palace and remain there as long as you can"

Gabrella smiled, "Thank you Altor for your concern but I will be fighting alongside my people"

Gabrella looked at Faria "Find a way to get those children out of here, we must assume help is on the way but it will take time"

Faria nodded, unfurled his wings, and flew away.

"Well general, shall we see what unholy creatures we can kill"

Altor smiled as they both took flight to the wall.

The Horde was about a mile away, but closer than that were the spiders, just out of arrow range about every fifty feet all along the length of the walls.

"Crafty beggers" Altor sighed

"I don't see how they can get over the walls in sufficient numbers to create a breach," Gabrella said

"They must have a plan, they certainly have the numbers" Altor replied surveying the advancing horde

The Horde was about half a mile away when out of the mist and through the uniformed ranks ran hundreds of screaming, snarling creatures, they closely resembled velociraptors with arms, they were covered in light jet black armour and they all carried a small round shield and a short scythe-like sword.

They ran towards the line of spiders along the wall.

"Wait" shouted Altor to the archers on the wall, "wait"

Suddenly the spiders span around and fired the same black thread from their abdomens up to the tops of the wall, pinning the end to the floor they continued to repeat this creating bridge-like structures from them to the top of the walls.

The creatures were soon bounding up these lines to the tops of the wall

"FIRE!!!" Altor shouted

Already a couple of creatures had made the top of the wall, but all along the wall, the defenders were holding their own.

Gabrella noticed the threads hit the wall below where she stood, she tried to hack at them with her sword but it seemed to do very little damage, a creatures head appeared snarling above the wall, all teeth and saliva, she severed its head with one stroke.

The sheer numbers of creatures soon made the defence of the wall look pretty impossible. Two more creatures appeared and Gabrella blocked an arcing slash from one creature and thrust her sword through the second, two arrows pierced the second and they both fell from the wall.

Gabrella took a step back and looked along the wall, in a couple of places the Horde now held large sections of the wall. She shouted to Altor "We must fall back" as she gestured along the wall.

Altor turned, his eyes locked with Gabrella's, a creature appeared behind him at the wall and thrust his blade through him, Altors eyes widened with a look of panic and he fell to his knees, two creatures jumped on him hacking and snarling. Gabrella turned away spread her wings and leapt from the wall, she landed below by the signaller.

"Sound the retreat," she said and took off once again so her troops could see her, she flew about twenty feet in the air her sword held high in defiance "Back" she yelled, "fall back"

All along the wall, her troops rose into the air, some were pulled back down by the creatures who seemed to have an ability to jump high. Most of the troops were now in the air just a few feet above the wall, a strange whistling sound started from in front of the wall, getting closer and louder.

Gabrella squinted against the sun to try and see what it was, just as the sun was blotted out by hundreds of arrows. It took the retreating troops totally by surprise, she looked in horror as hundreds fell dead or dying back onto the wall to be pounced on by the creatures.

The few survivors joined the rear guard with Gabrella and flew to the crystal bridge where Stello waited.

They reached the bridge quickly, the wounded were taken into the palace the rest of the troops from the walls joined the ranks behind the fresh troops.

Stello and Faria waited as Gabrella landed beside them. "Altor?" Faria asked, Gabrella just shook her head.

"How goes the evacuation," Gabrella asked Faria

Faria looked uncomfortable "We still haven't figured out how to get them out"

"We still have some time, it will take a while to get enough troops up and over the wall," Gabrella said

"We may have to take them over the mountains," Faria said

To the rear of Arcandru stretched the mountain range of the Icleesials, the mountains were so high that no Seraph had been able to fly high enough to get over them.

"We cannot send children to the mountains," Gabrella said "There must be another way"

The ground beneath their feet began to shake and tremble.

"What is it?" asked Gabrella

"Part of the wall is coming down" A scout from above shouted

"Damn" Stello exclaimed," I thought we had longer"

"Stello, command the remaining troops, give us as much time as you can" Gabrella said

"Faria, get two hundred who fought on the wall to the rear of the palace with the civilians"

Faria and Stello embraced each other nodded to the Queen and left.

The city was laid out as such that everything led here to the bridge before the castle, there was an open courtyard before the bridge to which all the avenues led.

Gabrella saw Stello arrange troops in the courtyard in an arc along the front of the bridge with archers at the rear and along the bridge.

Gabrella could hear the marching feet getting closer, she knew the wild creatures from the wall had now been replaced by the more organised troops.

She raised her sword above her head "My people, today we do not fight to defend this city, we are fighting for our people to survive, for our way of life, for good over evil. Not all of us will see the new dawning of a day but we must make sure that our children do, that our way of life survives." She raised her voice and shouted out "We fight now as the light fades before us, but we will not fade into the night, we will burn this unholy scourge from our realm, we will shine bright. Let our voices ring out in the darkness, let them know fear, FOR ARCANDRU!!"

Horns blasted, and cheers erupted from the troop's men and women side by side, Gabrella flew to the entrance to the palace just as the first ranks of the horde lined up on the opposite side of the square.

"FIRE!!" Stello shouted and the archers released their silver arrows that arced across the courtyard into the ranks of the Horde. Many fell but were straight away replaced by more and they continued their march forward.

Gabrella turned and entered the palace. Faria was waiting. "I have a plan," Gabrella said

"We are going to make a run for it," Gabrella said "I know some of us won't make it, but I think it's the only choice we have"

"How?" asked Faria

"The left hand side of the wall has been left fairly isolated, I will lead a hundred and fifty soldiers at the wall and try and draw them away as much as we can. You must then lead the civilians out, fly as high and as fast as you can away from here and head for Hanoria"

"Its madness, that will never work" exclaimed Faria

"Do you have a better idea?"

Faria shook his head

A messenger flew into the palace " Your highness they are at the bridge"

"Right we go now," Gabrella said.

There were a few thousand civilians and Gabrella knew they would be a massive flying target, she was just hoping some would escape.

She could hear the fighting raging on the bridge and she wondered if Stello still stood. She turned to Faria, "Goodbye my friend, I hope the wind carries you to safety"

Faria nodded "Goodbye my Queen"

Gabrella readied her troops, the civilians were mainly in the gardens at the rear of the castle, but they had also taken up positions on every window and balcony of the palace to try and escape.

Gabrella nodded and she flew out of the palace followed by her escort, the flew silently close to the floor hoping to avoid detection, so much of this plan relied on luck. They skimmed across trees and rooftops until they reached the wall, then they flew almost vertically straight up. As the appeared above the top of the wall they blasted their horns and flew down along the wall, killing the few troops stationed atop the wall.

Gabrella saw the breach in the wall and headed for it, she noticed the horde on the outside of the wall was following her along, she hoped Faria had started the exodus.

Back at the palace, Faria watched as his Queen flew along the top of the wall killing creatures as they went. He gave the signal and thousands of wings beat a soft strum as they took flight, gaining momentum as they flew. He saw children, men and women of all ages flying as fast and as hard as they could.

It was working the first few were beyond the wall, it was going to work. He looked back to his Queen and gasped.

Gabrella had flown straight down into the breach with her guard and they had stopped the flow into the city. They stood there, wings raised to the sky fighting this unnatural foe. They seemed to glow as more and more of the horde pushed forward. The brightness was almost blinding but slowly one by one they began to fall until Gabrella could be seen with just five remaining guards at her side.

Faria couldn't pull his eyes away.

Gabrella was tired, her arms ached from all the fighting, she had been cut a few times but nothing serious. She knew most of her guard lay dead around her, she chanced a glance at the palace and saw the exodus was working. A piercing screech echoed above the noise of the battle, Gabrella turned to see a creature in black pointing at her escaping people, she threw her sword, it cartwheeled around and around coming to rest in the visor of his helm, his cry stopped dead as he fell to the floor.

Weaponless Gabrella felt the first blow pierce her left shoulder, then her left thigh. Two arrows thudded into her chest and she dropped to her knees. She looked up to see a face of pain and hatred raise an axe above his head and she felt no more.

Faria saw his Queen fall and saw the Horde turn back towards the escape

"GO, GO, GO" He shouted as he took off

The sky was full of escapees trying to find the best route away from the city, then he noticed his people dropping from the sky, a small boy fell to his right a black arrow in his stomach.

"Nooooooo" he shouted as more and more fell

He noticed a group of about fifty had begun to fly up the face of the mountain, he knew no one had ever been able to fly that high but as he looked no one was getting away across the plain.

He beat his wings and began to climb the face of the mountain, he soon reached the group as he noticed about twenty were children, they were aiming for the clouds, surely sanctuary was in the clouds.

After what seemed forever he began to see the first wisps of clouds around him, he slowed down and allowed the group to vanish from sight.

He hovered here and turned to look at the city, he could see none of the civilians had made it out, bodies were stacked high along the wall like a giant pin cushion covered in arrows. He let out a sob as he saw motionless children lying broken on the walls. There were still a few cries of pain and anguish but the fighting had stopped, he could see the bridge had fallen, the great city of Arcandru belonged to the Horde. He blinked the tears away as he turned and continued his ascent.

The Great Battle

Silari looked down at the table, "Both cities had fallen so quickly, no one saw Faria or his group again, a few had managed to escape the city, troops who had been out on patrol and a few dwellings outside the city about three hundred in all and they met us on the plains of Allinon"

"It is here we had decided on a plan"

Silari looked at Straven "You should continue"

Straven nodded "My people studied magic in all its forms and the wisest of them all came up with a plan to banish the Hellions to a different realm where they could do no more harm"

"We would draw them onto the plains, the entire Horde and there we would cast the mightiest spell ever used and transport them to this other realm"

"It was designed to be a living thing in its own right and expand as needed, as bad as the Hellions were we all hoped they could be saved and returned to how we had known them, we would construct several portals across the land which would allow us to monitor the situation"

"Like Jacks gate," said Ben

Straven nodded "Yes exactly, each gate would have three seals, three locks, if you will and guardians, would be placed at each seal to protect them, the guardians were volunteers from the remaining realms, they gave up homes and families to sit waiting as statues in case they were needed"

"We knew that magic was getting harder to use and taking a greater toll on those who used it but we had no choice"

"About three days after the fall of Arcandru our scouts picked the Horde up entering the plains, we prepared for battle, the remaining survivors from Arcandru begged us to let them fight. And so the free people lined up against the monstrous Horde of Thrall"

The Horde spread itself across the plain, shrouded in a black mist, it rolled along like the waves lapping at the edge of the shore. Closer and closer it got until it came to a silent halt, no shouting, no screaming nothing but eerie silence.

Facing them were the combined armies of the other realms, at the rear stood Silari, Straven, Kron and their advisors.

"We cannot see their numbers" growled Kron "Or their formations"

"Maybe we can do something about that" Straven said nodding to his advisor

His advisor ran off to a group of about thirty men and women withstood in a circle meditating. A short conversation was had with one who nodded and left the circle followed one by one by the others.

They walked until they were in the midst of the army, they stood in a line both hands on their ornate staffs. They closed their eyes and the staffs began to glow, they raised them above their heads, small blue bolts of electricity crackling around them. A gentle breeze began behind them, slowly getting stronger and stronger.

By the time it hit the Horde it must have been travelling as it thudded against them making some stumble back a few steps. The mist began to be forced back, slowly at first then quicker and quicker getting thinner as it was blown away. Eventually, the mist was pushed back and disappeared.

Straven gasped and looked at Silari and Kron, "How is that possible?"

The Horde was huge and was four times the size of the combined force before them. Rank upon rank of creatures in jet black armour all varying in size and shape.

"My people have started the incantation but it will take us some time" Straven looked to the others.

"Ha let us go teach these Hellions a lesson in fighting," said Kron

"May Selendrial be with us all" Silari said as she mounted her white horse

"I will see you soon my friends," Straven said turning and walking away

Kron reached his troops and strode purposefully to the front line, he walked about ten feet past the front line and stared at the Horde, he swung his huge axe around as if he were warming up all the while keeping his gaze fixed forward.

He heard his second in command begin to chant "Kron, Kron, Kron, Kron", this spread out amongst his troops like ripples in the water, getting louder and louder, echoing around the plain. A horn blasted from the left and was answered from the right.

Kron smiled and turned to face his troops, he raised both hands and let out a huge battle cry.

He turned and ran towards the Horde his people took up the cry and rushed after him.

The Kandars charged at the Horde, as they got closer the middle section dropped back as if inviting them in. Arrows then arced over to pepper the onrushing Kandarians, however, the Kandarian's skin was thick and many arrows bounce off, this made the battle cries even louder.

Kron could see the trap unfolding before his eyes so just as they entered the now vacated space he spun to the left and crashed into the ranks of the Horde, his troops followed his lead and as they met it was like thunder, the crash of metal on metal, the cries of pain, the screams from the Hellions as the creatures now attacked.

Straven lined up his troops who were mainly archers and quick on the heels of Kron they fired volley after volley into the massed ranks of the Horde. Straven could see that the right side of the Horde was starting to close in around the Kandarians, he looked to the Elhuri, their ranks of cavalry sat waiting for something, couldn't Silari see what was happening.

He had no choice, he split his force in two and charged the first section at the right flank of the Horde, as they ran they continued to fire volley after volley into the mass of black before them, once they were close enough they pulled the two short swords from their backs and flew into the enemy.

The Hanori fought hard alongside the Kandarians, it was difficult fighting as everyone was so close together but it seemed like they were getting the upper hand, they seemed to be forcing the horde backwards. Volley after volley was still sailing over their heads from his remaining troops. Suddenly they stopped and Straven knew this meant the arrows had been used, a horn sounded from behind and the rest of his troops rushed to the fight.

Straven found himself side by side with Kron, he was covered in blood and swinging his axe left and right cleaving two or three Hellions at a time.

Suddenly the Hellions began to turn and run, Straven couldn't believe it, had they won anyway? He signalled for his men to hold formation, he saw Kron raise his axe signaling his troops to hold.

They cheered as the Hellions broke before them running away with what looked like fear in their red eyes. Then as the scene in front of him began to clear he saw it for what it was, a trap. The fleeing Hellions disappeared through ranks of more troops with what looked like spiders at the front. There mounted atop his huge beast sat Thrall.

Straven looked around him and then noticed how many of his people lay dead or wounded, ice cold fear ran through him, he looked around at Kron whos eyes just blazed with defiance.

The spiders moved forward and fired a black thread from their abdomens, it flew at the ranks of the troops in front spearing men and women as it went. Straven felt the crackle of energy behind him, he turned his head to see some of his magic users raising their staffs. They fired bolts of blue lightning that blocked or deflected most of the deadly threads, some still got through and there was nothing anyone could do about it.

Thrall shouted an order, his voice rolling like an avalanche across the plain. His troops charged forward. Straven and Kron braced themselves for the charge, as they closed a wind seemed to come from behind and Straven ducked as the Seraphs flew over his head firing silver arrows into the onrushing Horde, then the Horde was upon them, thrashing and snarling, these were fiercer and stronger than the others. Straven saw his troops falling quickly and he noticed that they were starting to encircle them.

The Seraphs landed to the right of them and held them back, they fought as if they were one being wings used to knock them over as another ducked underneath to slash and stab, it was the deadliest dance he had ever seen.

Kron's forces were being outflanked and he knew it, he pulled a horn from his belt and blew it, a long resonating blast that was answered from somewhere behind.

Then the earth began to shake and thunder rolled down from behind, the Elhuri were charging.

Line upon line of regimented cavalry charged with lances raised, the horses were large powerful war horses, armoured at the front and rear, a silver glistening cascade rode across the plains. Silari was in the middle, her great horse champing at the bit to join the battle.

They wheeled out to the left flank then turned back into the Horde. They hit the Horde full on, a huge explosion as the cavalry charged into the ranks of the Horde. Their lances piercing through the jet black armour, they crashed further and further into the ranks, passing the fighting Kandarians.

Suddenly horses began to fall and Kron saw the spiders were now shooting their threads into the ranks of the Elhuri horses, some riders fell with the horses, others leapt from the saddles into the ranks of the Horde fighting with their golden swords and small golden shields.

That's it Straven thought that's everyone, no more help.

He noticed Thrall himself was moving towards the battle, then the hairs on the back of his neck stood up and the air started to crackle around him.

This is it, he thought.

It's happening now. "Fall back" He shouted and blew his horn.

They tried to fall back but the fighting was so fierce it was impossible.

A small orb of light appeared amid the Horde and began to spread outward, enveloping Thrall but also some of the troops from the other realms. Straven turned and began to run followed by his troops, he hoped the others would do the same.

He looked around to see the orb envelope all the Seraphs along with some of Kron's force and a few Elhuri. The orb covered most of the Horde, there was a blinding flash as a shockwave boomed out from the orb knocking everyone over.

All that was left was a scorched mark in the ground. Straven hadn't got time to think there were still some Hellions left, there was still a battle to win.

Straven could see some of his troops had also disappeared in the blast of the orb. All around everyone was getting groggily to their feet and as they did so the fighting began again.

There were small pockets of Hellions left, these were soon dealt with by the combined force of the realms, the Hellions were confused and disorganised, there was no surrender, they did not try to retreat, they fought until the last one fell.

Straven stood surveying the battlefield, so many had died, he saw Kron and raised a sword in greeting, Kron nodded back. Straven was exhausted, his blue tunic was covered in blood and dirt, he sank to the floor and sat there, his eyes filled with tears as he contemplated the loss before him.

Reality

"Had it worked?" Jack asked

"Yes it had worked" Straven replied

"We initially had no way of knowing if it had or not, the magic users were exhausted and couldn't create a spell to see if it had, unfortunately, a lot of our people had been caught in the blast" Silari paused "all of the surviving Seraphs were gone, the only ones left on the field were already dead"

"So when did you find out?" asked Ben

"Some weeks later we finally managed to muster a spell that allowed us to travel briefly to the other side" Straven looked at the children one by one "We travelled to your world, what we found was that a side effect of the spell was that every creature transported lost a lot of their memories, they retained some but not enough to remember their past, their memories were almost dreamlike. A very large number had not survived the transportation, just a few from each realm that had been at the battle, unfortunately, Thrall was one who survived."

Straven looked down at his hands "We could not transport our people back, we had to leave them, all we could do was observe"

Silari spoke "We found that as we travelled to your world it created a portal that could not be closed, so we had to create a gate with guardians to protect each gateway"

"Like the one in Jacks garden, with the statues," Grace said

"Exactly" Straven replied "As we observed your world we found at first the realms split apart to make their homes, the Seraphs were the fewest in number as the years went on we saw less and less of them. Thrall and his Hellions could not change who they were and began to try to destroy everything around them, he had no magic so could not create anymore but he seemed to be able to influence weak minded individuals."

Straven looked at Kron "They hunted down Kron's people first until non survived, they became a thing of myth and legend in your world, the giants"

Grace gasped "Of course, Silari's people must be elves"

Silari nodded "My people also disappeared from your world but lived on in your stories. Straven's people seemed to adapt best to the new world, although we did see the occasional one still able to practice some degree of magic it too was eventually lost"

"Ha" Kron snorted "Only reason they did so well was that they bred like rabbits"

Straven laughed as did Silari, the sound somewhat unnatural in the tent.

"Yes my people thrived in the new world and grew to outnumber Thrall and his Hellions, they eventually disappeared into the earth and began to influence your world from below"

"From below? Is that why we call it Hell?" Ben said questioningly

"Yes" Silari replied "Your names for Thrall vary but I think the most famous is the Devil or Satan"

"WOW, that is crazy," Ben said

"Who were the ones in our history who could do magic then?" Grace asked

"AH," Straven said "You have an enquiring mind, well there have been a few. It has been hundreds of years since the last as you concentrate on your science. I think the last one we know of was Merlyn"

"What!!" Shouted Jack "You are joking that's just a myth," he said as his words trailed off with realisation set in.

"The Seraphs?" Ben began

"Yes you call them angels, we do not know where they went, but occasionally when things are really bad one or two of them will appear to help your kind out" Straven smiled

"So Thrall is the one that causes the evil in our world?" Jack asked

"To some degree yes, he suggests things from what we can tell and some take up the suggestions some don't" Straven looked solemnly at Jack, "We think that he has somehow realised our world exists and he has found your portal so we need to stop him"

Straven paused and looked from face to face "Jack, Grace, Ben, unfortunately, it is your task to stop him"

"What can we do?" Jack asked

"We are not exactly sure, we knew of the Kitari Selendrial told us, but the way it talks to us now is vague and full of questions. We knew you were arriving but not when or who" Silari explained

"We were chased by some shadow things" Ben blurted out

Straven's headshot round "WHAT!!" he shouted, "You wait until now to tell us, child!!"

"Straven" Silari admonished him

"I'm sorry, forgive me, please explain"

Ben looked a little shaken at the outburst "We were chased through a park but we managed to get away, then before we went through the gate the guardians were fighting"

Kron banged his hand down on the table, pushed back his chair and stormed out.

"Kron wait, excuse me, children, I must attend to this straight away" Straven also stood and followed Kron out of the tent.

"Sorry" Ben whispered

"Its ok" Silari replied, we are all very much on edge lately.

"There's nothing we can do," Jack said

"There is I am sure of it, or you would not be here, unfortunately, I do not know what that is, that is why tomorrow we travel to the tree," Silari said

"What?" Grace asked

Silari clapped her hands and once again Phoebe entered "Take our guests to their room, make sure they have everything they need"

"Of course your highness" Phoebe turned to them "Follow me please"

Jack, Ben and Grace all rose and followed Phoebe from the room.

They followed her down a corridor and into another room.

As they entered the room Jack was amazed how big it was, there were three small rooms off it each with a bed inside. On the floor were luxurious fur rugs and piles of pillows, in the middle, was a table low down on the ground covered in food and drink.

"These are your rooms," Phoebe said "Please have what you need, if you need anything else there is a small bell on the table for you to ring"

"So we have to stay here then?" Grace asked suspiciously

"Yes please do not leave your quarters, there are fresh clothes in each room for you if you desire" Phoebe then turned and disappeared out of the room pulling down a flap of material over the doorway.

"I'm starving," Ben said jumping onto the cushions by the table, he grabbed what looked like a chicken leg stared at it shrugged, and began to eat

"Shall we?" Jack asked Grace gesturing with his hand

Grace smiled and sat down next to the table.

"So what we thinking," Ben said through a full mouth grabbing various foods and piling onto his plate

"No idea," said Jack

"It all seems so far fetched, but here we are," Grace said

"I doubt there is anything we can do," Jack said "Perhaps I should try to talk to Silari"

"You think?" Ben asked

"Worth a try I suppose," Grace said

Jack looked at the little silver bell, he reached out and took it in his hand and rang it.

Phoebe appeared almost immediately.

"Can I see Silari please?" Jack asked

"Of course, just you Jack?" Jack nodded "Follow me then please"

Jack followed her along a different corridor to another room

"Please wait here," Phoebe said as she vanished inside through the curtained door.

The curtain was pulled back "You can go in"

Phoebe smiled as she walked past Jack, Jack entered the room. It was a smaller room with sofas in it, each one was covered in a kind of fur, a fire crackled in the middle but no smoke came from it.

Silari was sat on a sofa staring into the fire. Jack closed the curtain behind him and the movement broke Silari from her thoughts.

"Ah Jack, you wanted to speak to me? Please sit down"

Jack sat on the sofa next to her.

"What can I do for you?" Silari smiled a gentle smile of kindness and compassion

"I er, I don't" Jack began

Silari stood and came and sat next to Jack, she took his hand in hers "It's ok, go on"

"I can't help you"

"Why do you think that Jack"

Jacks hand involuntarily gripped his leg

"I erm, had a fall, I have a, er my legs not better yet"

Silari smiled again at him "Jack you are chosen, not by me, by Selendrial herself"

"But I" Jack wanted to say a hundred things but nothing seemed to want to come out, he knew as soon as this conversation was over so was his part in this.

"Please Jack, everything is fine," Silari said squeezing his hand

"I have a condition" Jack blurted it out

"A condition?" Silari asked

"Yes," Jack looked down at his legs and pulled his hand away from Silari.

"My bones aren't as strong as they should be, they break easily"

Silari took his hand again "Jack that does not matter, you are Kitari, you are chosen"

Jack raised his head and locked eyes with Silari, he saw nothing but compassion and kindness, he felt tears fill his eyes.

"I'm not going to be able to help, its too risky, if anything happens"

"Jack my child, we all have something that defines us, that makes us who we are, whether it is good or bad, its how we use it that makes the difference. Do not let this be you, do not be a condition, be Jack, be the strong young man you are. You should be proud of yourself and how you cope. You cannot see it but it has made you strong in other ways.

I see compassion in you, empathy for others you are not the condition Jack Knight, you are Kitari, you are chosen for a reason. Be proud, be strong and let your strength guide you"

Jack stared into her eyes, he couldn't break his gaze, he had never felt like this before, he had always thought his condition ruled his life and yes it had stopped him doing some things but Silari was right it had made him who he was.

"Thank you," Jack said

"It is my pleasure, do not think you cannot help, you have a large role to play yet. Now go join your friends and get some rest"

Phoebe entered the room to take Jack back, Jack stood and followed her out. Just as he got to the door Silari said "Oh Jack, I think you should tell your friends"

Jack felt himself nodding as he followed Phoebe out.

He got back to their room, Ben and Grace still sat on the floor, Ben was still eating.

"Are you ok?" Grace got up and came straight over to Jack.

"Yea I'm ok"

"You need something to eat," Ben said smiling

Jack smiled back

"Come sit down tell us what happened," Grace said taking Jacks' arm.

They both sat down at the table, "What did she say?" Grace asked looking worryingly at Jack.

Jack took a deep breath "She didn't say much, I erm just needed to tell her about something"

"What?" Grace looked at Jack

"I said to her that there was no point me going anywhere"

"Why?" Ben said

"I have a medical condition and I'm not gonna be any use, in fact, I could be more of a hindrance than any help"

"What's wrong with you?" Ben said

"Ben!" Grace exclaimed

"It's ok" Jack found himself smiling

"I have a problem with my bones, they break easily"

"How easily?" asked Grace

"Well I first broke my leg when I was two since then I've had twelve other breaks, the last one not long ago"

"Oh Jack, I didn't know," Grace said

"Cant you drink more milk?" Ben said

"No its not calcium it's the fibres that aren't strong enough, I have type 4"
"How many types are there?" Grace asked

"A few of the others are a lot worse"

"Worse than yours and you've had twelve breaks" Ben gasped

"So you see, I'm not going to be any help at all"

"Don't be silly Jack, we made it this far together we arent splitting up now!" Grace said smiling

"Yeah buddy, we are in this together, want some chicken?" Ben offered a chicken leg to Jack

"Well I hope its chicken" Ben said looking at it

Jack and Grace both laughed and for a long time, Jack felt like he had real friends again.

Selendrial

The next morning they all got dressed into the clothes that had been left for them. All three of them were dressed in light green shirts with a dark green leather vest with gold buttons, dark green trousers and brown boots.

As they stepped out of their rooms ben said "We look like Robin Hood" and they all laughed

They were still laughing as Phoebe entered. "Ah good, your ready follow me please"

As they followed her Grace said, "How long will it take to get there?"

Phoebe reached the door and gestured for them to go through, as they passed through they heard her say "We are already here"

They stepped through and out into the sunshine, the warmth from the sun hit them and birds were singing. The air smelt sweet with the scent of a million flowers.

Silari stood waiting for them in an elegant green and silver dress, she wore a thin silver band around her forehead.

"Welcome Kitari to Selendrial" she raised her hand and gestured behind them, they turned to follow her gaze and were amazed to see a huge tree behind them.

"Its smaller" Grace said

"Yes it is smaller than when you saw it last," Silari said sadly

Even though it was smaller it still stood hundreds of feet tall, they could see the crack in the trunk and the silver shimmering trunk seemed dimmer than they remembered.

"Come it is time," Silari said to them

An ornate coach pulled up, it looked like it was made from tree roots all twisted together to form a round shape, each side had two windows and a door, there were strands of silver woven into the twisted wood making it gleam in the light. They climbed inside this was luxurious and elegant with large cushioned seats. It was pulled along by two beautiful pure white horses.

As they travelled along Jack looked out of the window, all he could see was green luxurious meadows filled with flowers and trees of all description, birds sang and swooped through the air.

The coach came to a halt and they all got out, Silari walked up to the tree and placed her forehead against the trunk and began to say something none of them could make out. She stopped and took a step backwards and turned to look at them.

After a few moments, Jack said "Should we do something?"

"Selendrial will speak when she is ready," Silari said

A part of the tree's trunk began to shimmer and blur and the three of them stared open mouthed as a doorway appeared in front of them.

Jack saw a frown cross Silaris face

"Where does what....." Her voice trailed off as she turned to look at the tree.

"That," said Ben pointing to the doorway

"I don't know it never happened before," Silari said in wonder

They all tried to look inside but as with the tent, you could see nothing at all.

"Selendrial is waiting children," said Silari

"What you're not coming?" asked Jack

Silari shook her head a gestured the children forward.

Jack looked at Ben and then Grace, neither of them moved just stared straight ahead. Jack took a step forward thinking they would follow but they remained where they were. Jack continued to take a step at a time until he was a step away from the doorway, he looked back at Ben and Grace smiled and stepped through the entrance.

As he stepped through he again became a bit disorientated and his vision was a little fuzzy, slowly it cleared to reveal a corridor winding up into the tree. It was illuminated by streams of silver light running along the walls. He took another step forward just as Grace appeared closely followed by Ben.

They were blinking crazily to clear their vision.

"Well can this place get any weirder," said Ben

"It's quite beautiful," said Grace smiling

"Well there's only one way to go," said Jack and he turned and made his way along the corridor.

Strangely Jack felt at ease as the three of them walked along the winding corridor slowly climbing upwards. After what felt like ages as Jacks's leg had begun to hurt slightly they reached a door.

The door was similar to the gate in his garden with the tree carved into it and embossed in silver, Jack looked for a handle but there was non, he gently pushed on it but nothing happened.

"Great well that was a waste of time," said Ben "Let me try" Ben pushed on the door, gently at first then he rammed it with his shoulder

"Ben!!" said Grace "What are you doing?"

"Trying to open the door obviously," he said with a smirk

"Let's all try together," said Grace

They all positioned themselves by the door, Jack and Grace with their hands on the door Ben with his shoulder pressed against it.

"After three" began Grace "One, two" Ben was already pushing hard with his shoulder, as Grace said three he put his hand on the door to steady himself.

The silver tree on the door flashed brightly and it swung open.

Ben fell forward and landed with a thump on the floor, he jumped up shouting "I'm ok, I'm ok"

The room was round and fairly large, there were seven chairs around the outside, one was larger and more ornate than the others. In the middle of the room was a large stone, protruding from the stone were seven swords, each sword had a silver blade and a golden hilt. Each hilt had a different animal on the end.

They stood there looking around the room.

"Do we get a sword then?" asked Ben

Jack shrugged, "Shall I try?" Ben continued

"No" Grace replied

There was a low hum beginning to vibrate from the walls, slowly getting louder. The air began to feel charged and small bolts of lightning flickered around.

"Here we go again" sighed Ben

The noise got louder and the air more charged until suddenly there was a loud crack like lightning followed by a flash. None of them was prepared for it so the light blinded them for a while, slowly their gaze cleared, their eyes went wide as they noticed a figure sitting on the largest chair in the room.

It was a woman, she had dark skin and long silver hair, she wore an emerald green dress. Jack noticed she had no shoes on her feet, he looked at her face, she was beautiful and had a look of peace on her face even though her eyes were closed.

She opened her eyes and looked at each of the three children and smiled, the most beautiful, serene smile filled with love and happiness. Her eyes danced with specks of silver.

"Welcome," she said smiling "I am Selendrial"

Selendrial

"You're the tree?" asked Grace

"Ah" she smiled "I am but a part of the tree, please sit"

The three children sat next to each other on the chairs more or less directly opposite.

"Silari said the tree was Selendrial," said Ben looking puzzled "all in good time, would you like food or drink?"

"Hell yeah" exclaimed Ben

"Ben!!" said Jack and Grace together

Selendrial smiled and waved her hand, a round table appeared with a hole in the middle where the stone stuck through. On the table was all sorts of food and drink, which Ben soon began to tuck into.

"Are you not the tree?" asked Jack

"As I said before I am but a part of it, my brothers, sisters and I reside in the tree, the tree is our father"

"What!" said Ben spluttering through a mouthful of food "We are sitting in your Dad??"

Grace punched Ben on the arm

"OW!"

"Hush," said Grace

"Anu is my Father and he created everything, he created our world and then my brothers, sisters and I. I have three sisters and two brothers. My brothers are Adam and Geddron, my sisters Rhea, Leto and Sulis"

"Are they all here now?" Jack asked looking around

"Some are, some are not"

"You see our father left us here, he does not speak to us any longer, he has transcended away from us leaving us to look after his creations. For a long time we explored the world, we explored everything and everywhere. Each of us became fascinated with different aspects of this beautiful existence. We were happy, happy together as a family"

Selendrial paused as if lost in thought, lost in distant memories.

"Then they appeared, we assumed our father had created them for us, six races, six races one for each of us to look over and keep safe. We each chose a race, no one selected the same, our father knew us so well. We watched over them all and kept them safe and well"

"Silari never mentioned your brothers or sisters," Grace said

"They do not know of them, they do not know of this which I am telling you now"

"What? Why?" Jack said

"There was no need, they had the tree, we selected a few from each realm to live here at the tree and to these, we revealed my name and my name only. We did not require worship or gifts or homage, just peace and prosperity"

"So what happened?" Ben asked with a wry smile

"Ben!" said Grace

"What? Something always happens, no one can be happy forever"

Selendrial nodded at Ben "You are correct. My brother Geddron, he chose the Hellions as his realm to watch over. They were an amazing people full of life and energy, they created beautiful artworks and their homes were the most beautiful in all the realms."

"Geddron my brother, ha it has been a while since I spoke his name, he was the most inquisitive of us all, always out searching and exploring and always laughing. It happened quite suddenly, we noticed his moods beginning to change, less laughter and more prone to anger. He seemed darker somehow."

"Anyway he accused the other realms of encroaching on his realm and trying to take from him. Obviously, it was all ridiculous, but he wouldn't listen"

Selendrial closed her eyes and waved her hand, over the stone appeared what looked like a swirling pool of water. The water slowly settled to reveal the room they were now sitting in, Selendrial sat in the chair next to the one she was sitting in now. A figure walked in dressed in black, his long black hair shining in the light, his clothes seemed to be made of shadows and almost swirled around him. He was tall and imposing and powerfully built, then the chairs began to fill one by one.

"Brother," Selendrial said to the black figure

"Sister" Geddron almost spat the word out

"What is that you wear?" Selendrial said pointing to a sword hanging from his belt

"It is for my protection"

"Who do you think means you harm brother?"

"Ha, you all want what is mine"

"Please sit little brother, let us speak" replied Adam. Adam had long blond hair, his face was strong and imposing, he had green eyes that danced with gold. He wore a simple tunic across his broad frame, his arms and hands were huge and imposing.

"I cannot, I have things to attend to"

With that, he shimmered and disappeared.

"He grows worse" sighed Rhea she too had golden hair which was held back with a silver band. Her face was pale, her cheekbones were as fine as her delicate chin, her eyes were blue with flecks of gold and her lips a deep red. She also wore a simple tunic of silver and gold on her slender frame.

"I do not understand what is wrong with him and now he brings a weapon with him, hear of all places" added Adam with a hint of anguish.

"We need our own weapons," said Leto. Leto looked very much like the Kandarians, she had short brown hair, her face was broad, her eyes a dark brown flecked with gold, yet still, it held a beauty there. Her physique was strong and powerful looking, more akin to Adam than her sisters.

"We do not" replied Adam, "I have nothing to fear from my brother"

"Alas, I fear that is no longer our brother," said Rhea

"I agree with Leto" the final figure spoke

"But Sulis you can't mean that," said Adam

"I am afraid I do," said Sulis, she was slender and beautiful just like Rhea, her hair was as black as ebony. Her eyes were almost catlike finishing at a point, they were a steel grey colour and flashed with silver.

"I agree," said Selendrial

"I do not know how to make a weapon" exclaimed Adam

"But our people will," Selendrial said

"So we got each realm to fashion us each a sword, each one different but each one special in its own right. We observed as each one was made and then we took them from each realm and imbued it with a part of each of us.

Finally, we created a sword between us, each of us crafted a part and then we combined it with our magic" Selendrial spoke as they watched the swords come into being.

"The swords were placed into the stone so that only we could withdraw them, and we hoped we would never need them"

Selendrial sighed "The last time we were all together in this room was a very long time ago, we didn't realise how bad Geddron had become, we should have watched him more closely. Our little brother, the smiling laughing inquisitive bundle of joy was no more"

The water suddenly came to life again and they were back in the room. They were all there except Geddron.

A black mist appeared near to the stone in the centre of the room, it swirled and danced with crackles of red and slowly a figure appeared. Geddron stood there, dressed from head to toe in jet black armour, his eyes danced with red flame. He removed his helm and his face was pure hatred.

The faces of his brothers and sisters were in complete shock.

"Geddron?" Sulis whispered, "What has become of you?"

Geddron laughed "Why do you all look so shocked, do you not love me anymore"

"Of course little brother, now and until the end of time," said Adam as he stood

Geddron took a step back and almost stumbled over the stone

"What is this? Do you seek harm to me brothers and sisters" his voice was full of loathing

"Of course not dear brother, we are just worried," said Selendrial

Adam took another step forward and Geddron drew his sword "Stay back big brother, I have no time for your games today"

"Stop it now," Leto said to Geddron

Sulis stood up and moved towards Geddron "Brother do not be afraid, we mean you no harm"

Geddron spun around, Sulis eyes went wide and she gasped. Geddron looked down his sword had pierced his sister's stomach.

Geddron looked down at the sword then at the face of his sister "no" he whispered. Sulis started to fall and Geddron grabbed her, he lowered her down to the floor.

"Noooooooo" Adam bellowed from behind, Geddron spun around.

Geddrons face was a mask of sorrow and regret a tear ran down his cheek.

"Adam no!" shouted Selendrial as Adam rushed forward.

Instinctively Geddron thrust his sword forward stabbing Adam in the chest, Adams eyes filled with tears "Oh little brother" and crashed to the floor.

Selendrial, Rhea and Leto all grabbed their swords from the stone and flew at Geddron, the fighting was fierce, a flurry of blades and blocks and counters. Slowly they seemed to be getting the edge over Geddron when suddenly he smiled and launched a vicious attack, he knocked Rhea to the floor stunned and threw Selendrial against the wall.

Rhea attacked and it looked as though she may win when Geddron flicked his wrist and her sword flew from her hand. Rhea fell to the floor and Geddron stood over her sword raised.

"Nooooooo" it was Adam who shouted "No more" he raised his hand and in a blinding flash Geddron vanished.

The whirling pool in front of them vanished abruptly.

"I lost a sister and both brothers that day" Selendrial managed somehow to speak through her tears.

Jack looked at Ben who had stopped eating and then Grace whose eyes had filled with tears.

"We do not know exactly what happened next, but we think Geddron consumed Thrall turning him evil and then set about twisting and deforming all of his people. Then he attacked the two realms that reminded him most of his brother and sister."

"Why didn't you help them?" Jack said softly

"We were trying, we had given the Hanori the idea for the spell to banish them, however, we created the other world, your world and it took so much of our power we had very little left"

"We did not know that in creating that world we had also created a life, a human life and could not comprehend how you would thrive."

"So Thrall or Geddron whoever it is, is in our world?" Grace asked

Selendrial nodded "Yes, when he was banished there his power was very low his army was all but destroyed, some of the people from our world were also trapped in your world, but very few in number and they soon died out."

"So our ancient civilisations would have lived with the people who were stuck there?" Grace said

"Yes you still talk about them today in your books, giants were the Kandar, wizards were the Hanori, elves were the Elhuri and the Seraphs are your angels."

"But there is no such thing as magic," said Grace

"Tell Dynamo that," said Ben

Grace rolled her eyes.

"There was once, but it too died out, the last was Merlyn in your world. You replaced it with your science and they cannot occupy the same realm at the same time" Selendrial explained

"So wheres Geddron now?" Jack asked

"As you know he took his Hellions deep underground, it is where your word Hell comes from. He learned he could influence you, humans, without showing himself, all the while waiting and growing in strength"

"Er waiting for what?" Ben said biting an apple

"To return home and finish what he started," Selendrial said

"Once he is strong enough Geddron and his army will conquer your world and then he will turn his gaze to us, he must be close because he is already attacking the portals," Selendrial said with concern

"Hang on a minute," said Grace "The army of Geddron?"

"What?" asked Jack

"Army of Geddron, Armageddon!" gasped Grace

There was a stunned silence from the children as they contemplated what Grace had just said.

"What is Armageddon?" Asked Selendrial

"Only the end of the frickin world" blurted Ben

"What can we do?" Jack asked to no one in particular

"You are the Katari, you are the chosen, you will restore order and balance to our realm" Selendrial answered

"What about our world?" Grace asked

"To that, I cannot say, we created your world yes, but" she looked away from them "but we did not look after it as we should, I am sorry"

"Its ok everyone calling us chosen but we are three kids and Jacks, well Jacks erm delicate," said Ben

"Thanks," said Jack wryly

"No problem," said Ben the reply going straight over his head.

"Bens right, what can we do?" Grace said

"This room is for the Katari, those swords are for the Katari" Selendrial explained

"Well someone cant add up," said Ben

Jack shot him a stare and Grace kicked him in the leg "What now?" Ben exclaimed

"I will explain it as best I can to you," said Selendrial

"When we realised what was happening in the other world we decided between us to try and hinder Geddron as much as we could. Rhea and Leto went to your world to observe. Every time evil tried to take over your world we helped to stop it. Our powers were useless over there but we helped when we could with influence and ideas. At first, they would be gone for a while then they would return, but alas I have not seen or heard from my sisters for a very long time"

"That's cause of all the crap everywhere, no one likes anyone anymore" Ben explained

"My sisters did what they could like I said we tried to set up a Golden Age with the help of Merlyn and Atoir"

"Arthur," said Ben

"Sorry?" Said Selendrial

"Ben for goodness sake!" sighed Grace

"I'm just saying it was Merlyn and Arthur, he was not French!"

"Please carry on," said Jack to Selendrial

"Yes of course, but Geddron stopped us this time, what a beautiful realm it could have been. After this, we decided that we would be unable to stop him alone but had no idea what we could do. Then we all had a dream, we are sure Anu spoke to use, we dreamt of seven warriors pulling swords from this stone and they would create balance and order. They would be chosen when needed most and we would know when the time came who they were. The Katari"

"So there is seven Katari?" Asked Jack

Selendrial nodded.

"And do you know who the others are?"

Selendrial shook her head "I can guide you as to where to go to find them, but that is all"

"I'm sorry but we can't do anything even with a sword," Jack said

"Do not underestimate yourselves, you are chosen, you were always chosen, this path has been set for you hundreds of years before you were born," Selendrial said

"You must each take a sword, I do not know which sword belongs to who, but you will know which is yours. The five around the outside are our swords, belonging to each of us each with some of our powers and strength contained. The seventh is the sword that will lead the Katari"

"And what happens if we pull a sword out?" asked Ben

"I do not know" replied Selendrial

"Sooooo who wants to go first?" asked Ben

"I will," said Grace quietly

Selendrial raised her hand and the table, food and drink disappeared.

"Aw," said Ben

Grace stood up and moved over to the stone, she looked at the swords, they were all similar except from the animal at the end of the hilt. There was a horse, a panther, a tiger, an eagle, a dragon and the one in the middle was a lion. She reached out her hand and instantly felt a pull towards the swords.

Grace gasped

"You ok," said Jack leaping to his feet

"Yes, yes I'm fine sorry," said Grace

She reached her hand out again and closed her eyes, she felt her hand brush against a sword, then another on the third time electricity coursed up and down her arm. She reached down caressing the hilt, she knew straight away it was the horse one. She closed her fingers around the hilt and slowly began to pull it from the stone.

Jack watched as Grace pulled the eagle sword from the stone, once it was clear lightning arced across the room, the air crackled around Grace. Jack and ben watched open-mouthed as Grace began to change, she began to grow older and taller all the while this happened the light around here grew in brightness and intensity until it was too strong to look at.

"Grace!!" Jack and Ben both shouted at the same time.

Jack stood there blinking trying to clear the blinding light from his eyes, eventually, it began to fade, and there before him was Grace, but not Grace. It was Grace as a young woman and boy had she grown, she was at least seven feet tall. Her hair was long and she wore a green tunic and brown leather boots, at her waist was the sword in its scabbard.

She opened her eyes and smiled.

"I am so next," said Ben

"Wait," said Jack "Grace are you ok?"

"Yes I'm fine, it is all clear now, when I drew the sword everything was explained to me"

"Right I'm doing it," said Ben

Before Jack could say anything Grace had sat down and Ben was striding over to the stone. He stood there and closed his eyes, doing exactly the same as Grace. His hand eventually stopped and came to rest on the tiger one. He slowly pulled it from the stone and the light show began again.

Eventually, the light faded and Jacks gaze began to clear, there stood Ben, easily as old as Grace now was but he was even taller easily eight feet and he was huge, his arms, shoulders, hands were enormous.

He wore a blue tunic with the sword hanging at his side.

He opened his eyes and tried looking at himself.

"Oh hell yeah I'm ripped he said pulling up his shirt"

"Look at this Jack" Bens voice boomed "pow, pow," he said flexing his muscles.

He bounded over to Grace and sat down beside her with a huge grin on his face, his hand resting on his sword hilt.

"Jack" Selendrial urged.

"I don't know," said Jack. How can I possibly do this he thought, why do I need bigger bones to break.

"Jack, do not be afraid, all will become clear" reassured Selendrial

Jack walked over to the stone and stared at the beautifully made swords, I can't do this he thought but found himself closing his eyes. Instantly he felt a pull forwards as if something had taken his hand and was moving it forward. He felt a sword brush against his hand, not that one, he felt another and straight away electricity shot up his arm. This is the one he thought, he slid his hand down and grabbed the hilt, taking a deep breath. There was a blinding flash and he found himself sitting under a tree in the blazing sun, birds sang overhead, a small stream bubbled past just in front of him. The smell of flowers and grass filled his head, he closed his eyes and breathed in deeply.

A voice shocked him out of his thoughts

"May I sit?"

Jack spun his head round to see a tall figure standing beside him, he could not make out his face as the sun was blinding him. Jack just nodded.

The figure sat beside him "Hello Jack, I am Adam"

Instantly Jack recognised him as Selendrial's brother, "But your"

"Yes I am dead, or dead as you think of it, but none of us really die Jack, we just move on"

"Where am I?"

"We thought this would be easier for you whilst the transformation takes place"

"Transformation? You mean like Ben and Grace"

"Yes exactly, I have much to say but you must listen and pay attention"

Jack nodded

"Grace has been chosen to represent the Elhuri, she knows what she has to do I have spoken to her already. Ben is to represent Kandar he also knows what is expected, they both have an idea now of what they are capable of but some learning must happen as you go"

"Who do I represent?" Asked Jack

"Jack you are special, you have been given the highest honour but the greatest burden. The Lion sword chose you, you represent Anu and will be the leader of the Katori."

"I can't, I'm not strong enough," Jack said looking down at his feet

"Jack your strength comes from inside, do not worry about the weakness of your body for whilst you are transformed this will no longer affect you"

Jacks eyes shot up and gazed into Adams daring him to say that again.

"Don't mess with me!" Jack said with a hint of anger

"Jack I am not, magic is a powerful thing and it will protect you whilst you are transformed. If you journey back to your own world you will not be able to transform only unless magic returns to your world."

"I, I can't believe it" whispered Jack, unable to control his emotions

"Now you must listen, for our time is short. The sword grants you many powers, when you draw the sword you will gain magical armour to cover your body. The sword can be changed into whatever weapon you wish, you just have to will it. Your powers are stronger together and will be at their height once the six are together."

"Six?"

"Yes, you three must find the others for the swords. Two are in this world, you must look for the signs to guide you, one is in your world, it is up to you whom you find first"

"You must find the others and bring them here to retrieve their swords, then and only then can you face Geddron. The fate of our world and yours rests on you"

"Am I going to be, er bigger when I go back?"

Adam nodded "Yes, it will seem a bit strange at first but you will adapt quickly"

The sun seemed suddenly brighter and Jack blinked against it

"Our time is up young Lion king, I wish you luck in your quests, farewell"

The light blinded Jack and he closed his eyes. Immediately he was back in the room trying to clear his vision and boy did he feel different.

His vision slowly cleared and he looked down at his feet which were a really long way away, he held out his hands, they were huge. He could see he was wearing a silver and green tunic with the sword at his waist.

He looked over to Ben and Grace who were both smiling.

"This is the dogs!" said Ben

They all laughed a familiar but very unfamiliar sound.

Jack turned to speak to Selendrial but she was no longer there.

"She vanished when you pulled the sword." Explained Ben "I can't believe you got the main one, you jammy git"

Grace stood up and moved over to Jack "Are you ok?"

Jack knew exactly what she was asking "Yes I'm fine," he said with a grin.

Ben cottoned on "No way, you mean your not, you know fragile. I mean you certainly don't look fragile"

"No," said Jack with a sense of elation, he wanted to jump, run, or even just fall on the floor to try it out.

"Do you know about the others?" asked Jack

They both nodded.

"Any ideas on how to find them?"

They both shook their heads.

"Two in this world and one in ours," Ben said out loud

"I say we find the ones here first, get used to these," she said holding her arms up as if showing off a new coat.

"The swords that are left belong to the Hanori, the Dwafen and the Seraphs" Grace stated

"Do you remember how some of the Dwafen went into the mountain and some of the Seraphs went up into the mountains?"

"Yeah" Jack and Ben answered

"Well perhaps they survived, perhaps we need to go there to find them"

"To Arcandru and Stonehaven?" Jack exclaimed

"Well, it's a start" agreed Ben.

Revelation

The three friends made their way back out of the tree, on the way out they decided not to tell Silari and the others about Anu and the gods just yet.

They strode out into the brilliant sunshine and saw Silari, Straven and Kron awaiting their return. As they left the tree and shout went up and swords were drawn and spears pointed at them. At first, they were a bit confused until Jack realised how different they looked.

"Wait, it's us Silari" Jack shouted holding out his hands

A confused expression crossed Silari's face before realisation sank in and the guards were stood down.

"How is this possible" Silari said to them.

"We have much to discuss and very little time" Jack almost commanded as he spoke

Silari, Straven and Kron all bowed and ushered them to a table and chairs set up in the meadow.

Jack explained what had occurred inside the tree and the tasks that now lay ahead of them.

"We are going to Arcandru and Stonehaven to look for the last of the two peoples" Jack explained

"There is only death there," said Silari

"We must go there and see for ourselves" replied Grace

"You will need a guide" Straven stated "I will take you there"

Jack nodded and turned to Kron and Silari

"You must prepare for war, for no matter what happens war is coming to your world and ours"

Jack felt as though he had changed, not just on the outside but now he felt a sense of responsibility, a real sense of urgency. For the first time in a while, he thought of his parents and hoped they were ok.

Straven strode from his tent to his horse, loading his equipment and supplies, as he looked up he saw Kron striding over to him.

"Straven" Kron nodded in greeting

"Kron, how goes the preparations?"

"Well, messengers have been sent but we do not know where to muster so we are gathering on the great plains as before" Kron paused looking troubled

"Do you trust these children" he emphasised the children as he spoke.

"Children" Straven chuckled looking over to where Jack, Grace and Ben were stood talking to Silari.

"You know what I mean" Kron chided

"Yes, yes I do, their hearts are pure and look at them, if that doesn't make you believe in them I don't know what will"

Kron grunted, shrugged and walked away.

Jack looked up to see Straven coming over, he nodded a greeting.

"We will be ready in an hour" he informed them

"Good" Jack replied

"I have a question" Ben blurted out "Right we have these new bodies that apparently can do cool stuff, but we don't know what or how to even fight with a sword"

"I think that we will know when we need to" answered Grace

"But I've not used a sword since Junior school" Ben exclaimed pulling his sword from its scabbard.

As he pulled it clear a silver tree appeared on his chest and glowed brightly, his body was slowly covered in armour, finally, his head was covered with a helmet with the tiger ornament at the front and a white plume flowing from it.

"Hell yeah!! I'm like Iron Man" he shouted swinging his sword.

"But can you fight" Kron had appeared from his tent holding a large sword

"I er" Ben stuttered as Kron let out a roar and charged. Jack and Grace went to step forward but Straven grabbed their arms.

"We all need to know," he said to them.

Kron rushed at Ben and swung his sword, Ben parried the first blow but he was unprepared for it so staggered back. Kron rushed again, Ben sidestepped away and swung his sword, Kron blocked easily.

For all the shouting it was soon obvious Kron was going easy on him and Ben was growing in confidence. They cut and thrust and parried, backwards and forwards, until Kron smiled, he swung an overhanded blow, Ben dodged it but Kron feinted the other way and tripped Ben over. Kron raised his sword and ben raised his arm in defence, suddenly a shield grew from his wrist and took the blow. Ben rolled away and sprang to his feet crouched in a defensive posture now with a shield and a sword.

Kron charged swinging a blow which Ben blocked with his shield, the block spun Kron around, as he turned back to face Ben he stopped dead, Bens sword was an inch from his throat.

Kron smiled then let out a booming laugh. "Well you can fight"

Ben smiled and sheathed his sword, immediately the armour disappeared. He turned to Jack and Grace

"You really need to try that"

Jack looked at Grace and shrugged, he pulled his sword closely followed by Grace and within seconds they were both covered in armour, Grace with the horse mantle Jack with the lion.

"Guess we are ready then," Jack said sheathing his sword.

"We got to Stonehaven first," said Straven

"Has anyone been there since you know the war?" asked Ben

"No one has ventured to Stonehaven or Arcandru they were taken over by the Hellions and some still reside there, they do not venture out from the walls so we just keep away" Silari explained.

"So there's gonna be things there?" Ben asked

Silari nodded, "I am sending ten men with Straven as an escort, too many will slow you down"

"Just one question," Grace asked "Those horse don't look big enough for us at the minute"

Grace placed her hand on the horse at the end of her sword and she felt it vibrate and get warm. She resisted the urge to withdraw her hand.

"Grace your hand," Jack said

She looked down to see it covered in a strange glow, then she felt the sword move, she took her hand off with a small yelp and looked at the sword. The horse was moving, slowly at first, then she realised it wasn't the horse on the sword it was as though the horse was inside trying to get out. It wriggled and squirmed until the head was out as soon as a leg was out it leapt from the sword, as it leapt it grew in size to the biggest pure white horse she'd ever seen.

The horse was plenty big enough now for Grace to ride, it had a green blanket on its back with a horse logo embroidered on in silver, then a silver saddle and reigns. The horse stood there shaking its head and mane, whilst stamping its front leg. Grace walked over to it and placed her forehead on its forehead, the immediately calmed down and Grace was able to leap up into the saddle.

"Well I'm ready," she said exuberantly

"I'm so doing mine next" Ben shouted excitedly.

He grabbed the tiger on the hilt of his sword and the biggest tiger ever leapt forward, complete with a silver saddle and reigns. Ben yelled and jumped on its back, the cat roared and leapt into the air and ran off at an amazing speed.

Within moments they were back, Ben laughing his head off "This is so damn cool"

They both then looked at Jack.

Jack looked down at his sword, seeing the lion carved into the handle, he stared at it, his hand hovering over it before he grasped it.

The weird sensation of heat, electricity and the carved lion starting to move, within seconds a huge lion leapt from his sword, it landed with a huge roar than thundered around the camp. Jack walked over to it and placed the palm of his hand on its head, he felt connected to it as though they were one. He moved around to the side keeping his hand in contact with the huge cat before leaping into the

178

saddle. The lion reared up and let out another huge roar.

Jack turned to his companions "To Stonehaven" he shouted and the cat leapt forward followed by the rest of his companions.

The road

They had been on the road for two days, during those two days they had passed many people answering the call of the muster and travelling to the great plains. They had ridden through deserted villages and towns. As they got closer to Stonehaven the air became a lot quieter and a sense of foreboding came across them all.

At the end of the first day, Ben had learnt that not only do they get covered in armour when drawing their swords but also their animal companions. Ben charged around for hours on his tiger who he'd called Tony much to Graces disgust. Ben had said he loved frosties so it was a grreeatt name. Grace had walked off muttering he was an idiot.

Grace had called her horse Silvermane as she thought it sounded powerful. Jack had decided to call his lion Ragnar as he was a fan of the show Vikings, this also made Grace tut.

Straven called them to a halt on the brow of a hill.

"There's a small town down in the valley over the next hill we will be able to see Stonehaven. We will make camp in the town tonight I do not want to be in Stonehaven at night" he warned

Jack nodded and they moved down into the town. They entered in twos Straven and Jack, Grace and Ben followed by the escort troops.

They rode down the main street, the place was deserted and had been for some time, some of the buildings were boarded up others looked like people had left in a hurry.

"This is Stode and has been empty since Stonehaven fell" Straven spoke with hushed tones. They stopped outside a large building in the middle of the town. The exterior would have been a brilliant white one time of day, but now it was a dull grey overgrown with vines, all the windows were boarded up, across the boards there seemed to be scratches or claw marks, everyone noticed them but no one said anything.

"We will stay here for the night," Straven said dismounting from his horse

"You are kidding!" Ben exclaimed "It looks like a house from scooby doo"

"We will be safe here until morning," Straven said calmly

They all dismounted, Jack, Grace and Ben all returned their mounts to the swords and followed Straven inside. The inside was as bad as the outside, the downstairs seemed to be one big room with a stairway going up from the rear wall.

Straven posted two guards on the front door the others set up beds around the room. Jack, Grace and Ben moved to one corner and set up their sleeping mats. Jack heard a whoosh and looked round to see Straven had started a fire in the hearth, the heat and light warmed the room, pushing back the shadows and lifting the mood.

Straven called the Captain of the escort over "I think we should keep two on the door all night but rotate them regularly. "Yes sir", "Oh and Captain tell them if they see or hear ANYTHING then they wake us straight away" The Captain nodded and moved over to where the troops were eating, he spoke to them then disappeared outside to speak to the others.

Straven pulled some chairs around the fire and sat down. Jack and Grace went and sat with him, Ben went to join the game the soldiers were playing on the other side of the room.

"How many people lived here?" Grace asked

"Oh about three thousand including the outlying farms, they used to trade with the Dwafen from Stonehaven" Straven replied

"What were the Dwafen like?" Jack said staring into the fire

"They were a proud, but fiercely loyal people. They were the best craftsmen in the whole realm and also had the best army along with the Seraphinans, that's why they were given the job of guarding the border. When both fell and so quickly it was a great shock to us all"

"So the Hellions came here?" Grace looked a little alarmed

Straven nodded, "But they have not been here for a long time. I think maybe we need to all get some rest tomorrow will be a hard day"

Straven got up and walked over to the troops, they responded with a yes sir and proceeded to their beds. Ben came over and plonked himself down on his mat next to Grace.

"I was winning that game too"

Jack lay down and pulled the covers up to his neck and closed his eyes. It seemed to take an eternity to go to sleep. No sooner as he had it seemed like a voice in his head shouted: "Get up now!". He sat bolt upright and grabbed for his sword, it was still dark and the fire had died down.

Everyone else was still asleep, so he looked around the room straining his ears to listen. There was no sound, it was eerily quiet, he heard a rustle outside then silence. He thought about waking the others but thought they would be mad if it turned out just to be a dream.

He stood up and walked to the window at the front and tried to peer through the crack in the boards, he couldn't see anything at first only darkness, then something moved across the window, a black shape that caused him to recoil back. Another noise outside this one slightly louder, he thought the sentries were moving around a lot and hoped they'd not seen anything.

He put his hand on his sword and moved to the door, he grasped the handle and slowly turned it. He began to pull the door open but stopped, something wasn't right. Jack peered through the crack in the door, he was sure he should be able to see the guards but he couldn't see anything.

He took a deep breath and opened the door wider, enough so that he could see along the front of the building. The guards were gone and so were the horses, he looked down, is that blood he thought. A sudden movement across the street caused his head to snap up and he stared into the darkness, he knew this was wrong.

He swung open the door pulling his sword, his armour covering him in seconds. "Get up, get up" he roared as the darkness across the road exploded into a flurry of shapes as the Hellions attacked.

Ben and Grace shot up to see Jack in full armour standing in the doorway with the darkness outside moving in some weird ways. They jumped up pulling their swords, covering themselves in armour, and rushed to their friend's side.

As they arrived Jack had moved out onto the porch and was slashing left and right and these creatures from hell, jet black all teeth and claws, snarling and slashing. Ben leapt into the fray followed by Grace, the three of them fought side by side blocking the doorway giving the others time to get up. Slowly they began to move forward pushing the enemy back. Jack felt his sword squirm in his hand and knew Ragnar wanted to join the fight, he grasped his sword with both hands covering the lion allowing Ragnar to leap into action, he was covered in armour but still allowed him the freedom of movement he needed. He was closely followed by Tony and they began to cause terrible losses to the enemy.

Straven and the escort suddenly burst into view, Straven cast a ball of light into the air giving them the first real view of the enemy. Jack wasn't sure if that was a good thing because there seemed to be hundreds of them.

They all fought side by side, gradually they were drawn out into the street and surrounded, the escort troops slowly began to fall one by one. Straven was using his magic as best he could but it was having minimal effect on the enemy.

Jack saw six of the company fall.

"Ben, Grace! We need to do something fast!" Jack shouted over the bedlam of the battle.

Jack then felt his sword squirm in his hand again, he gripped the handle with both hands, he felt the handle grow longer and watched as his blade grew into a longsword, the blade burned a blue colour and as he swung it, the blue light arced out as he swung not just killing the ones at the front but also three rows of them. He carried on swinging the blade in massive arcs causing chaos in the enemy ranks.

He noticed Bens sword had split into two and he was swirling and dancing with the two blades a very deadly dance into the ranks of the enemy.

Grace's sword had grown into a spear with a blade at both ends and she was scything her way through them.

The enemy then began to falter the push became less and the mass began to thin.

"We've got them on the run" Ben shouted above the noise.

Within a few minutes, they had gone, vanished back into the darkness, leaving just their dead behind.

Jack looked around, Grace had hunkered down onto her knees breathing heavily, Ben was stood hands on hips his chest rising and falling in rapid succession. Ragnar and Tony were just ripping the last remaining hellions to pieces.

"Straven," Jack said looking at him, Straven nodded "We won't see them again tonight"

"Casualties?" Jack asked. "Twelve dead, four wounded" Straven said solemnly.

"I don't think we should stay here" Grace stated

"We won't have to," Straven said pointing off to the left.

They all looked as the sun rose slowly over the hills, they had fought all night.

The City of Stone

It was decided that the remaining troops would escort the wounded back home and the four of them would continue onto Stonehaven. They bid their farewells and departed after breakfast.

The four companions continued on the road to their destination.

"I'm sorry aren't I," Grace said out loud

"Eh, what?" Ben replied

"Its Silvermane shes peeved I didn't let her out to fight last night, I tried to tell her shes not got teeth or claws like Ragnar and T, Ben you really need to change his name, you cant call him Tony it's just not right"

"Yea, it doesn't really fit does it?" agreed Jack

"Ok, ok, Tony, you arent Tony anymore your name is Leonidas"

Jack frowned at Ben

"You know, for Sparta!!" he shouted

"Oh lord," said Grace sighing

"Well it's better than Tony I suppose" Jack agreed

"A lot of the time I have no idea what you three are on about," Straven said.

They rode for a few hours before they began to climb the hill, they stopped at the top.

"I give you Stonehaven" Straven gestured with his hand

"It's huge" exclaimed Jack

"How did they take that?" Ben asked

"No one has ventured any farther than this hill since Stonehaven fell" Straven sighed deeply

"There is no way to sneak in, we have to go for the main gates and hope we can somehow get in unseen"

"I can't see that happening," said Grace "It's not like they don't know we are coming"

They made their way slowly towards the walls, as the got closer the sheer size of the walls became obvious. They rode along the outskirts of the wall, keeping close to the base hoping to avoid detection.

Jack could see the main road into the city appear in the distance and knew they were close. As they got to within a few hundred feet Straven held up his hand

"I will go and scout ahead" He nudged his horse and trotted up to the gate, a few feet from the gate he stopped and dismounted then walked slowly to the gate and disappeared.

"I hope he's not gone long it's creepy out here and too quiet," Jack said breaking the silence.

After about ten minutes Straven appeared, got on his horse and rode back to them.

"There is no sign of life, unfortunately, all the bridges to the next level are down so will need to find a way across"

They all proceeded to the gate, one gate was hanging off its hinges against the wall, the other was nowhere in sight.

Jack was in awe of the scale of this city, he could see clear signs of battle, a sword or helm here and there, but not as many as he expected.

"I think this city is not as unoccupied as was thought" Straven whispered "Everything pretty much has been gathered up or destroyed"

They emerged through the gateway into the interior and saw the chasm that greeted them.

"Wow this place is immense" Ben gasped.

"How could it have fallen so quickly?" Grace asked

"No one knows, there were no survivors to tell the tale" Straven replied in hushed tones.

"How are we getting over that?" Ben gestured to the space in front of them.

Ragnar growled and began to paw at the ground, followed by Leonidas and Silvermane began to stamp her hooves.

Jack looked at Ragnar and placed his hand on his head, "They can jump it"

"What?" Grace spun around "Jump that?"

Jack shrugged, "If we do this then it seems this is where we part Straven"

Straven nodded "I will return to the gathering and report on your progress, good luck my friends may Selendrial be with you always"

He embraced each of them in turn, jumped onto his horse and rode away, the three friends stood there listening until the horse's hooves could be heard no more.

"Me first" Ben cried as he leapt onto his tiger and disappeared down the main gate tunnel. Jack and Grace looked at each other.

Ben came charging out of the tunnel at full speed, the tigers front paws hit the edge of the ravine and leapt, it arched through the air and landed safely on the other side. "Now that's what I'm talking about" shouted Ben across the ravine.

"I'll go next," Grace said climbing onto her horse. She followed the same procedure as Ben and made it safely to the other side. Jack leapt onto Ragnar, "Cmon let's go" he said. The big cat bounded down the tunnel, skidded to a halt and turned. It stood there for a few seconds then burst forward gathering speed as it went, they broke free from the gloom of the tunnel as the edge of the ravine got nearer and nearer. Then take off, they soared across the chasm landing with a skidding halt on the other side.

"This way" Ben ushered them through a gateway and out the other side.

Plants had started to reclaim this area of the city, vines and creepers climbed the walls and buildings. Clearly, this was where the civilians of the city lived, streets led off from here with houses and what looked like shops all abandoned and crumbling.

"I don't suppose it matters which street we take," Grace said

"Be my guest" Ben gestured to the streets leading away.

Grace urged her horse forward and they followed her down the street.

They rode slowly down the street towards the citadel, their eyes constantly aware of every shadow, window and door, a lot of buildings had collapsed, the road was broken and uneven in places. Jack wondered what it would have been like to ride down here when the Dwafen were alive and not this tomblike place it was now.

They finally emerged from the buildings into an open space and the citadel arose before them, it was a breathtaking building and they all sat there staring up at its vastness.

"So what now?" Jack said looking for inspiration

"I don't know" Grace replied

"Guess we go inside," said Ben

"We can't take our rides in there we will have to return them to our swords" Jack suggested

"Ok," Grace said dismounting, they all thanked their rides as they shrank and disappeared into their swords.

Jack drew his sword, covering himself in armour "I'm being prepared" Ben and Grace did the same and followed Jack up and into the citadel.

They entered through the main entrance whose door had been ripped from its hinges and lay splintered and in pieces inside. They entered a huge room with high ceilings all intricately carved depicting various animals our Dwafen people.

"This place is enormous, how on earth do we know where to go, we could get lost in here" Ben sounded exasperated.

"This way," Jack said, he didn't know why or even why he thought it was this way it just felt right.

They followed Jack down a long corridor which eventually led them to a walkway outside the citadel. Arches were carved into the side letting you see the mountain outside, a river ran along the side of it flowing fast, the water churning as it went.

Jack looked outside and could see that the light was failing.

"I think we need to find somewhere to rest for the night, its gonna be dark soon"

Ben and Grace nodded, they followed Jack as he moved cautiously down the corridor. Jack stopped outside a large heavy wooden door, he reached his hand out and grasped the handle, it clicked as he turned it. He pushed and the door moved, thankfully it was unlocked. He pushed the door open slowly and stepped inside, the room was fairly large, it had no windows but a small fireplace was situated in the far wall. The walls were covered in racks, some of the racks still had weapons hanging from them.

"Must have been a weapons room" said Ben

Jack saw that the key was in the lock on the inside of the door and the door also had two internal braces that could be locked into place.

"I think this will do," Jack said to the other two. "I will get the fire going and then we can lock and brace the door"

Not long after the light began to fade quickly, they had lit the fire and the door was now closed and locked. They'd found a few blankets so were now sat together around the fire, listening to the crackle and spit of the flames, whilst listening intently for any noise outside.

"Are we safe in here?" Grace questioned.

"As safe as anywhere here I think" replied Jack.

They sat there in silence for a while before Jack spoke: "I wonder if my mom and dad are ok?"

"I'm sure everyone is fine," Grace said unconvincingly, "Well I hope so, I hope my dad is ok"

"Just your dad," asked Jack

"My mom died last year, she was killed on the way home from fetching my brother from his friends, a car mounted the pavement and hit them both" her eyes filled with tears and her voice began to break, Jack and Ben both put an arm around her. Grace tried to smile but a small sob escaped.

"It's ok," Ben said softly

"Charlie was six, he'd been to a birthday party. My mom died there, they tried to save her but couldn't. Charlie fought for a week after the accident, my Dad and I stayed at the hospital, we never left his side, I was holding his hand when he died, he had the most beautiful blue eyes, his hair was always uncontrollable and he was always smiling and laughing. I miss his laughter so much" Grace sobbed uncontrollably and buried her head in Bens shoulder.

They all sat together until Grace had stopped crying "I'm sorry" she said

"Don't be" Jack said caringly.

195

"The woman in the car was drunk, she didn't even go to prison. My dads not been the same since"

"I'm sure he's fine," Ben said reassuringly

"What about your family," Jack said to Ben hoping to distract Grace from her grief.

"Ah now that's a long story, I have three brothers and two sisters. I haven't seen any of them since I was three and we were put into foster care, my parents by all accounts were a waste of space. It would be good to see my brothers and sisters, but I have no idea where they are at the minute. I'm not sure if Chas and Dave know and aren't telling me"

"Er Chas and Dave?" Jack said trying to hide a smile

"Yea my foster parents, they are great, they really are but I'm not great to them and its not their fault at all"

"Yes but, Chas and Dave," Jack said with a giggle

Grace chuckled a bit and said, "Is it the Chas and Dave?"

"I have no idea what you mean" snapped Ben defensively

"No, no I don't mean anything, Chas and Dave were singers my grandad used to play their music" Jack blurted out.

"Yeah right" snorted Ben

"He's right I've heard of them too" agreed Grace

"Oh I will ask them about it when I get back" Ben
paused "If we get back"

Jack knew they wouldn't be the ones he knew of but
thought it best to drop it now.

"How do you cope, with your condition? If you don't
mind me asking" Grace said to Jack

Jack hated talking about it, and about himself.

"I er just do I guess. There are some a lot worse so I
guess I just get on with it"

"I've seen a couple of kids making fun of you at
school, sorry I didn't say anything," Ben said
sheepishly

"It's ok I'm used to it, they are just idiots who I'm
sure cry over a cold"

"Do you get bullied a lot?" Grace asked gently

Jack didn't like how the conversation was going, as
much as he had grown close to them he didn't want
to open up yet, plus it seemed weird talking about it
in his new body.

"Some, I don't let it bother me"

There was a noise at the door, a small scratching sound.

"What was that?" Jack said suddenly

They all got up and drew their swords. They stood together side by side watching the door and waiting.

Jack had no idea how long they had stood their for before they decided it was all clear as they had heard no more sounds since.

"We should rest, or try to get some rest," Jack said to them

They agreed and settled down on the blankets to rest.

Discoveries

Jack awoke to see light coming under the door, he sat up and roused the others. Thankfully they had all managed to get some sleep.

Jack rummaged through the bags to sort some food for breakfast, provisions were getting low and they would definitely need water soon. He shared the food out between them and they ate breakfast in silence.

After breakfast, they all got ready and pretty much assumed the same positions as the previous night, side by side facing the doorway.

"I will open it, so get ready," Jack said unlocking the door and lifting the two braces. He took the handle and turned, there was a loud click and the big heavy door swung open as he pulled.

There was nothing the other side, just the corridor and an archway to outside.

"C'mon let's go," Jack said stepping through the doorway and carrying on up the corridor. The corridor continued down the side of the palace wall, there were a couple of doors they tried but all were locked. Finally, they came to a tunnel that led into the mountain itself, there was little light in there and the air did not smell good at all.

"We need to go this way," Jack said to his friends, he said it almost like a question and was happy when they both nodded. As they stepped inside the tunnel they noticed how it had been carved out of the mountain, it wasn't hacked or hewn it was beautifully carved. There were columns and archways of intricate design, carved murals on the walls depicting what must have been stories from their history.

It was breathtaking in its beauty, but also held a sense of foreboding.

The light began to fade as they moved further into the tunnel, as it did their swords began to glow illuminating the tunnel with an eerie glow. They walked further and further into the mountain, they passed a few what looked like dwellings, they were I total disarray and starting to crumble.

They eventually came to what looked like a small town, the town was situated in a cavern in the mountain. As they approached they could hear the rushing of water and it was a lot lighter here.

As they exited the tunnel into the huge cavern they could see the town was situated on a piece of rock that looked like it floated in the middle of nothing. A bridge spanned the gap at the front and rear of the town, A huge waterfall cascaded down the side of one wall disappearing far below them. As they looked up they could see the sky, the cavern stretched straight to the surface which allowed natural light to illuminate the town.

"Now that's impressive," Ben said in awe

"Let's go, we shouldn't stand around here it doesn't feel right," Grace said moving to cross the bridge.

Ben and Jack followed into the town. It looked as though each building had been carved from a giant rock, they were stunningly beautiful, every carved pillar or relief was smooth and covered in detail that would be impossible to do.

"How did they do this?" Jack asked

"Let's have a quick search of a couple of buildings see if we can find anything useful" Ben suggested

"Yea good idea" Grace agreed

They split up and each selected a building. Jack selected a large building on the right side of the street. He walked in through the open door, chairs and tables were strewn all over the place, along one wall was what was clearly a bar. This must have been a pub Jack thought, he went around behind the bar, there were tankards and drinking horns scattered around and plenty of broken stuff, he kicked a few things around with his foot looking for anything interesting.

A loud scream suddenly filled the air. Jacks head snapped up and he ran to the door and out onto the street, closely followed by Ben and Grace.

"What the hell was that!" Ben almost shouted.

"There" Grace pointed down the tunnel, they could see movement, they started to take a few steps backwards slowly.

Then they burst from the tunnel, it was a swarm of teeth and claws, the Hellions had found them.

"RUN!!" shouted Jack turning and running away from them, followed by Ben and Grace. They soon cleared the town and were across the other bridge to the other side.

"NOOO" Grace shouted.

The tunnel the other side went a few feet into the mountain and then stopped, it was clear a cave-in had occurred some considerable time ago.

"We fight" Ben bellowed spinning round to face the screaming horde.

Jack and Grace turned to face their enemy. Ben pulled a second sword from his, Jack placed both hands on his and his sword grew into a longsword, Grace began to spin and twirl her double-bladed spear.

The horde was closing, they were just a few feet away, Jack chanced a quick glance at his friends and then they were on them. The fighting was frantic and fierce, the three friends cut a deadly dance through the horde. They severed arms, heads, legs but still, they kept coming, more and more bodies were starting to pile up, the floor was getting slippery with blood.

Jack felt his sword twitch and knew Ragnar wanted out, he slipped his hand onto the pommel and Ragnar leapt forward with a huge roar, Grace and Ben did the same Leonidas and Silvermane soon joined the battle. It seemed to be working the animals were tearing and stamping their way through the horde, amazingly Silvermane now had wings and was using them to beat the enemy down.

The horde began to fall back, slowly at first then they turned and ran back.

"YES!!" Ben shouted leaping onto Leonidas as he relieved a monster of its head.

A huge roar echoed through the chamber and suddenly from the other tunnel four huge giants emerged, all twisted and gruesome, clad in black armour and carrying huge axes

"Oh shit," Ben said

"Over here"

A voice shouted to them from over by the waterfall, they looked and could see an opening had appeared and a man of very small stature was waving them over.

"Let's go" Jack shouted as he jumped onto Ragnar, Grace leapt onto Silvermane who immediately took off and flew to the opening.

Leonidas and Ragnar both leapt from the edge their claws cutting into the rock face as they tried to make their way to the opening, they had leapt about half the way. Arrows began to ping against the rocks around them.

Grace had made it easily into the opening and had vanished inside, Jack and Ben both created their shields and tried to cover themselves and their animals as best they could. Leonidas made it first and leapt the last bit into the clearing, Bens face appeared calling Jack on.

The arrows were growing in ferocity and it was starting to sound like rain against Jacks shield, they were so close now.

"Go Ragnar" Jack shouted, Ragnar responded with a huge roar and leapt the final bit, gliding through the opening they both ended in a tangled heap on the floor. Jack watched as a huge stone was rolled over the opening, he heard the screams from the horde die out as the last bit closed.

Jack stood and looked at the, well what was clearly a dwarf before him, "Welcome friends, my name is

Bodil I am to take you to Gars he has been waiting for you"

Eiserwelt

They followed Bodil down a corridor, the corridor was smooth on both sides and the roof arched over, the walls were a pale blue with varying shades of blue running through them. Their footfalls echoed around them as they walked bouncing back off the smooth walls.

"What is this place?" Jack enquired

"This is Eiserwelt the last remaining stronghold of the Dwafen" Bodil replied

The corridor opened out into a cavern, in the far wall was a huge closed gate, the gate was made up of thick pieces of wood and huge iron braces. Above the gate in archways chiselled out of the rock could be seen guards standing on duty, all clad in armour.

"This is the gate to Eiserwelt, this is where the remnants of the Dwafen have lived since the darkest day. Please follow me" Bodil ushered them forward as the gate began to swing open almost silently.

Standing the other side were about twenty armed soldiers, all armoured from head to toe and carrying weapons. As the group approached they parted into two columns either side of the road.

The three friends walked between the ranks of the troops and followed Bodil along the road. The road swept down in a gentle curve, pillars had been carved intermittently along both sides of the passageway, the pillars were a deep blue colour and were adorned with intricately carved depictions of creatures and events. The walls glowed with natural light illuminating everywhere.

They came to a crossroads, straight in front was another gateway, this door was open and you could see that it opened into a large space beyond. Left and right the road curved upwards and disappeared.

"Left and right leads to the barracks where the troops are housed," Bodil said

He beckoned them forward and they followed through the gate. The area opened up into a huge cavern, the size of it was breathtaking, there was a vaulted ceiling more intricate and beautiful than any cathedral they had ever seen. Huge pillars were carved into the walls covered in an array of animals.

But it was the noise that was most noticeable, the area seemed to be a huge market, where people moved from stall to stall buying goods they needed. Each stall was different and sold a variety of items from food to weapons. They were shouting and haggling and laughing as the three friends followed Bodil inside.

Slowly one by one the people began to notice them and stopped to look, slowly the noise died down to a few murmurs as everyone stared at them.

"Well this isn't awkward much," Ben said through his teeth

"My kin" Bodil bellowed "behold the Katari"

A cheer erupted from the crowd, that got louder and louder, the acoustics amplifying its power to a deafening roar.

Jack, Grace and Ben shuffled a bit on the spot embarrassed by the reaction.

"No pressure then," Grace said.

The crowd parted as Bodil lead them forward, but the cheering continued, they could see more and more people appearing drawn by the commotion. A few tried to pat them on their backs but because of the height difference, it ended up as pats on the behind, after a couple of yelps from Grace this stopped.

They finally exited the chamber on the other side and the cheering gradually died down.

"I wasn't expecting that," Jack said shocked

"Your arrival has been foretold but many thought it would never happen, Gars will explain everything"

"Where are the houses? Where do people live?" Grace asked Bodil as they entered another tunnel.

"Off the main chamber we have just come through are doors that lead to the living areas, they aren't really houses but dwellings carved into the rockface on many levels. It's up to you how big a home you want depending on how much work you want to do. All you have to make sure is you don't end up appearing through someone else's bedroom wall" Bodil said chuckling.

The road began to narrow slightly and eventually finished at a staircase. There were hundreds of steps leading upwards.

"This leads to the palace, not far now," Bodil said leaping up the first few steps.

You could not make out the top as it curved around to the right, the walls both sides looked more like pearls than rock, they shimmered with a thousand different colours.

They made the climb up the staircase, as they reached the curve they finally saw the entrance. The entrance to the palace was a hugely carved dragon's head and arms, it was carved so that it looked like it was emerging from the rockface, mouth wide open ready to breathe fire. The dragon itself was silver with green eyes. Jack found it weird that as fierce as it looked its eyes almost carried an air of kindness.

Bodil strode purposefully into the dragon's mouth followed by Jack, Grace, and Ben.

There were guards just inside, but they just stood there as they walked past, their faces grim and expressionless. There was a small well furnished room the other side of the entrance with a lavishly ornate staircase leading up to a set of gold doors.

"This way" Bodil said as he ascended the stairs, he got to the top and paused in front of the gold doors waiting for the others. "This is the crystal throne room, our Lord is waiting here to speak to you"

He took a deep breath and pushed open the doors.

The view before them was breathtaking, the walls were made of crystal, with two rows of crystal pillars following the path to the throne. A guard stood at every pillar in ornate golden armour, holding a shield and a large two-headed axe. A royal blue carpet started at the doorway and lead through the throne room to the throne, on the throne sat a man, he was maybe five feet tall, he was as broad as he was high, his hands were large and gripped a sword that he held blade down between his legs. He had a long beard with flecks of grey, his face was stern but his eyes looked softer and more caring.

They followed Bodil until they were facing the King. "My Lord" Bodil said bowing "The Katari"

All three of them did varying bows none of them very successful.

The King stared at them, he gazed into their eyes one by one.

"You are but children, I can see it in your eyes," he said in a deep gravelly voice

"I am supposed to believe you are the chosen ones, the ones to lead our people back into the light"

He sat back in his chair "I expected more"

Jack knew he had to say something but he didn't know what to say, they needed to somehow reassure him, of what he didn't know himself.

"Your majesty" Ben started, oh no thought Jack turning to stare at Ben

"We've come a long way, but we're not really sure where we've been. We've had some success"

Grace groaned and Jack rolled his eyes "He's reciting take that" Grace sighed in Jacks's ear

"Yes your majesty we have had some success along our way, but it has been difficult" Jack butted in hoping to shut Ben up.

"We didn't ask for this ourselves, and we are still learning" Grace continued

"But if we can help, we will, and if we can make a difference somehow then we will do that also" Jack assured him

Gars stared at them all again "Perhaps I judged too hastily, you must be tired and hungry. Bodil will show you to your quarters and we will speak tomorrow when you are rested"

"Thank you," Ben, Jack, and Grace said bowing and they followed Bodil out of the throne room.

As they left the room Grace turned to Ben "Take That!"

"My dad is a fan, the first thing that popped into my head" Ben replied shrugging.

Meeting

The following morning they were taken to a smaller room with a table and chairs in it. They sat down and shortly after the King and four others entered and sat down.

"Good morning I hope your rooms were adequate," Asked the King

"Yes sire, thank you" replied Grace

"We will commence with the meeting, introductions first I think. Bodil you know he is my chief advisor" The King gestured to his left "This is Egil he is the captain of the palace guard, the other two are Halvar and Torben my generals, my son Viggo will join us soon"

They all nodded in greeting

"I am Grace, this is Ben and Jack"

"Now where to start" the King began

Grace briefly described what had happened to them including the meeting in the tree, the others watched with an increasing sense of awe on their faces.

"So we aren't sure why we are here just that someone here must come with us" Grace finished

There was a prolonged silence before the king spoke.

"That is some journey you have had, we too have been on a journey since we watched our world crumble around us"

"We came here, the last remnants of the Dwafen people, whether we came to rebuild or just to die I was not sure of for a long time."

He looked down at his hands rubbing them together.

"We all watched nearly everyone we know, family, friends all died on that day, we had no choice but to run here and never return. It was years later when I received a vision in my dreams of the Katari who would one day save us, after that day the feeling changed here, I think for the first time we started to hope, hope that one day we may be able to return home"

"It is not the home you left I'm afraid," Jack said softly

"Walls can be rebuilt," Bodil said

The door swung open and a younger man stormed in "Father you called for me" he said dragging out a chair and plonking down on it.

He had long brown hair and a short brown beard, his face was rugged yet handsome. He was powerfully built and had an air of arrogance about him.

"Yes I did, this is my son Viggo" The King introduced his son

Grace, Ben and Jack all nodded.

For the first time, Viggo noticed them, "Who are they?" he said sitting more upright.

"They are the Katari" The King replied

Viggo's mouth dropped open "I thought you were losing it father, but they are real?"

Viggo reached out his hand to Jack "It is my pleasure"

Jack clasped hands with Viggo and immediately felt the air change, it became alive with electricity. Lightning began to dance around the room. Ben and Grace stood up as the rest of the people and the room began to shimmer and distort.

There was a blinding flash and a roar as the energy built into a crescendo.

As their vision began to clear they saw they were back in the room inside the great tree and their sat on a chair was Selendrial.

"Welcome travellers, welcome Viggo son of Gars. I am Selendrial daughter of Anu and you have been chosen"

And then there were four

Viggo stood there blinking and staring around the room with his mouth slightly open.

"Are you ok?" Grace asked

"Takes some getting used to," Jack said

"Hang on a minute, is it just me or is no one else wondering why we couldn't she couldn't have just zapped us there in the first place" Ben exclaimed "I mean, its taken days, we've had to fight, sleep on the floor, be thirsty and hungry and we could have been zapped there"

"I'm sorry, but to reach your destination first you must complete the journey," Selendrial said

Ben rolled his eyes "That from a fortune cookie". "Ben!" Grace gasped, Jack couldn't help but smile.

"Where are we?" Viggo stuttered out

"You are inside the great tree" Selendrial replied

Viggo's face went paler still, "If this is Selendrial and your Selendrial"

"We will explain all that later" Answered Jack.

"You have been chosen Viggo son of Gars, you are a Katari, the burden of all worlds is now yours to bare" Selendrial walked over to the stone in the centre of the room.

"You must choose"

"Choose?" Viggo said

"A sword, approach the stone, close your eyes and let the sword choose you" Selendrial instructed

Viggo approached the stone, he closed his eyes and held out his hand. He moved from hilt to hilt, he hovered over the dragon sword for a while then moved to the others. However, he moved back to the dragon sword and grasped the handle. He pulled the sword from the stone with a blinding flash.

Their eyes began to clear and there stood Viggo, he was taller than before but still nowhere near as tall as the others, he wore a beige tunic with a dragon emblazoned across his exceptionally broad chest, he had aged slightly but not as noticeable as the others.

"Wow, I feel great. I know a lot more now than when I woke up this morning"

"Pull your sword out," Ben said excitedly "It's the best bit"

Viggo drew his sword and was immediately covered in silver armour.

"Haha, that is impressive" Viggo bellowed. He replaced his sword and the armour vanished.

"Now there are four of you, but time grows short and you must hurry to find the other two" Selendrial warned. "Your next part of the journey will be hard and take courage, strength and bravery"

"Where do we have to go?" Viggo asked

"You must travel to Arcandru"

Viggo's mouth dropped open once again "But that city is dead"

"You must seek out Faria and the people in the clouds, that is all I can say, I will return you to Eiserwelt and you can travel from there"

Ben sighed, "Can't you just zap us straight there"

Selendrial smiled and the electricity started again, the lightning flashed around and then a blinding light. They found themselves back in the room they had left, the others at the table looking stunned then gasping as they noticed Viggo.

"My son, what has happened" Gars words stumbled out

"Father I have been chosen, I am Katari now. We do not have time to explain everything we must travel to Arcandru and look for the survivors"

"There were no survivors" Gars answered

"That's what they said about you lot" Ben blurted out.

"We need some supplies and a way out of here that's not back the way we came in" Jack explained

"There is a way out that is rarely used, the passage of Einar but it leads into the cursed lands" Gars stood up opened a drawer, and pulled out a rolled up parchment, he spread it on the table.

"This is a map of our lands, here is the passageway that leads into Hellion, then you have two choices, go straight across to Arcandru or travel south along the mountains to the border with Kandar then up through Seraphina"

"I don't think we have the time to go the long way" Grace declared

"Then we will go across Hellion as fast as we can," Jack said

"It is probably three days hard ride" Gars stated

"We will do it in two" Ben bragged.

"We will prepare some supplies and you can leave in the morning" Gars instructed his men to gather what was needed. "I will see you escorted to your rooms and you can get some rest"

The next morning they were escorted through the city to a small cave, the cave seemed untouched stalactites and stalagmites pierced the ceiling or erupted through the floor, they were of all different colours and sizes. A small path had been cleared through the cave to an opening on the other side, this opening was protected by a huge door. The door had several large metal bolts securing it from the inside.

Gars was waiting for them "Welcome, through this door is the Einar passageway, it spirals down onto the cursed land, once you pass through this door I do not know what will await you" he turned to his son and embraced him "My son, may your journey be fast, true and without interference. Be strong, be brave and I will see you soon"

"Thank you father"

Gars signaled for the door to be opened. The heavy door began to creak open, a gush of wind echoed up from the darkness beyond, the air smelled stale and old.

Jack moved forward and the others followed, each of them holding a torch to light the way.

The passageway was more of a tunnel, it looked like it had been cut from the mountain by a drilling machine, Jack had seen a program on the channel tunnel and it looked very similar. They walked in silence descending downwards with the tunnel.

The silence and the darkness gave jack time to think about his parents again, he hoped everything was ok at home he realised how much he missed them and fought to control his emotions. He started to think how much had changed, he knew his condition was still there but it was funny how easily he had forgotten it, he had spent his whole life wondering what it would be like to do things normally, not exceptionally, not like some superhuman, just normally like every other kid that's all he ever wanted. His life had been constant what-ifs from as early as he could remember, he hoped as he got older it would become easier but it just through up newer problems and the breaks impacted more heavily on his life.

He stumbled slightly in the dark and Grace grabbed his elbow to steady him

"Thanks" he couldn't say anything else because Grace's hand slid down his arm and held his hand. He was confused and his heart was going like it would soon be running off down the tunnel without him, it seemed so loud in his ears he was sure everyone could hear it.

A dull light appeared in the distance, he wasn't sure how long they had been walking for, he'd been lost in his thoughts now he was lost in the gentle, warm touch he could feel on his hand.

"There is that the end?" Ben whispered

Grace loosed Jacks' hand, Jack turned and their eyes locked. A smile spread across Grace's face as she lowered her eyes, Jacks smile was a bit more stupid looking with a massive grin. Ben burst passed them

"C'mon lovebirds" he laughed as he strode past them followed by Viggo.

Grace laughed, at Ben but more at Jack's shocked face. "Let's go Jack" Grace laughed

Jack followed them out of the tunnel and into the blinding light of day.

They stood there for a while looking around letting their eyes get accustomed to the light. They were about fifty feet from the base of the mountain, stretched out in front of them was a vast wasteland of rocks, dirt, and very little vegetation. The air smelled bad, it smelt of death and decay.

"Wow that smells worse than my dog" Ben exclaimed

"It is a fouls stench" Viggo agreed. "How do we cross this land without transport"

"Oh your gonna love this" Ben said

Leonidas leaped from Ben's sword with a roar, Viggo jumped back in surprise as Ben leapt upon his back.

Jack and Grace followed suit, soon Ragnar and Silvermane stood there waiting.

"Who do I share with" Viggo asked

"You have your own" Jack said "Place your hand on the Dragon head on your sword and wait"

Viggo placed his hand on his sword and felt the movement start, he resisted the urge to pull his hand free. Viggo watched as a huge dragon appeared from his sword, its scales were a deep blue, its claws and horns a shining silver, its eyes an ice-cold blue. It landed stretched out its wings and let out a roar.

On its back was a saddle, it turned to look at Viggo and beckoned him onto the saddle. Reluctantly Viggo climbed aboard, as soon as he did the connection was made.

"You have to name it," Grace said

Viggo gazed at his dragon "I shall call you Throdin"

The cursed land

They set out across the land towards Arcandru, Viggo and Grace flew ahead as they could see for miles from the sky and warn of any dangers. Jack and Ben raced onward as though the horde itself was on their tail.

After a few hours of riding Grace and Viggo returned.

"There is something ahead, a few houses of some sort" Viggo explained

"We couldn't tell what they were from so high up" Added Grace.

"Can we go around?" Jack asked

"If we do it will add hours onto the journey, it looks deserted" Viggo replied

"Ok you two fly overhead, Ben and I will scout forward as far as we can and decide what to do"

That decided Viggo and Grace took to the air.

"Right Ben lets do this"

They started toward the settlement, as they grew closer they could see it was a small village, it did look deserted although the buildings did not look derelict.

"What do you think?" Jack nodded at the village.

Ben shrugged "what choice do we have?"

Jack pulled his sword, followed by Ben and they made their way down to the settlement. Jack looked up and could see Grace and Viggo circling above, obviously, they hadn't seen anything to concern them.

They reached the outskirts of the settlement, it looked like a town from the old cowboy films but it couldn't be, not here. They walked further into the town and stopped dead outside a large building. On the front of the building was a sign it read Saloon.

"What the?" Ben said shocked

"It cant be" Jack sounded shocked "I'm going to have a look inside"

"Be careful" replied Ben.

Jack dismounted and walked up the steps to the saloon and went through the swinging doors. Inside was exactly how he thought it would be. Round tables were situated around the room, a long bar against one wall with bottles of alcohol behind.

Written on the mirrors behind the bar was Tombstone.

Jack walked over to the bar, sat on the bar was an old leather-bound journal, it had the initials DH on the front, he picked it up and returned to Ben outside.

"Well?" Ben asked

"You aren't going to believe this but it says Tombstone in there"

"What as in the gunfight at the ok carrol?"

"The what?"

"You know Wyatt Earp, Doc Holliday, Chas loves the Kurt Russell film said I needed to see it as its movie gold"

"Yea I guess so. It looks like everyone left in a hurry, but I found this book"

"Think we should look around more?"

"We are starting to lose the light so we need to make camp somewhere"

Jack signaled to Grace and Viggo, they came down and landed next to Jack

"Is that a saloon?" Grace almost shouted

"Yea from Tombstone apparently," Ben said, "You know the one?"

"Yes vaguely" Viggo looked puzzled "It is a place in our world from many years ago, it certainly shouldn't be here"

"I've found a journal so it may give us some answers but we need to find somewhere to make camp"

"I spotted a small crop of rocks not far from here, I think I saw a cave there, that may do" Viggo suggested.

"Ok lead the way" Jack instructed.

They found the cave Viggo had spotted, it was about forty feet up in the air. Grace and Viggo flew Ben and Jack up, they returned their mounts to the swords and set up camp.

They wouldn't risk a fire but Viggo had some small rocks that gave off light to illuminate the cave but could not be seen from the outside.

They sat around eating their meal for the night and Jack reached for the book

"DH"

"What?" Ben said

"It says DH on the front" Jack replied

"You don't think it's Doc Holliday, do you? Now that would be some weird shit"

Jack opened the book and began to read.

Monday 24th October 1881

That Clanton is gonna be heading for a reckoning, Wyatt sure has had enough of all the threats. I know I'm gonna be drawn into this as he's pretty much my only friend. We will see what tomorrow brings but this ain't gonna end well for someone.

Tuesday 25th October 1881

We are in hell! Last night we were taken, part of the town was taken to hell. I woke up with the biggest lightning storm ever, the last flash was that strong it bought the daylight with it.

I've checked outside and we aren't in Tombstone anymore, part of the town is now here wherever here is. It's a miserable, desolate place and nothing we can see for miles around. There's about two hundred of us here, we don't know what happened to the rest of them, or the rest of the town.

Wednesday 26th October 1881

They came in the night, the demons from hell, a few of us managed to hide, our guns wouldn't work, not a one. They took most of us, there's about fifteen left, I'm not afraid to say that I am scared, I know they will come back at some point.

"That's it nothing else"

"The last date is the same date as the ok carrol fight" Ben said knowingly

"How did they get here? It sounds like a portal of some description" Grace mused

"However it happened it didn't change our history, that event still happened," Ben said

"I don't know but we need to try and get some rest, I will take the first watch," Jack said

They all settled down to try and get as much sleep as their minds would allow.

Morning

Jack sat at the entrance to the cave watching the sunrise, he could hear the others sleeping behind him, he heard a scuffle behind him as Grace came and sat next to him. She didn't speak, just linked her arm through his, and put her head on his shoulder. They sat there in silence watching the sunrise over the mountains, the golden light slowly washing the darkness away.

Yes the land is barren and sparse but it is just land thought Jack, it doesn't look scary or foreboding, it is just the land. For a moment he was lost in his thoughts and the feel of Grace next to him.

He pulled Grace in closer to him and smiled, even in all this nightmare this was the happiest he had ever been.

"Wow you pair are doing a great job of lookout," said Ben from behind.

They both jumped up as if they had received an electric shock.

Ben stood there smirking "You guys" he laughed, Jack and Grace both burst out laughing.

Viggo emerged from the cave "What's going on?", this made them laugh even more,

"You lot are strange, very strange indeed" he went back into the cave shaking his head.

Ben turned and followed Viggo back inside, Jack took a step to follow and Grace grabbed his hand, he turned around and she pulled him towards her and kissed him.

"I know what you're doing" Ben shouted from inside, they both smirked and returned to the others.

They ate a small breakfast and packed up all of their things.

"We should see Arcandru by the end of the day," Viggo said as they sat on their mounts readying themselves.

"We need to ride as fast as we can, I can't help but feel time is running out for both worlds" warned Jack

"Right then let's go" Ben shouted as Leonidas took off with a roar, followed closely by the others. Viggo and Grace were soon in the air and soaring overhead.

Ben looked up "I think I have wing envy" which was followed by a snort from Leonidas "Sorry pal, I wouldn't change you for the world"

They rode along together, both lost in their own thoughts, across a barren wilderness of rocks and mountains. Occasionally the wind blew and kicked up so much dust they had to slow down as they could not see that far ahead, but still, they continued onwards.

"Do you think we can do this?" Jack broke the silence

"We don't seem to be doing too bad so far" Ben replied

"Do you feel like you are losing your old self? I feel like I'm not the me that came here, apart from the obvious differences" Jack asked

"We have been through a lot, it's going to change us all, I think we've all had to grow up faster than we would have liked"

Jack thought this was the first serious conversation he'd had with Ben "What's happened to you?" he laughed.

Ben smiled "Can't joke all the time buddy. I know Grace and I draw our strength from you"

"What no way!"

"Jack what you have been through and how you've handled it, well I know I couldn't have. We draw our strength from you, I'm proud to have you by my side and call you my friend"

"I er, same here, but I look to you both all the time"

"I guess that's why we are such a good team then" Ben smiled

There was a shout from above, they both looked up to see Grace and Viggo flying down to them signaling them to stop.

Jack and Ben stopped and waited, Viggo and Grace landed.

"Arcandru is just over that hill" Viggo explained

"It is huge," Grace said in awe.

"What's the plan then," Ben said and they all looked at Jack.

This was the first time Jack realised how much he had been making the decisions and how much they were relying on him.

"Is there a way we can get up to the walls without being in the open" Jack asked

"There's a gully that runs from the hill to within a few feet of the wall" Viggo explained

"The problem we have is getting in, there's a huge hole in the wall but I am guessing that's the place we are more likely to run into trouble"

"So we fly in?" said Grace

"It's the only way" Ben agreed

"I can take Jack on Silvermane with me and Viggo can take Ben"

"Sounds like a plan" Viggo agreed, "We will have to walk along the gully though to make sure we aren't spotted"

They reached the hill and returned their rides to the swords and slowly made their way down to the gully.

"The only problem we have is we can't see what's above us" Jack whispered

The gully was about twenty-five feet deep and ran in a zig-zag fashion along the plains up to the walls. They had no way of knowing how far they had to go as the corners were that sharp it made you lose your sense of direction and distance.

Eventually, the walls began to loom over them.

"Wow," said Ben as they all stopped to look at the walls.

They were hundreds of feet high, smooth, and white. In areas the wall had started to crack and crumble, some plants had started to grow out of these cracks giving a splash of colour to the drab surroundings.

"I do wonder how we are supposed to stop Geddron if these huge fortresses couldn't" Grace mused.

They reached the end of the gully and Viggo climbed up to see what was around.

"I can't see anything, we are about thirty feet from the wall"

"We've got two options, we fly from here or we try to make it to the wall and go up that way" Jack suggested.

"Just in front of us part of the wall has crumbled, there's enough cover there for us to get to the wall before we fly," Viggo said

"Right let's do that, we will get to the wall and hopefully that will give us enough cover to make the ascent," Jack told them "I will go first, follow me one at a time"

Jack clambered up the end of the gully and stuck his head above the edge, he scanned around straining his ears for the slightest noise, all he could hear was the whistling wind and all he could see was the empty plains and the huge walls.

He leaped out of the gully and sprinted to the fallen wall, trying to keep as low as possible, within seconds he was behind a huge block of stone. The stones had fallen creating a small concealed area with enough gaps to see clearly along the length of the wall.

He turned back to the gully and signaled the next one.

Viggo's head popped up and then he was sprinting towards Jack, he reached him in no time.

"Great place to hide," he said entering the makeshift cave.

Grace came next, leaving Ben the last to make the run.

The wind began to pick up, it was blowing dust-up in clouds along the length of the wall towards where the hole had been made.

Jack leaned out to beckon Ben across, as he leaned out he heard something on the wind and held out his hand for Ben to stop. Bens' head dropped down slightly at the gesture.

What was that Jack thought as he strained his ears to try and listen past the wind, there it was again, it sounded like a blast on a horn, he could also hear thunder in the distance. He looked along the length of the wall and a dark shape began to emerge slowly from the now entrance to Arcandru.

"What the hell!" Jack said

"What?" said Viggo and Grace in unison rushing to the side of the shelter to peer through the cracks

"Oh no!" Viggo said in almost a whisper

"It's the horde," Jack said with dread.

Emerging from the shell of Arcandru was an army, rank upon rank of armoured troops in black and crimson armour. Marching in unison away from Arcandru.

"They don't look like anything we've encountered before," Grace said

"Ben," Jack said suddenly realising his friend was still in the gully. He looked over at Ben he was staring at the army which would get very close to where he was soon enough.

The wind began to blow in gusts, kicking up more and more dust, Jack knew this was his only chance. He waited until a large gust almost blocked out the sight of the troops and signaled Ben to move.

Ben sprang out of the gully and sprinted towards Jack, Jack watched for anything that would signal he had been seen. Ben was feet away when he tripped, he flew forward and rolled into Jack knocking him over.

"Ta-Da!" Ben said jumping to his feet

"You're an idiot sometimes," Grace said helping Jack up

"We can't risk flying up now, we are going to have to sit and wait it out," Viggo said staring at the army marching out.

They watched for hours as line after line of soldiers emerged, some on huge beasts that looked vaguely like elephants and rhinos. The creatures that accompanied them were twisted, gross things, they

236

looked like an affront to nature a vile concoction of everything that is evil and wrong.

"We need to warn Silari and the others somehow," Grace said

"They will have scouts posted, they will see them coming" Viggo replied

"The light is fading do we try and go now?" Jack asked.

"Too risky, none of us have been here before, we'd best wait for morning" stated Ben.

They all nodded and settled down for the night. None of them slept, any sleep was haunted by the marching army of the Horde.

Ascension

The next day, as dawn approached they gathered their things together and readied themselves to make the ascent to the top of the wall.

"When we get to the top we need to find somewhere we can look around, if we fly around too much we are likely to be seen" Jack explained

"If there's anything left inside," Ben said referring to the exodus of the enemy.

"Right let's do this" Jack stepped outside.

Grace and Viggo released Silvermane and Throdin, the two creatures stretched out their wings. Grace and Viggo mounted first followed by Jack and Ben.

"Hold tight," Grace said to Jack as he put his arms around her waist.

With a few beats of their wings, they were airborne flying up the face of the wall to the top, closely followed by Throdin. As they crested the top of the wall a huge tower rose to the right of them.

"There" shouted Jack "to the tower"

They flew up the side of the tower to a large balcony that was big enough for them to land on. They landed on the balcony and Jack jumped off.

"Quick everyone off, Grace, Viggo recall them" Jack was giving orders as he sprang from Silvermane's back.

They all jumped to the floor and Silvermane and Throdin were recalled.

"Inside quickly" Jack ushered them through the balcony doors and into the tower.

They found themselves in a large round room, the door leading out was a heavy wooden door and was bolted and barred from the inside. It looked like it was once a bedroom but whoever had lived here had left in a hurry, tables were turned over, drawers were pulled out, clothing was strewn around the room.

"Now what?" Ben said

"We need to decide where to go next" Viggo replied.

"Do we go to the palace?" Grace asked

"No that will be the last place there are any survivors" Jack answered.

"We can't just wander around this place hoping to find something because what we find will probably be not what we want to find" Ben stated.

Jack stepped into the doorway of the balcony and looked out over the city, looking for a clue, anything that would give them an idea of where to go.

Then out of the corner of his eye, he saw a flash, he turned his head and stared. There it was again, near to where the wall joined the mountains behind.

"There Look" Said Jack pointing

They all crowded into the doorway to see.

"Viggo, your eyes are better than ours can you make anything out?" Asked Jack

Viggo stared intently at the flashes "I don't believe it"

"What? What is it?" Grace almost demanded

"It looks like Seraphs, fighting" Viggo stuttered.

"We need to get there and fast" Jack exclaimed

"Viggo, Grace its time to fly"

Throdin and Silvermane were set free and they mounted again. They took off from the tower and swooped down so they were flying along the top of the wall, trying to keep hidden as much as possible.

As they got closer Jack could see what looked like a small group of angels battling creatures from the Horde along the top of the wall, they were swooping in and out cutting and stabbing the creatures who tried to grab them in vain. They were vastly outnumbered but seemed to be winning. Just then at the rear a small group appeared with bows and let off a volley of arrows, two of the Seraphs fell to the floor and were immediately jumped upon by the creatures.

"Ben" Jack shouted "There!" Jack pointed at the archers and Ben nodded.

"Get us in close I'm going to jump" Jack shouted to Grace

Grace and Viggo swooped down and Ben and Jack leapt from the mounts drawing their swords. Their armour had covered them before they landed amidst the archers.

Jack killed two in quick succession, Ben was doing the same cleaving a pathway through the creatures. Jack saw Grace and Viggo land just as they finished off the archers, the creatures were confused they had no idea who this new enemy was. The four friends fought together cutting down creature after creature.

A blow landed on Jacks's helmet and sent him dizzy, he fell to one knee, straight away Ben was by his side pulling him up. "No time for a rest Jack"

Ben pushed Jack and he stumbled but an arcing sword carved through the air where he had been stood, Ben dispatched him with one blow.

Jack was still stunned but now Grace and Viggo were also by him fighting side by side. Ben spun round and severed the head from a rather large creature that had just raised a large axe above his head.

A Seraph landed by the group "This way, there are too many"

The Seraph gestured to the mountain behind them "We will fly you up but you must get closer"

They fought slowly along the top of the wall to the mountainside, every step was a small victory. They carved a way through the enemy, blocking and cutting, sending some creatures spinning from the wall. Viggo blocked a blow that was heading for Ben which threw him off balance, Jack grabbed his arm and used his weight to stop him from falling.

They were within a few feet of the wall now, they had killed so many creatures but the numbers seemed to be growing. Ben had split his sword into two and was now spinning his blades like a windmill of death, no creature could get close to him.

"We need to go now" shouted the Seraph

"Grace, Viggo, go me and Ben will hold them off" Jack yelled.

Jack placed both his hands on the handle of his sword and it grew into a longsword, he began to swing it in great arcs carving the creatures before him. He saw Grace and Viggo being lifted into the air.

"Ben!" Jack shouted "We need to go now"

Ben nodded, a Seraph swooped down and grabbed Jack under his arms and lifted him, he watched as another did the same to Ben. They rose about ten feet into the air, Jack looked up to see where Grace and Viggo were. As he looked back a black shape leapt from the throng of creatures, Jack watched as it reached out its long claws towards Ben.

"BEN!" Jack bellowed a second too late as the creature's claws somehow pierced the armour around Bens's leg.

Ben shouted out in pain, the extra weight forced the Seraph to drop suddenly, the creature was yanking on Bens's leg.

Jack heard Grace and Viggo shouting from above just as the Seraphs grip loosened and Ben fell.

The next few seconds happened so slowly, Jack watched in horror as his friend fell in what seemed like slow motion to the floor. Then he vanished beneath the creatures.

"Nooooooo!" Jack shouted and wriggled free of the Seraph holding him, he leapt into the creature's sword above his head.

Grace screamed as she saw Ben fall, then again as Jack leapt after him. Then her eyes opened wide, she looked at Viggo whos eyes were also wide and staring along with the Seraphs holding them.

As Jack fell he screamed, a cry of pain and anguish and vengeance, his sword began to glow blue, electricity sprang from the blade, he landed amongst the creatures like a bolt of lightning a huge shockwave rang out knocking the creatures over, the next few minutes Jack slaughtered the creatures around him, it was not a battle they stood no chance. He swung his blade left to right blue lightning arcing out from the blade killing four or five at a time, within moments he had killed half and the others began to run. Jack continued until none were left alive, then, and only then did he return to Ben.

He looked at his friend, his eyes were closed his helmet had been ripped from his head, he was covered in blood and his breathing was labored. He cradled his friends head gently in his lap, Viggo and Grace knelt beside him, Grace was crying they both took his hands.

"Oh, Ben," Grace said through her tears.

Jack couldn't speak, this couldn't be happening not now. Ben opened his eyes and looked at Jack

"Aw buddy looks like this is where we say goodbye" his speech was stuttery as he grasped for each breath

"Ben, it's ok," Jack said

"We kicked some ass didn't we?" he said closing his eyes

"Ben it's gonna be ok, you just need some rest" Jack felt stupid for saying it but it was all he could say.

"Grace?" "I'm here Ben," she said squeezing his hand. "Look after him and Jack keep her safe"

His breathing started to slow and a tear rolled down his cheek "I'm scared Jack"

Jack cradled him close as tears ran down his cheeks.

They sat there and held their friend as he took his last breath and slipped away.

Grace sobbed uncontrollably and was comforted by Viggo who also had tears in his eyes.

"I'm sorry but we must go," The nearby Seraph said "Bring your friend we will take care of him"

"Go where?" Jack managed to say

"Up, we have to fly up the mountain"

"Throdin will carry Ben," Viggo said

Viggo and a still sobbing Grace called forth Throdin and Silvermane, the Seraphs looked on with a stunned expression.

Viggo climbed aboard Throdin who moved toward Jack and Ben, Jack gently laid his friends head onto the floor and stood up. Throdin carefully picked Ben up in its claws and took off, the Seraphs took wing also and began to ascend the mountain.

Jack stood and watched his friend's lifeless body being carried into the air, he bent down and picked up Ben's sword, he turned to Grace who sat upon Silvermane.

"Jack" she held out her hand and he leapt behind her, wrapping his arms tightly around her waist. Everything had changed now, everything.

Heavensholme

As they ascended Jack was lost in his thoughts, he blindly watched the mountain face sliding by, listening to the flap of wings. No one spoke, there was no noise, they broke through into clouds which gave everything a dreamy feel to it, a sort of out of body experience.

The clouds began to thin out, Jack could make out a dark shape that seemed to be protruding from the mountain. As they reached it the cloud cleared and he could see it was an outcropping of rock, they flew around it and over it, the top was flat and smooth. He saw the Seraphs had landed and they were taking Ben's body from Throdin.

Ben and Grace landed next to Viggo who was just sat watching them Take Ben's body towards the mountain. Jack followed them with his eyes, he noticed an opening in the mountain, there were two doors open, obviously to protect the entrance. Each door had a large silver wing that glistened in the sunlight.

Jack and Grace dismounted and stood with Viggo watching them carry Ben inside.

A seraph walked towards them, he wore a light silver and blue armour with a sword at his side, his face was beautiful, angelic almost with piercing blue eyes.

"Welcome to Heavensholme I am Candel General of the army of Heavensholme. Firstly must I say how sorry I am about your friend, he will be taken care of"

"I want to see him" Jack stated

"My Lord Faria would like to speak to you"

"I will see Ben now!" There was no mistaking the authority and determination in his voice

"Of course, please follow me" Candel turned and made his way inside, followed by Jack, Grace, and Viggo.

As they walked through the great doors Jack noticed a large room either side of the entrance with what looked like soldiers in each one. The floor was pure white as were the walls, the roof was a pale blue with wisps of white, it was almost as though you were looking at the sky. Along the walls every so often were pictures of from what Jack could tell Arcandru, it did look a beautiful city, once.

They reached a room where the door was closed, he was a heavy thick-set wooden door with an arched top. Candel paused in front of it "He is at rest in here, take as long as you wish"

He opened the door and pushed it open, then he stepped aside to allow them to enter.

The room was small but stunningly beautiful, Jack gasped as he entered. The walls and floor were painted so realistically, on the far wall was the great tree, looking around the room was as though you were stood in that exact spot. You could smell the grass and the flowers, feel the warmth from the sun.

In the middle was a stone table, Ben's body was laid upon it and covered in a silver sheet. They had cleaned him up and he looked as though he were asleep.

Jack walked over to him and could feel the tears welling up again, he was joined by Viggo and Grace. Grace clung to Jack's arm as they looked at their fallen friend. Jack pulled out Ben's sword and placed it on his chest.

"We should say something," Grace said

Viggo stepped forward and placed his hand upon Ben's chest "My brother, never have I known a more ferocious warrior or a more trustworthy friend. Rest now from this war and I hope we will meet again soon"

Grace went next "Ben, I will miss your laughter and your smile, I will miss you constantly getting on my nerves, I will miss your strength, your courage, and your friendship"

She stepped away and stood next to Viggo taking his arm as Jack stepped forward.

"What can I say that hasn't already been said, you accepted me for who I am, you will never know what that meant to me, you kept our spirits high and always looked for the positives in everything. I will miss your appetite for life and anything edible. I will miss my best friend, sleep well my friend"

Jack took a step back to his friends. "What now? Is that it? Is it all over?" he asked to no one in particular.

Then he felt the hairs on the back of his neck rise, he could feel the electricity in the air.

"Jack?" Grace said

"What's happening?" Viggo said looking around the room

The energy continued to build until a blinding flash, as their eyes cleared a woman stood at the head of Ben's body her hands on either side of his face.

"Selendrial!" Jack exclaimed

The door burst open and Candel and two guards rushed in "What's going on?" he shouted.

"Candel, I am Selendrial and I have come to take Ben home" Selendrial answered.

The Seraph's stood there open mouthed.

"Selendrial where are you taking him?" Grace asked.

"Do not worry, I will look after him, this part of his journey is now over another part awaits him"

"What do we do now?" Jack asked

"Continue with your quest Katari for you are our only hope"

The energy began to build again, flashes of lightning danced around Ben's body, a flash and they were gone.

"I think you need to explain things to Faria as soon as possible" Candel said

Jack nodded, still in shock and trying to come to terms with the loss of his friend.

"Follow me and I will take you straight to him, he is waiting for you"

They followed him along several different corridors all twists and turns, they didn't pass through any large spaces just corridors, but it still felt as though you were outside. They finally reached a crossroads, straight in front was a small passageway with two soldiers guarding it, at the end of the passageway was a round door, the door was open and led into a larger room.

Candel walked past the two guards and into the room, followed by Grace, Viggo, and Jack.

The room was fairly large, like the room where Ben had been the walls were painted with an outdoor scene, the roof of the room curved over, and although it was also painted to resemble the sky it glowed as if light was shining through it, as though the rock was wafer-thin.

Once again Jack could smell grass and flowers. There was a row of troops either side of the walkway some male some females all in the same armour as Candel.

At the far end of the room on a raised platform was a solid round table, sat at the table were two men and two women.

"My lord Faria, the Katari" Candel introduced them.

Faria stood and walked around the table to them, he shook their hands in turn "Welcome travelers, firstly may I say how sorry I am for your loss but I feel we have much to discuss and not a great deal of time to do it. Please sit" he gestured to the chairs at the table and returned to his seat.

"let me start by introducing everyone here, Candel you've met, he is my General and also happens to be my son, this is Cerebal, he is the warden of my city. This is Kara, she is the head of my security and finally Syr my chief advisor."

They all nodded a hello, "I am Jack, this is Grace and Viggo"

"Viggo is a Dwafen name is it not," asked Faria

"That is correct I am from the survivors of Stonehaven"

There were gasps all around the table.

"We didn't think anyone had survived," Candel said in shock

"No one thinks any of you survived either" replied Grace

"It is true we have not left here since that dread day, we only ventured out today because we saw the army leaving, obviously there are still a few of the foul vermin left," Faria said

"We are here to find someone to join us, to hopefully fulfill a prophesy and stop the Hellions once and for all" Jack explained.

"Whom do you seek?" asked Syr

"That is the problem, we do not know" Viggo answered

Unexpectedly Grace stood up, drawing all eyes to her.

"Grace" Jack said to her

Grace had a funny expression on her face, as though she was staring into space.

"Grace" reiterated Jack.

Grace began to walk around the table, Jack and Viggo stood up followed by the others. Syr was sat closest to Grace, but she walked around her, next was sat Kara who was now stood with her hand on her sword.

"What's going on?" she asked concerned

Jack noticed how beautiful she was, but she also had a look of strength and determination, her blonde hair was almost white as it fell down her back in a plait.

Grace stopped in front of Kara and held out her hand in greeting.

Viggo and Jack looked at each other with a knowing look.

Grace stood there with her hand held out in greeting, eventually, Kara hesitantly reached out her hand and took Graces.

The crackling electricity began immediately, lightning dancing around the room, building to a crescendo of static, noise, and a blinding light.

As Jack's eyes began to clear the first thing he saw was Kara looking frantically around the room, blinking quickly as if to remove the last residue of sleep from her eyes, she looked like a cornered rabbit.

"Kara it's ok" Jack reassured her.

Grace went over and placed her hand on her arm "It's ok, your fine"

"Where, are we?" she stuttered

"You are perfectly safe my child, I am Selendrial" a voice sounded from behind them, causing Kara to spin around and crouch ready for an attack.

"Selendrial? But you're a tree" Kara exclaimed

"All will become clear soon enough" Selendrial explained. "please sit" she gestured to the chairs around the room.

They all sat and Selendrial explained to Kara all she needed to know about Anu and the war.

As Selendrial was speaking Jack again felt the sense of loss, the feeling that Ben was no longer here. He glanced at the stone in the middle of the room and noticed Ben's sword had been returned to its place. His eyes filled with tears, uncontrollably the grief washed over him. He felt Grace put an arm around his shoulder and they held each other and cried as they remembered their friend.

Jack felt a presence in front of him and looked up, through tear-filled eyes, he saw Selendrial standing there, a look of love and compassion on her face.

"My children, do not weep for your friend it is just a part of his journey, be glad you had him in your life even if it was for the briefest of moments. He is at rest now"

Jack pulled himself together, as Grace sat back in her chair he saw Viggo his face full of sorrow and sadness, Kara sat opposite looking concerned.

"I'm fine, I'm sorry," Jack said, no more words were needed.

Selendrial turned again to Kara "My child it is time to choose your destiny, please select a sword"

Kara stood and moved to the stone in the centre of the room, she reached out her hand and hovered over the remaining swords, her hand stopped over Bens, both Jack and Grace let out a little gasp before she moved on, finally stopping over the eagle sword. Her hand slid down the hilt of the sword, her hands gently grasping as she pulled it free.

The energy started immediately, surging and crackling around the room, building in intensity until a blinding flash. As their eyes cleared there stood Kara, in a white tunic trimmed with gold, two wings emblazoned across her chest, the sword in a scabbard at her side. She had grown also and was now nearly seven feet tall, however, the most noticeable change was her wings had gone.

"My Wings!" Kara exclaimed

"They are still there, the magic has hidden them, but if you need them, concentrate and they will return" Selendrial assured.

Kara's face took on a look of concentration and her wings unfurled from nowhere, she flapped them slightly before they again disappeared.

"Take out your sword," Viggo said enthusiastically

Grace and Jack both smiled.

Kara drew her sword, immediately she was clad in white and gold armour.

"That is pretty amazing," Kara said returning her sword.

Selendrial spoke "You are now Katari, your quest is drawing closer to its conclusion. You have one more soul to find and this will be the hardest one. Jack, Grace you must journey back to your world to find the last chosen one".

It was the first time Jack had thought of home for a long time as if that part of him had somehow been repressed.

"Home" Jack whispered.

"I will not return you to Arcandru, you must leave her and seek Silari and Straven they will help you return home. Be warned, the end of your world is close, your magic will not work there until Geddron returns. Kara, Viggo you must travel with your friends to their world it is as different to ours as night is to day so prepare yourselves. Kara my magic will allow you to hide your wings there so you may move about freely other than that you are on your own" Selendrial finished speaking and sat back down.

"Good luck and hurry for time is short" with that she disappeared

"So what is your world like?" Viggo asked

"We will fill you in as much as possible on the way," Jack said "C'mon we have some people who are going to love to meet you"

Home

They emerged from the tree into the brilliant, blazing sunshine. Birds swooped and dove across the sky, birdsong echoed around. The scent of flowers and the smell of grass assaulted their sense of smell.

It seemed like a lifetime ago the three of them had stood in this spot before entering the tree, another pang of loss hit Jack like an arrow. He looked at Grace and smiled.

"There's a camp over there" Viggo pointed.

"Right let's go," Grace said leading the way.

They followed Grace to the tent, it was strange as they had expected to be spotted before they reached it but it seemed deserted.

"Hello" Jack shouted, but no one responded.

"Well that's weird," Grace said to Jack.

"Let's look inside," Viggo said striding to the entrance.

They reached the entrance to the tent and again Jack shouted, again there was no reply.

They stepped inside and went through into a room, inside the room was a table and chairs. On the table food and drink had been laid out.

"This looks pretty fresh," Kara said

"Maybe whoever's tent this is will be back soon" Surmised Viggo

"Well I am starving," Grace said sitting down at the table.

"I don't suppose they will mind," Jack said as they all sat down and began to eat and drink.

"What is your world like," Kara asked

"That's a tough one to answer, it is a complicated world where a lot of people do not get on with each other, there is a lot of conflicts and there have been many, many wars" Jack replied

"Wars? Over what?" Viggo asked

"Land, religion, oil. Lots of things" Grace replied

"There is no magic in our world, we have science"

"What's science," Asked Kara

"Science is finding how things are made and how things work, then using that to make new things" Grace tried to explain "for instance you get around using horses, in our world, we have machines that move us around along land, water or through the air"

"Wow your world sounds strange," Viggo said

"Erm hello" a voice sounded from behind them and they all span round.

"Phoebe!" Grace exclaimed

"Oh it's you, oh wow you've changed, where's Ben"

"He, he didn't make it" replied Jack "Phoebe this is Viggo of Eiserwelt and Stonehaven and this is Kara of Heavensholme and Arcandru"

"You're a Dwafen and a Seraph?" she said excitedly

They both nodded.

"Where is everyone" Jack inquired

"Gone to fight, an army appeared in the north, our forces were converging on the plains so they are holding there waiting for the attack. I was entrusted with staying here hoping you would return"

"We will stay here tonight and then we are to journey back to our world" Jack explained

"There are beds for you and I have plenty of food," Phoebe said smiling

They sat and finished their meal explaining to Phoebe all that had happened and then went to their beds.

That night Jack couldn't sleep, he was thinking about Ben and about going home and going back to being normal Jack again. Could he do what needed to be done without magic, and more importantly with his condition again.

Eventually, sleep did take over and he slept until morning when Viggo roused him.

They got all their things together and took as much food and water as they could carry and set off to the clearing from which they had arrived.

They finally reached the avenue of trees from which they had all arrived, to Jack, it seemed a lifetime ago, again as he looked down the avenue his thoughts turned to Ben and how he would explain it to his family. Grace come up and stood beside him "It seems so long ago"

"I know, I was thinking the same"

Jack turned to Phoebe "You must go to Silari and the others, tell them what is happening, tell them to do the best they can, I have a feeling things are about to get a lot worse"

Phoebe nodded, "Good luck to you all, hopefully, we will meet again soon" with that she turned and ran back towards the tent.

"Right then, this is it, let's go," said Jack

Jack, Grace, Viggo, and Kara set off down the avenue of trees, it was still an amazing sight but somehow seemed a little duller.

They eventually arrived at the clearing, there stood the stone arch at the one end.

They walked over to the archway, Jack was expecting something to happen, but nothing did.

"What do we do?" Kara asked expectantly

"We don't know we came the other way" Grace replied

Suddenly Jack felt a vibration against his chest, he put his hand in his chest pocket and pulled out the key. The key was glowing as before.

"I'd forgotten about that" Grace said staring at the key

"I'm fairly sure it wasn't there earlier," said a surprised Jack

"We need a keyhole"

Together they inspected the archway for the keyhole, it was Kara who found it eventually and seemed so obvious after it had been noticed.

Jack placed the key into the hole and turned it.

Lightning flashed around them, there was a roar of energy, every colour flashed before their eyes. Jack heard the others shouting, he had forgotten what it had been like getting here. Once again it felt like they were falling, the lights, the noise was too much to bear. Again Jack felt himself losing consciousness, he fought against it but in the end, darkness overtook him.

The End

Jack slowly opened his eyes, he blinked several times trying to clear his vision quickly, the roaring in his ears was slowly starting to fade away. He looked around the others were still out on the floor, there was the gate in his garden closed again. He was home.

He got up and immediately felt pain in his leg, it was then he noticed he was back to being Jack, the others had also changed yet in his dazed state it hadn't registered. He still had his sword at his waist, he drew it out and nothing happened. This may be even harder than I thought.

The others started to come round first Viggo, then Grace, then Kara. Viggo looked at them and said, "You are just children!"

"Great this is going to go well" Kara exclaimed.

"What's wrong with the sky?" Grace asked

Jack looked up, the sky was dark almost dusk-like with hints of red. The clouds swirled across the sky as if they were being blown by the strongest wind, but there was no wind anywhere.

"We need to get to the house" Jack urged them

"The lions are gone" Grace noticed.

Just then they heard a rustling sound, they all drew their swords ready to face what was about to emerge. Slowly out of the undergrowth a panther emerged, it was badly injured.

"So you have returned finally, I am Joken and the last of the guardians"

"The last?" Jack gasped

"The gateway was attacked as you left by the creatures from Hellion, my brothers and I fought a long time before they were either dead or they decided to flee"

"My parents!" Jack shouted

"They are fine, they were of little interest to them now they have found the gate, they do not know they cannot get through without the key"

"I need to see my parents," Jack said "I need to go home too" Grace agreed.

"I will stay at my post until you return"

"I can help with your wounds," Kara said kindly

"Ok, Grace you and Viggo go to your house, find your father and bring him here. Kara, once you are done here come to the house" Jack gave the instructions and they set off along the path to the house.

They eventually got to the back door of the house.

"See you soon Jack," Grace said hugging him tightly and she left with Viggo through the wide-open gate.

Jack took a deep breath and opened the back door, "Mom, Dad" he shouted

"In the living room," his mom shouted back.

Hearing her voice again made a million emotions come rushing all over him at once, he wanted to run to them and tell them everything, he knew they would never believe him. How was he going to explain all this to them, he rested his hand on his sword, he'd have to take that off at least for the time being.

He removed his sword and leaned up some boxes in the utility room. It was a box that had been here since they moved in, as he leaned his sword he was sure he saw some small dashes of lightning slide down his sword. He was going to open the box but thought he'd come back later and have a look.

He walked into the house and felt like he had been away from home for months, home, was it home yet even though they hadn't been there long. I guess home is where your family is so yes this was home.

He walked into the living room, strangely his parents were both sitting watching TV, they never watched TV.

"Mom, Dad," Jack said as he entered, resisting the urge to run to them and fling his arms around them.

"Jack, have you seen this? The weirdest thing is going on in Georgia" his dad said without taking his eyes off the TV.

Jack sat on the other sofa, "Hang on when did you finish this room"

His parents both looked at him strangely "Weeks ago" said his mom

"How long have I been gone?" Jack said without thinking

"Gone where son?" asked his dad

"It doesn't matter, what's happening in Georgia then?"

"Not sure if its some sort of terrorist thing or what, apparently there's heavy fighting in Georgia"

Jack felt a chill run down his back, the BBC news was on the TV, the presenter was interviewing a reporter who was in Sochi"

"Graham can you give me the latest on what's happening?" the newsreader asked

"Well it seems like a terrorist force of some description had been planning an attack, it seems they had been preparing in a cave network near here called Krubera Voronja, apparently it is the deepest cave known on earth"

"Do we know who is responsible yet?"

"As yet there are no confirmed reports or anyone admitting responsibility, hang on I am just getting reports that Tbilisi has fallen, this doesn't sound like an attack it sounds like an invasion"

"Graham thank you, keep us updated as much as you can. We have been told that the prime minister has called an emergency meeting of the Cobra committee and that will take place in the next hour. We will keep you updated as events unfold"

"What the hell is going on," Jacks Dad said

"I don't know, but I don't like it," said his mom

Jack knew he had to try and say something but he had no idea where to start.

"Erm Dad"

"Yes pal"

"I need to try and tell you and mom something but you probably won't believe me"

"Of course we will honey, you know you can tell us anything" assured his mom.

So Jack began to tell his story, trying to make it as short as possible but keeping the important things in.

Jack finished with "and I think what is happening in Georgia has something to do with it"

"Is this one of your comic books?" his dad asked

"No dad its"

"Breaking news from Georgia, we are getting fresh reports that it is indeed an invasion and the invading force has now moved into Southern Russia and Eastern Turkey" the news reporter's voice shocked them all back to the TV.

"Russian and Turkish forces have been mobilised and are heading to the affected areas. NATO troops in Europe are being put on high alert, as yet we still have no news as to who is responsible"

"Shit its world war 3" his dad exclaimed.

Just then Kara appeared at the door holding Jack's sword "Hi I thought you may need this" she said offering him his sword.

"Who's this? More importantly, who's is that sword?" his mom almost shouted.

"This is Kara who I told you about, and the sword is mine as I also told you about"

"Don't get cheeky with me young man" admonished his Dad.

"Did you listen to what I have been saying at all?" Jack asked

"Of course, something about swords, trees, gateways in the garden," said his mom

"And lions and maybe a dragon, maybe," said his Dad

"Oh for goodness sake, will you ever listen to me!" Jack was getting fed up.

"You never listen, you say you do but you don't"

"Jack, honey we do listen" assured his mom

"But you don't believe me?"

"Well it is a bit of a stretch son" offered his dad

"Kara, can you do the thing?" Jack asked

"The what?"

"You know the thing we can't see?"

"Oh, I don't know I will try?"

Kara began to concentrate, her face was a picture of concentration and resolve, but nothing happened. Five minutes past with the three of them watching Kara pull a variety of faces and make a variety of noises.

"No nothing!" she said breathlessly.

"Stupid wings!"

At that point, her wings unfurled and stretched out across the room.

Jack's parents shot up and stared, they looked at Kara, then Jack, then each other and back at Kara.

"Oh my," said his mom

His dad looked at Jack "Sorry son, I guess we had better listen to you again, properly this time"

Jack again told them what had happened, told them what he thought was happening in their world now and how bad it could be.

"Oh boy!" his dad's face was shocked as was his mom's. Kara had just managed to conceal her wings as there was a knock at the door.

"I'll get it," Jack said jumping up and heading to the front door. He opened the door and there stood Grace, Viggo and another man who he assumed was Grace's dad.

"Hey," Jack said

"Hey, this is my dad" Grace replied

"Hello sir, pleased to meet you," Jack said offering out his hand.

"Please its Andrew or Andy will do, I think I have a lot to thank you for. For getting my daughter back safely"

Jack smiled unsure of what to say "Please come in" he took them through into the living room.

"Mom, Dad this is Grace, Viggo and Andrew" Jack introduced them

"These are my parents Joe and Emma"

"Please call me Andy," he said offering his hand to Jack's parents.

"So what's the plan?" Viggo asked

"I don't know," Jack said and for the first time, he had no clue.

Suddenly the TV drew their attention

"We have breaking news coming in," the newsreader said

"Turkish forces are currently holding a line across their border with Georgia, in the north Russian and

Ukrainian forces are holding a line through Volgograd, Luhansk, Donetsk and Mariupol. Armenia and Azerbaijan are being reinforced with Iranian forces. Not much is coming out of the areas already lost and reports from the frontline are sketchy and a little crazy.

Whatever force this is are extremely well trained and well equipped, it is being compared to the German Blitzkrieg of World War two"

"This is not going well" Jack's dad sighed

Jack needed some water so got up and went to the kitchen, followed by Grace, Viggo and Kara.

"Anyone want some water?" Jack asked and they all nodded

"What are we going to do?" Grace broke the silence

"I have no idea where we find the other person or what we can do about what's happening," Jack said

"We are in this together, do not feel the need to take this on alone Jack" Viggo said

"But I don't know where to star………hang on, maybe I do" Jack rushed out of the kitchen and into the living room, he picked up his sword and left.

"Jack is everything ok?" his mom shouted after him

"Yes mom I'm not leaving the house" he shouted back.

The others followed him into the utility room. He stood facing the piles of old boxes and drew out his sword. The sword immediately began to glow blue, it got brighter the closer it got to the boxes.

Jack turned to the others and smiled "Let's get these boxes open"

There must have been about fifteen boxes of varying sizes, most were full of junk or old books, but the final two at the bottom each contained a wooden chest.

The chests were dark wood, about a metre long, half a metre high, and the same wide. They had large gold hinges on with a large golden clasp locking the lid shut. Engraved on the lid was the tree carving they had seen so many times before, this was covered in silver leaf.

Jack tried to move the one box but it was very heavy, Viggo, however, managed to drag them both out, they studied them and they were both identical.

"How do we open them, because that is not a keyhole?" Grace sighed

"Let's get them into the living room, I think we are going to need some ideas to get these open" Jack suggested.

Between them, they half carried, half dragged them into the living room, to some bewildered looks by their parents.

"What are those" Jack's Dad asked, "And where did you get them from?"

"They were in those old boxes in the utility room, we need to get them open" Jack replied.

"I will get my tools," his dad said leaving the room

They all turned their attention back to the TV.

"We are about to go over to ten Downing street where the prime minister is about to make a statement"

They watched as the prime minister stood solemnly outside number ten, ready to address the worlds media.

"Good afternoon, at approximately eleven am this morning a military force of unknown origin invaded parts of Georgia, this force then moved north into Southern Russia and South into Armenia and Azerbaijan. Turkey currently is holding a frontline approximately ten miles from its border with

Georgia. We have reports that Iranian forces have moved north to assist in the defence and that forces from the middle east including Israel have been sent north to aid

Turkey.

There were audible gasps from the amassed reporters.

UK and NATO forces are on high alert, with a rapid response force being sent to Ukraine as we speak. We are currently trying to assess the situation and to find out exactly what is happening in the area, we will be sending special forces teams into the area to try and gain what intel we can.

We will try and keep you updated as much as possible. Thank you"

Jack's dad returned with a box of tools, saw everyone's faces "Have I missed something?"

"The world's gone to shit!" Grace's dad said

"Dad!" said Grace

"Let's get these boxes open, quick" Jack said

Viggo stepped forward and opened the toolbox, Jack and the others took a step back knowing somehow he was the best man for the job. He took his time examining the chest then looking through the tools.

He tried every tool in the box pretty much a hammer, a chisel, a bigger hammer, a drill nothing worked nothing even left a mark.

"Well that's not going to work," Viggo said

"The key must be around here somewhere," Grace said, "Where was the key to the gate?"

"Erm hanging up by the door," Jack said ironically

"Ah!" Grace sighed

Jack drew his sword "This helped finding the boxes perhaps it can find the key"

"Hang on a minute," Kara said looking at the lock then at Jack

"Perhaps the sword is the key, it looks about the same size"

Viggo shrugged "Give it a go"

Jack offered his sword up to the lock on the chest, his sword began to glow brightly. It slid easily into the clasp on the chest, then there was a loud click as the clasp unlocked.

"Try the other one," Grace said excitedly.

Jack did exactly the same and the same thing occurred the clasp sprang open.

"Let's see what we've got," Jack said sheathing his sword.

They opened the chests, in one were three large leather bound books, in the other was six large stones, three blue and three white, laying between the stones was a rolled up parchment.

"Let's see if there is anything in these books that can help," Jack said taking out the first book.

He sat back on the sofa with the book on his lap and opened it, you could tell straight away it was old, the pages felt delicate between his fingers, and it smelt old and musty when he turned the page.

"Anything?" Grace asked

"It looks like a diary or an account of something" Jack answered and he began to read

"We have been here for months now, trapped in this new world, trapped with the few Hellions that made it through. They are very few and thankfully we outnumber them at the moment, no one has seen Thrall since the spell.

There are a few of us from each race, the Seraphs are the fewest in number along with a few Dwafen, the other races are represented equally.

We have built a place for us to live and named it Gobekil Tepe, we are having to fashion crude tools and weapons as magic seems very limited here. Hopefully, we can go home soon."

"It's written by the lost ones," Viggo said "The ones caught in the great spell during the banishment of Thrall"

Jack flipped a few pages forward "It has been years now and we are managing to thrive, well the Hanori seem to be more suited to this world than the other races, the Dwafen and Seraphs are even fewer in number now.

We have had a few skirmishes with the Hellions and have pushed them back north into a series of caves, it has been a few months since any were seen. It seems that they are trying to get back to the place we crossed over, we guess they have a way of getting back from there we don't know about"

"What was the name of the settlement again?" Grace's dad asked

"Erm Gobekil Tepe, why?" Jack asked

"I've heard of it, I'm sure I have seen a program about it," he said taking out his phone "Yes here it is" Then he stopped looked at the TV then back at his phone.

"What is it, dad?" Grace asked

"It's in Turkey"

"That answers that question then," Viggo said "That is definitely Thrall and his Hellions trying to get back"

"They need to be stopped from getting there," Kara said

"There is no way we can get there in time, and I don't see what we could possibly do against what looks like a very large army" Jack replied "We need to read through these and see if we can find anything else out. Grace you take one, Viggo you take the other and Kara check out that other chest. Let's hope we can find the answers"

Major James Stewart was sat in the passenger seat of a jeep, heading North through Turkey to the border with Georgia. Driving was Sergeant Alistair Smith, in the rear sat Corporal Andy Duncan and Privates Jason Grainger and Paul Simpson. They had been operating in northern Syria when the orders had come through to drop everything and head north.

They were part of the elite British special forces the SAS.

It was to be a purely reconnaissance mission and to gather as much intel as possible, they had been given the go ahead to engage any hostile forces but the priority was to report back as much information as possible.

The Major knew very little of what was happening as nothing seemed to be coming out of the warzone, this was very worrying as in this day and age it was easy to get battlefield intelligence and relay it where it needed to go quickly.

He knew the entire British armed forces were being mobilised along with all NATO forces, he knew the Russians were fighting side by side with Ukrainian forces, which just a few days ago would have been impossible. But the strangest thing was the fact Turkey, Israel, Iran and several Arab nations were also all fighting side by side.

Who could it be he thought, the Chinese? Why would they want to get on the wrong side of the rest of the world?

"What's our eta?" the Major asked.

"We are half an hour from Kars which is a few miles behind the Turkish frontline" the Corporal replied.

They were trained not to address by rank, even though in the field they followed orders they fought as one and addressed each other by name only just in case of capture.

In the distance, they heard a series of explosions and seven jets flew over heading in the same direction.

"Slow down Ali" James ordered "Let's have a look at what's going on"

They pulled over to the side of the road and got out their binoculars, James stood on the roof of the jeep with Andy looking into the distance. They watched the jets fly in low towards the city, as they watched, what looked like black lines shot up from the ground spearing through the jets within seconds five were down, the other two tried to climb away but were also soon destroyed.

"What the hell was that," Andy said

"I've never seen anything like it" James answered

"Hang on what's that," Andy said pointing down the road

They both looked, all they could see was a blackness moving down the road towards them, slowly as it grew closer they began to make out what it was. They lowered their binoculars, looked at each other then looked again.

282

"What is it?" asked Jason from below.

"It looks like hell" Andy said

"We need to go now," James said jumping from the roof, they all jumped in and Ali started the jeep up.

"Get us away from here now" James ordered

He swung the jeep around, "Paul get on that gun, the rest of you get ready this might get rough" James said.

Paul jumped into the back and swung the large mounted machine gun around to face the way they were coming from, the others picked up their guns and readied themselves for a fight.

"Who is it?" Jason asked

"Not who, what?" Andy answered "It looks like, like creatures, creatures from your worst nightmares"

"Are you kidding me?" Ali said

"I'm afraid not," James said

"They seem to be gaining," Paul said

They spun round in their seats to see they were gaining on them quickly.

"Go, go, go!" James shouted

Paul began to fire, round after round into the advancing horde. "They are goddam demons!" he shouted above the gunfire.

Jason and Andy were both now leaning out of the jeep firing at the advancing horde as they got closer and closer.

Jason watched as a creature resembling something from alien that was jet black and had claws and teeth of what appeared to be silver try to jump onto the jeep, it was cut down by Paul, they were just a few feet behind them now and there were a lot of them.

"This is getting too close!" Andy shouted "Ali put your foot down"

"It is down" he shouted back

They had all now opened fire, James was stood on his seat firing from the top of the jeep, he couldn't believe what he was seeing, Satan's demons seemed to be chasing them or it was an alien invasion.

Left and right they fired as the creatures were managing to get either side of them.

"There! Up ahead" shouted Ali

James looked around and could see a line of tanks and troops advancing towards them, "They are Israelis, head between those two tanks"

They drove between the two nearest tanks just as they opened fire with shells and machine guns, gunships flew overhead firing rockets and bullets into the horde of demons.

It was over, the few remaining monsters turned and fled back the way they had come chased by the gunships.

The jeep ground to a halt and they all just sat there stunned at what had happened and at what they had just seen. A jeep pulled up beside them an Israeli Colonel in the passenger seat.

"Who are you?" she said

James thought there was no point lying to allies "I'm Major James Stewart British Army"

"You're a long way from home Major"

"Just trying to find what the hell is going on"

"Hell is the correct word Major, I think this is the end of days, good luck" and she drove away her column advancing across the land.

"Right get that sat phone out we need to report this to London"

Discovery

Jack and the others had been trawling through the books for what seemed like an eternity. Kara had had no luck with the stones at all and the parchment according to Viggo and Kara looked like a spell.

"Listen to this" Jack started to read "The magic in this world is slowly fading, Thrall and the Horde seem to have disappeared underground, we have no doubt they will return, we are not strong enough to follow them and put an end to this once and for all.

We are learning how to create things using what is around us, the more we learn, the less magic there seems to be, we know we have no way of making it home now."

"These books must be chronicling the first people's life here"

Listen to this Grace read aloud "1492 we are starting to explore this world we now call home, amazingly we are finding other people in other lands, we don't know how this is happening but they are very primitive. We try to help where we can but sometimes we feel something is also working against us."

"Then further on it says. We have had terrible news from one of our emissaries Christopher who travelled to what we are calling the Americas came across a people calling themselves the Aztecs, they have traded peacefully at first. We have learnt that they somehow changed and they have killed a lot of people for no reason and now they have some terrible disease that is decimating the population.

We cannot allow this and cannot understand why this is happening, we have a feeling that Thrall maybe able to influence people we are not sure how but things are happening more frequently and this peaceful world is becoming a world of violence and war"

"1492 wasn't that the year Columbus discovered South America?" Jack said

"Yes, it was" answered his father, who was great to have on a quiz team.

"Keep reading, we need to find answers," Jack said "Grace flick forward a bit see if anything jumps out"

Grace began to scan through pages as she turned each one as quickly as she could.

"Hang on here's something, we have finally reached the conclusion that Thrall is influencing certain people, controlling them somehow and twisting them to create as much discord in the world as possible. There are few of us left now with the knowledge of our ancestors, who remember our homes. We try to travel the world as much as we can

287

and promote peace and love but our numbers are dwindling. We seem to eventually be persecuted where ever we go, Thralls hold over these people is strong."

"So he still managed to create havoc in your world," Kara said

"Oh wow, listen to this 1776 we have decided to create a group to keep these books and the one treasure we managed to bring from our world, a small number of people will be chosen to watch over our history and to keep us alive when we are gone. They will be entrusted to try to keep peace in this world to the best of their abilities, they have called themselves the Illuminati" Grace stopped reading and looked up.

"We have every conspiracy theorists dreams here in these boxes," Grace's Dad said

"Does it say anything else about the treasure?" Jack asked

Grace shook her head.

"Viggo, you have anything in yours?" Jack asked

"It is a record of your history but it makes no sense to me I am afraid, it just seems to be an awful lot of wars"

"There's another update on the news," Jack's mom said turning up the volume

"We have new information as to what is occurring, Russian and Ukrainian forces have been reinforced by NATO forces and are holding the line in Southern Russia. However Turkish and middle Eastern forces have been pushed back to Erzurum in Turkey, Mosul in Iraq and Al Hasakah in Northern Syria"

"We have unconfirmed reports from a Whitehall source that British Special Forces have encountered the aggressors and reported to number ten, but no news yet has emerged"

"They must be close to that Tepe place," Grace said

"I think I have something," Viggo said "1899 the Illuminati can no longer be trusted a few of us think that the rest have been turned by Thrall, they talk of a new world order, and the way they talk about creating it is wrong on every level. Wilhelm of Germany seems to be one of the main protagonists, his brothers have tried to reason with him but they all say he has changed somehow. A few of us have decided to take the chests and hide them for the safety of this world they cannot fall into the wrong hands"

"I can't believe what I'm hearing," Jack's Dad said "That date is near World War 1 find 1914 see what it says"

"Ok hand on," Viggo said flipping pages "1914, Wilhelm has done the unthinkable, he wanted to know where we had hidden the boxes, we, of course, would not say. He had Franz assassinated when we would not say, cutting our numbers down even more. Then using that as an excuse to start a war. The last thing he said was he would burn this world to the ground to find them"

"So much of our history must have been influenced by Thrall or Geddron," Grace said

"Go to 1918 see what that says" Grace spoke excitedly

"1918 we have managed to put an end to Wihelm's plan although the cost in life has been unimaginable, we are moving the boxes to England for safekeeping, there are more like minded people in this country and we have people in their government sympathetic to our cause" Viggo paused for a second "Hang on listen to this, we have moved the boxes to St Paul's Cathedral, they are being hidden in one of the tombs there, we still have access to update the books but at least we know that they and the protection stones will be safe, for now"

"They are protection stones," Kara said picking one up "I have heard of these but never seen them before, you place them around somewhere you wish to keep safe, say the spell and it becomes protected from anything"

"Well they aren't much good without magic," Viggo said.

"I'm sorry I'm struggling to get my head around this, magic, wars, demons, can it really be true, all of it?" Jack's mom said.

"Well that has answered some questions but we still have no idea what to do next" Jack sighed.

"After the first World War, it wasn't long after until the second, find the date Viggo" Grace's Dad asked

"And the date is?" Viggo responded

"Oh yes sorry I forgot 1939"

"Right here it is 1939, more terrible news coming from Europe another of our group seems to have been enthralled as we are now calling it. Adolf was a man to be trusted, he was resolute and unwavering but it seems he was also weak minded. Another war has been started in Europe, we know he knows the boxes are in England so we must do everything we can to prevent it. Winston has assured us that he will be able to convince the British people the dire need for action. We are trying to convince Teddy that his country needs to help too, hopefully, sooner rather than later" Viggo read aloud

"There's a lot then about the war, there's another bit about the boxes here. 1940 most of Europe is under Adolf's control he has called himself a Nazi and the vile things he and his people are doing has caused many a tear in our group. I am now the last survivor from the great spell I was Hanori, a magic user, how I wish for magic now, how I wish to help these people more than I can. I have had many names over my lifetime, I think Merlyn was my favourite, for a time there I thought we had created home, Camelot was the closest we ever got to being home.

The boxes are no longer safe here in London we are being bombed constantly, I know the British will not surrender but I hope their losses will not be too great in the end."

"There's nothing then until 1945, we are hoping beyond hope that the war is coming to an end the Allies are taking back Europe one piece at a time. Unfortunately, as we seem to be on the verge of victory something else happens, Josef has ceased all communications with our group, we have seen his forces working more on their own in recent weeks rather than with us, we fear he has been influenced, we are fearing for Nicholas and his family we have had no word for a long time now."

"So it seems our two worlds have been closely linked from the very start," Jack said to Viggo and Kara.

"It seems your world has suffered greatly from our banishment of the Hellions, it was not meant to be so, we had no idea life would occur here," Viggo said solemnly.

"Still nothing that helps us, we have had a history lesson that's it," Grace said sadly.

"There isn't much left in here now, there are a lot of empty pages" Viggo pointed out.

"Keep reading see if anything important jumps out" Jack instructed.

"Anyone want some tea?" Jack's mom stood up and clapped her hands "I think a nice cuppa will help, I know I certainly need one, nothing like a cuppa to soothe the nerves, anyone? Yes great I will sort it" and she dashed off into the kitchen.

"I'd better go see if she's ok," Jack's Dad said following her out of the room.

A series of loud clanking of cups and banging of cupboard doors followed, this culminated in a very loud "I'm fine thank you very much I'm making tea!"

Jack grimaced slightly as everyone looked at him.

"Ha parents" he chuckled nervously

Grace's dad was glued to the news on the TV, Grace, and Jack had placed their books back into the chest and watched Viggo as he continued to read.

"Oh my," he said after about five minutes

"What?" Kara asked

"Listen 1970, I do not have long left, I am the last one and I am looking forward to meeting my family and friends in the next life. Things in the world are fairly quiet now for how long I do not know. I get the feeling it is the lull before the storm. I will write when I can but it will not be often now.

Then it goes to 1971 I think this will be my final entry, grave news indeed, we discovered one of Thrall's minions in our group, we have managed to extract some information from him. His master's plan is to cast a spell at our arrival point, this as we have been told will negate the science the people on this world are so dependent on and usher in a new age of magic. We are hoping this is all rubbish as this world is ill prepared for the horrors that could unleash.

I cannot now in good faith trust our group once I am gone, so I have decided to hide these chests away from them, they will disappear until needed again. With my last bit of magic, I will make this happen."

"The arrival place is that Tepe place, that's where they are going, we need to warn everyone, we need to stop them," Grace said excitedly

"What can we do, no one would believe us, they could be already there for all we know." Jack sighed as his parents came back in.

"Then we need to prepare for when or if it happens," his dad said

"There's nothing else?" Jack asked Viggo

"No," he said flipping through the blank pages "Hang on there is something else, right at the back here"

"What's it say?" Kara blurted out.

"Katari you who have been chosen, you have the fate of two worlds to bear, I am sorry I cannot help more. Good luck, look for the signs for they will lead the way"

"Wow, that says nothing" Grace gasped.

"Erm, I think they have gotten where they wanted to go" Grace's dad suddenly blurted out. They all spun around to watch the tv.

"The latest updates seem to be that the invading force has set off some sort of EMP device centered on Gobekil Tepe which is the earliest known settlement on earth. Forces surrounding the area have reported all electronics have failed, what is more, surprising is that all weapons seem to also not be working. According to our science correspondent, the blast zone seems to be radiating out exponentially and has so far covered most of Turkey and shows no signs of stopping"

"I think its time to go," Jack's dad said

"Go where?" Grace asked

"We need somewhere safe," Jack said

"Zombie apocalypse," his dad said

"What?" asked Grace

"Oh yea zombie apocalypse, it's a plan me and dad have if there's a zombie apocalypse," Jack said enthusiastically.

"We will get in the cars call at the coop at the end of the road and get as much food and drink as we can, then we go to the water tower at Chase Green" his dad explained

"Why there?" asked his mom

"It is surrounded by two metal fences, it has one door a few windows and its solid concrete" his dad explained.

"Right, Jack you know what we need from here, all the camping gear. Everyone else load up the cars with whatever you think we will need and hope we get there before this thing hits"

Luckily Jack and Grace's dad both had large 4x4 vehicles and were big outdoor fans. Grace, Kara, and her dad disappeared to collect their stuff whilst Jack, Viggo, and Jack's mom and dad ran around the house grabbing everything and anything that may be useful.

The car was pretty much loaded up when Jack suddenly realised someone was missing "where's Merlyn?" he shouted.

His dad stopped what he was doing "I can't believe we forgot, he's down the road with the Smith's, long story we can get him on the way they only live a couple of doors from the coop"

They put the last few things in and slammed the back door shut.

"Jack give your mom the keys, she can start it up while we have one last look around and put the radio on"

Jack chucked the keys to his mom and dashed into the house, he heard the engine roar into life and Queen started blasting out of the radio, he smiled they all loved Queen and had had many journeys around the country to a soundtrack of Queen's greatest hits. As "Don't stop me now" faded away Jack had one last look around his room. "Will this be the last time I'm here?" he thought and felt strange how attached he was to this place.

Out of the corner of his eyes, he saw his crutches leaning in a corner and a slow realisation came over him. He sat down on his bed and exhaled deeply, if something was to happen now, there may not be any A&E to go to.

He felt his stomach tie itself in one massive knot, the feeling he got in the winter before venturing out onto icy paths or snow covered streets. He felt the dull ache in his leg again, as if it was just reminding him further.

He had spoken to a few other kids from around the world with the same condition through Facebook and knew they would all be going through the same as him now. He also knew how brave and strong all those kids are, every break, every operation is always dealt with determination, a positive outlook, and a smile.

He remembered speaking to a girl from America, she lives in Boston and was sixteen, Jack remembered her saying "The illness isn't me, it's not who I am, I won't be labelled by my illness, I will be myself and that is who people will know me as"

He stood up grabbed the crutches and headed back downstairs and outside just as the others turned up in the other vehicle.

Jack saw his Dad nod at him and smile as he chucked his crutches into the back of the car.

Grace's Dad leaned out of his window" I've got some tools just in case we need to break in"

"Good idea," said Jack's Dad "Right let's go"

Jack jumped into the back next to Viggo, his Dad got behind the wheel and they set off out of the street. It was only about a five to ten minute drive to the shop for supplies. Jack's Dad turned the radio up and they listened to the news as they drove.

"Reports are coming in that the armies of the world are in fact fighting some sort of creatures, we do not know where they are from but the government has declared martial law and is advising everyone to remain indoors and secure their homes.

The EMP blast that seems to have centered in Turkey has slowly been radiating outwards encompassing

Afghanistan, Pakistan, parts of Russia, Ukraine, Egypt, Libya and has reached Italy. Scientists are astounded at the scale of the device and say it is beyond their capabilities to produce such a device.

NATO forces are have pulled back and are holding a line along the German border and down through Austria. We are trying to get reports from our on site reporters but as to yet have been unsuccessful.

I will repeat the government guidelines again, remain indoors and secure your homes"

Jack's Dad turned the radio down, and they carried on in silence.

Berlin NATO frontline

Sergeant Josh Chambers peered over the sandbags into the distance looking for the enemy to approach. Josh was a Royal Marine Commando and was not used to sitting and waiting, usually, they were the ones taking it to the enemy.

This whole thing was messed up, there seemed to be very little leadership, he was here with twenty from his platoon, there were Spanish, Germans, Italians and he was sure he'd even seen some Russian troops along this wall.

The front line had been hastily erected but it was certainly going to do a job on anyone that came here, he did wonder how the enemy had been able to make such large inroads already but they were not being told much and had no access to the news.

Their orders were to hold at all cost, this was the line in the sand, this way NATO's last throw of the dice. America was sending more troops but they wouldn't be here until tomorrow, the bulk who were coming by sea would be a few days.

"Well, Marco what are you thinking?" Josh said to the man who stood next to him.

Marco was Italian and part of the Airmobile Brigade he looked like a tough nut and they had gotten on well since they had been posted together on the front line.

"I do not know Josh, I worry about my family and my country. I should be there not here"

"I know mate, hopefully, we can make a difference here and sort this crap out, then we can all go home"

"Have you heard anything at all? We cannot get in touch with our families in Italy because of the EMP"

"Nah, but I've never heard of an EMP with such a range"

Marco nodded his head in agreement.

"So where are you from Marco?"

"I am from Bologna in Northern Italy. You?"

"Liverpool mate"

"Ah I have heard of the football team"

"Who hasn't" Josh chuckled "Do you have family in Italy?"

Marco nodded and his face became sad.

"I have a wife and child, my son Gino is only six. I should be there protecting them not here. I fear for their safety"

"I'm sure they are fine pal"

"I would like to think so but last reports from my country are not good at all"

Marco began to play with a bracelet he had around his wrist.

"My son gave me this for my birthday" he smiled and Josh noticed his eyes fill with tears but he just as quickly regained his composure. "How about you?"

"Na mate, just my parents really, the army is my family at the moment"

They both stood there for a moment lost in their own thoughts.

There was a shout down the line and sirens began to go off.

"Get ready!" someone shouted

"Here we go then," Josh said "good luck Marco", he shook his hand as the other nodded and they both stood ready weapons aimed over the wall.

At first, Josh couldn't see anything, then in the distance, he could see a black shape stretching across the landscape moving slowly towards them.

There was a roar overhead as hundreds of jets suddenly appeared heading to the enemy, a cheer erupted from a bit further down as planes from all different countries shot forward.

The planes made up the distance in an instant and Josh watched as missile after missile was fired into the blackness, then his heart sank, his mouth dropped open and he looked wide eyed at what was happening before him.

As the planes reached the enemy and continued over them, they started to drop, drop from the sky like stones. Plane after plane dropped from the sky and exploded in flames, the horizon was a wall of fire.

"Why did no one eject?" Marco said next to him open mouthed

"It can't be that EMP surely we are out of range," Josh said

Another roar from behind as row upon row of artillery and tanks opened fire, rockets, and shells rained down into the distance adding to the wall of fire in front.

"No one is surviving that" he heard someone whisper.

The smell of burning drifted over towards them, an acrid smell of burning oil and fuel.

"Any visuals?" one of the section commanders shouted

"Negative, negative, negative" the word was issued down the line like some crazy kids game.

Josh strained his eyes to try and peer through the smoke as volley after volley of artillery fired overhead.

"There's movement" he heard the shout go up and again looked forward.

"Ready men" the section commander shouted.

Josh placed his finger on the trigger of his gun and peered down the sights, he could make out a few moving shadows that was it. He heard the crack, crack as the snipers situated down the line began to fire at the enemy.

Even though he'd just witnessed the failure of the airforce Josh had no doubt that the enemy would not get past them. There were some of the finest soldiers in the world here, he'd fought with a lot of troops from different countries in different campaigns over the years and felt that at this moment victory was at hand.

The crack, crack continued as did the shelling, the smoke across the front was getting thicker and making it more difficult to see any movement ahead.

Then there was silence, total silence descended upon them. Everyone was looking around confused.

"What is this? Have we won?" Marco exclaimed.

Josh shrugged. Then he heard orders being barked out down the line and they got closer and closer until his section leader shouted.

"Lay down blanket fire in front eight hundred yards"

"Strange," thought Josh but took aim

"Ready, aim, fire!" shouted the commanders

Josh pulled the trigger, nothing happened, he pulled it again, and again. He ejected some bullets and tried again, nothing.

He looked at Marco who was doing the same, all along the front no weapons were working at all.

The realisation slowly dawned on the men on the front line.

"Ok men, those of you that can fix bayonets"

"What!" thought Josh as he reached for his bayonet and fixed it to his rifle, he looked at Marco who was holding a knife.

"Here they come!" a voice bellowed from somewhere. Josh looked up and froze "Oh my god!"

"Dio Mio" Marco said his eyes wide "Hell has come for us my friend," he said

In front of them charging at NATO lines was an army of creatures, creatures that looked closer to dinosaurs than anything. Long back legs with huge claws, smaller front legs with claws that looked no less ominous. Their faces were hideous, eyes like a cats, elongated heads with a huge open mouth full of razor sharp teeth.

They moved fast along the ground and were screaming a blood curdling sound as they ran.

Josh saw grenades being tossed at them, but nothing happened it was like tossing rocks into the sea.

Josh stood and braced himself for the inevitable onslaught, this was going to be hand to hand on another level.

The creatures reached the line and jumped the last few feet into the massed ranks of troops. The first creature jumped straight over Josh's head, he watched it sail over him and land claws deep into the section commanders body, he screamed as the creature tore his arms from him and he fell down dead.

All around him the screams of the creatures were mixed in with the screams of the soldiers.

Josh managed to slice the belly of one creature and it fell writhing on the floor, he took a second to look for Marco and saw him lying dead on the floor, huge gash marks across his body.

This was going to be a massacre, he tried firing his weapon again but still, nothing happened, he knew he could not outrun them. He watched as two creatures looked directly at him and charged.

Here we go he thought he brought up his weapon and placed the butt onto his hip "Aaaaarrrggghhh!!!" he shouted as he charged at them. The first creature dipped its head to try and bite him, he sidestepped to the right and plunged his bayonet into the eye of the creature, the creature screamed and dropped to the floor. The impetus pulled Josh off balance and he stumbled, he felt the claws of the other creature sink deep into his back and then nothing.

He fell to the floor, he could feel no pain, he could not move at all, he guessed the attack had damaged his spine. Darkness began to encroach into the periphery of his eyesight like an early morning mist rolling across the fields.

He thought of home, his family, he hoped they would be ok and felt the pain of knowing he wouldn't' be there to protect them. His last thoughts before he finally slipped away were "I'm sorry I couldn't do more"

Hideout

The radio crackled slightly as they drove down the road towards the shop, they had seen no one, it was as quiet on the roads as they had ever seen it. No one was out walking, no one could be seen around their homes it was the strangest thing.

"Important news just in"

"Quick turn it up," Jack's dad said

His mom reached forward and turned the volume up.

"News in from Europe Berlin has fallen, I repeat Berlin has fallen. NATO forces have been decimated along the frontline. The prime minister is due to make a statement in about ten minutes, please stay tuned as we try to bring you more up to date information"

"Dad, what does that mean?" Jack asked

"I think it means we are on our own now," his Dad said solemnly.

Jack's Dad pulled onto the front of the Coop, Grace's dad pulled up next to them and they all got out.

"It's closed," Jack said. The shutters were down and the whole place was in darkness.

"Damn I was hoping the shutters would be up, we will try round the back," Jack's Dad said.

"We will go get Merlyn," Jack's mom said "I will take, Jack, Grace, and Kara"

"Ok," his dad said as the three of them disappeared around the back.

"C'mon it's only just down here," Jack's mom said setting off along the path.

They walked for a couple of minutes before they came to a driveway, the driveway had large gates across it, unfortunately, they were closed.

"Hello!" Jack's mom shouted up at the house "Hello Sam are you there? We've come to get Merlyn"

"I can't see that anyone's home mom"

"We are gonna have to go to the house," Grace said

"The gates are electric, they won't open without the buzzer thing," Jack's mom said.

"We are going to have to try, we can't get over the wall its too high," Grace said

Jack's mom tried to push on the gate, it wobbled but didn't budge.

"Jeez Sam why do you need these!" his mom exclaimed.

"Think we will all need to push, mom!"

They all positioned themselves by one gate and pushed, it moved slightly.

"That's it, its moving. Push!" his mom shouted excitedly.

Slowly with every combined push, the gate inched open a bit at a time, until finally, the gap was big enough for them all to squeeze through.

310

The house was a big detached house, very modern looking, they had fought tooth and nail to try and stop the coop from being built as they said it would degrade the area. They had however lost and they then proceeded to put up the wall and gates to keep the riff-raff out.

Jack wasn't sure how his mom and Sam had met, his mom said they had gone out a lot when they were younger. Jack liked her but she was very, very loud, her husband Tim was so quiet he wasn't sure if he spoke at all.

They made their way up the drive to the front door.

"There are no cars here" his mom observed.

They walked up to the front door and his mom rang the bell, nothing, she knocked, nothing, knocked a bit louder, still nothing, then the tried and tested method she opened the letterbox and bellowed "Sam!" through it. This also had no effect.

"Shit!" said his mom.

"Mom!" Jack said looking at Grace who was sniggering.

"Sorry" his mom chuckled "let's try round the back"

They walked along the side of the house in front of them was a large garage, the doors were open and were clearly empty. They turned the corner of the house onto a large patio area, in the corner was a hot tub complete with a roof.

They all moved to the windows at the back of the house and peered in.

"Anyone see anything?" his mom asked.

A series of nothings followed until Jack who was pressed against the patio doors said

"Yes, there, he looks like he's asleep in his basket"

They all crowded around and peered inside, yes it was definitely Merlyn. They began to bang on the glass shouting his name, eventually, he woke up, stood up, and just stood staring at them as if they had all gone mad.

"Now what?" Jack asked

"Smash it!" said Kara

"Oh no we can't," his mom said

"I don't think we have much choice" answered Grace

Kara began to scan the patio area and found a large stone, she picked it up "Stand back", she hurled the stone at the glass, there was a loud crash and it shattered into a thousand pieces.

They stood there for a while before venturing inside. Then the alarm began to go off.

"No ones in," said Kara with a straight face.

"Do we look for food now we are in?" Grace asked

"No let's get Merlyn and go, we need to get back to the others," his mom said.

They turned to leave through the broken door when Kara stopped them.

"Wait!"

"What is it?" Grace asked.

Kara drew her sword, instinctively so did Jack and Grace.

"There's something in the garden, in those trees at the back" Kara whispered crouching slightly.

"We need to move now slowly and quietly"

Kara slowly exited through the door, all the time facing down the garden, she then gestured the others to move. Jack went first, followed by Grace then his mom with Merlyn.

Merlyn started to growl, a low deep noise they had never heard him make before.

Out of the trees, three shapes slowly emerged, three black shapes. The heads were smooth and shiny almost like the shell of a beetle, their eyes were red and almost flickered with fire. They looked more insect or reptile like. Their mouths were slightly open revealing row upon row of razor sharp teeth.

"Go, go, go" Kara shouted

They began to sprint down the drive towards the barely open gate. An ear piercing scream echoed from behind and they knew the creatures were after them. Jack got to the gate first and spun around sword at the ready, his heart was beating out of his chest. He watched as the creatures came skidding around the corner of the house. They were the size of a man, they ran on their back legs but used the front to steady themselves. They had long necks and a short powerful looking body, their tails writhed around behind them like a snake.

But it was the teeth and the razor sharp looking claws that drew Jack's attention. Kara and Grace had both spun round also swords at the ready.

His mom looked at Jack, she was petrified. "Go," said Jack

His mom squeezed back through the gate with Merlyn and began to scream for the others to help.

The first creature was upon them it leaped straight at Kara, she stood there until the last second when she dropped to one knee and thrust upwards with her sword, she cut a long wound underneath the creature's belly, it screamed and dropped to the floor, the red eyes faded as though the fire had been extinguished.

The other two rushed at Jack.

"Jack!!" Grace screamed

Jack dodged to the side, one of the creatures went crashing into the gate and lay there stunned, the other turned to face Grace and Kara. Without thinking, Jack leaped forward and plunged his blade into the back of the advancing creature. The creature screamed and spun around throwing Jack off balance, the creature's arm swung around raking its claws across Jack's chest. Luckily the momentum of Jack's fall meant they didn't cut too deep.

Jack landed in a heap and his heart sank when he heard a loud crack, he knew what that meant, for a few seconds there was nothing, then the pain started in the bottom of his leg. The creature he'd stabbed was writhing around on the floor, his sword still protruding from its back.

Jack realised how close he was to the third one and despite the pain tried to drag himself away, it was slowly getting to its feet, its mouth opening slowly to reveal its teeth. He heard Grace and Kara running towards him. The creature stood up and roared, then its eyes went blank and it slowly sank to the floor.

As it fell it revealed Viggo behind it his sword in his hand, he smiled at Jack.

Grace and Kara got to Jack and knelt down, "Are you ok?" Grace asked

"It's my leg, it's broken" Jack replied

"We need to move," Viggo said "I will see if I can find anything to help move him"

His mom came rushing over "Jack are you ok honey?"

"Same leg, I think it's the same place as last time" Jack replied

Kara retrieved Jack's sword from the creature and asked for Grace's. She put them on either side of Jack's leg and wrapped her belt around them.

"That should help with the pain for a while," Kara said smiling at Jack "Oh, and thank you"

Jack smiled, then he rolled his eyes as Viggo came back with a wheelbarrow.

"This is all I could find"

They lifted Jack into the wheelbarrow, Viggo forced the gate open a little further and they pushed Jack back to the cars.

"What were they?" his mom asked

"Hellions" answered Kara

"I did not expect to see them just yet," said Viggo

"At least there were only three," Jack said thankfully.

They got back to the cars to see Jack and Grace's Dad loading food and supplies into the cars.

"What happened?" asked his Dad when he saw Jack in the wheelbarrow

"There were creatures," his mom said shakily.

"Are you both ok?" he said embracing Jack's mom, then squatting down next to Jack he took his hand "You ok kiddo?"

"Same as last time I think" Jack replied

"Damn," said his dad "You'll be ok, we've got painkillers"

"Let's get you into the car while we load the rest of the stuff in"

Jack's and Grace's dad got Jack into the back of the car with his leg along the seat. Grace got in by him and grabbed his hand "Are you ok?" she asked squeezing his hand.

"I'm fine, well I will be eventually, not going to be much use now though"

"Don't worry we will get everything sorted" Grace reassured him.

"Do you think there are more of them?" she asked

"There's bound to be, but there can't be too many here yet I wouldn't imagine"

"Ok, that's everything" Grace's dad shouted.

Grace stayed with Jack so Viggo and Kara got in with Grace's dad.

Jack's parents got into the front seats "Not far mate" his dad said turning around and smiling.

"It's the prime minister," his mom said suddenly

The radio crackled as they turned it up, Jack's dad signaled to the others in the other car to put the radio on.

"Good afternoon" the somber voice of the prime minister drifted through the speakers.

"I stand here today with a heavy heart, for what I am about to say will change everyone's lives, including all of those in government. As you may be aware an unknown force suddenly and without provocation has been attacking countries starting in Georgia. This force has now moved into Europe and has taken most of Germany now, we have lost contact with Italy, Finland, Sweden, and Denmark. NATO forces are now in full retreat through France and into Spain.

No solid intelligence has come out of the warzone as to who the aggressors are, however, we do know they seem to have a weapon of some description a sort of powerful EMP device that renders all weapons useless. Our forces are technically fighting with knives and bayonets.

The United Kingdom is preparing itself for an invasion that will probably happen soon, US troops crossing the Atlantic by ship have turned back, we are now on our own.

I have been told we have very little hope of regaining any of our troops from Europe and around the world.

We are asking any blacksmith's or anyone skilled in forging to make their way immediately to London, your country needs you.

Citizens of the UK I urge you to find secure places to stay, stock up on supplies if you can, stay together in groups do not stay alone.

We will be airdropping supplies, medicine, and equipment to all castles around the country, yes that is correct to all castles, if you live near or feel you can get to one within the next twenty four hours we strongly advise you too.

We will make as many updates as we can, but we are expecting all communications to be cut off soon. I wish you all luck, god be with you"

"Wow," said Jack's dad

"What?" asked his mom

"Well the PM has said a lot there without actually saying it"

"I don't understand," said his mom

"Well she says the troops are fighting with knives as weapons aren't working, then she asks for blacksmiths. They know they have the wrong weapons to fight these creatures, but they aren't going to have enough time to produce enough weapons for the army to stand a chance"

"So why ask then?" his mom said

"They are stockpiling, they are going to withdraw somewhere safe I'd say, maybe a castle as the PM suggested, they've been clever, they've said what needs to be said without trying to create panic"

"So what will the government do now?" Jack asked

"Nothing mate, they have pretty much just said we are all on our own now"

"Right here we are," said his dad pulling up outside a large concrete building.

It had a seven feet tall metal spiked fence around the exterior, a space of about ten feet, and then another metal fence about six feet tall. It was surrounded on three sides by trees, chase forest was a great local tourist attraction and was several miles deep.

The building itself was hexagonal in shape, about fifty feet high, and made of concrete, it had only one door in.

Everyone got out except Jack and Grace.

"The gates padlocked," said his dad.

"I've got some bolt croppers in the car," said Grace's dad.

He vanished then reappeared with a large pair of bolt croppers, they soon had the gates open and they moved inside the compound.

After a few minutes, Jack's mom came back.

"We have gotten inside, so we are going to drive the cars into the compound, unload all the stuff get the beds up then get you moved in and sort your leg" explained his mom.

The cars were driven inside, the gates were closed and locked with a new padlock and they began to unload everything inside.

"I feel so out of control," said Jack to Grace

"What do you mean?"

"Before we knew what we had to do, what we needed to do and we were capable of doing it. Now we are in survival mode with no idea what to do next, and well I'm now useless"

"Don't think like that Jack, your not, you just saved me and Kara, you did that without magic or armour you did it"

Jack felt his cheeks go a little red as he felt Grace's hand tighten on his.

"I wish Ben was here," Jack said

"So do I" agreed Grace

The car door swung open making them both jump

"You ready buddy?" said his dad

"I suppose," said Jack

He shuffled along the seat with his dad holding his leg.

"Think it's the Fibula again dad, it's not that painful"

"Will have you sorted soon buddy"

Jack and Grace's dad picked him up between them and carried him inside.

Inside was a large empty room with a few bits of furniture scattered around, there were stairs leading up to a second level. They had arranged camp beds, chairs, and set up a makeshift kitchen on one side.

They got him over to one of the beds and lay him down. Kara was stood there waiting.

The light was not great so they'd lit a load of candles and a few lanterns.

"Right," said Kara "let's see to this leg"

She loosened the belt and removed it from his leg, his dad took the swords away as Kara held onto his leg. She ran her hands down his leg gently squeezing as she went all the while looking deep into his eyes.

"I can feel no break, my guess is maybe a crack or you have aggravated your old injury. You need to rest"

"Here's some painkillers buddy," his dad said holding out some tablets and some water.

"We need to all get some rest tonight and we will decide what to do in the morning," his dad said "I have a radio so we will see what we can get on there and see if anything has changed"

Jack lay back down on his bed, he couldn't believe how tired he felt. Merlyn came and lay next to him, he reached over the side of the bed to stroke him and received a lick in thanks.

Grace had placed her bed next to Jack's and they both lay there lost in their thoughts. Sleep came quickly for Jack a surprise and a welcome relief.

New World

Jack awoke not knowing what time it was it seemed like everyone was still asleep, his leg was throbbing with the pain, the painkillers were wearing off. Normally he would shout his parents for some more but he didn't want to wake everyone up. It's not too bad he told himself trying to get comfortable in bed, it is hard enough in a proper bed without being in a camp bed.

He looked over the side of the bed to where Merlyn was curled up on a blanket, he raised his head and looked at Jack, looked into his eyes an almost knowing look. Jack frowned at his dog, but then Merlyn leaned over and licked his hand and the moment was gone. Merlyn settled back down on the floor, had one last look at Jack, almost as if to say you ok? Then lay his head down.

Jack lay there thinking, thinking of Ben, of what had happened in the other world. He remembered the freedom the magic had given him, the freedom to almost be normal, to not worry about running or jumping, about falling or slipping. A freedom most people would never feel would never be able to understand, but then to have it taken away and now this he thought looking at his leg, he felt as though his condition was punishing him or reminding him that it was still there. He had always laughed to himself when he heard people at school saying I wish I could run faster or jump longer or higher. To be able to run would be a dream come true, to have been able to have entered one sports day was a dream that never came true.

Wintertime was the worst, the season of dread the feelings of wanting to go and build a snowman, to have snowball fights or go sledging offset with the fear of one slip would mean hospital, so days were spent looking through the window either imagining or watching others enjoy what you could not.

He felt sad sometimes, he felt angry sometimes, sometimes he felt alone which is weird when you have a family but that's how it was, that's how it is. Sympathy and caring are great and your friends and family suffer too but in different ways, no one will ever know unless they have gone through it too.

He decided to try to move a little in bed as he did the pain flared in his leg and he let out a little yelp.

"Are you ok?" whispered Grace

"Yeah sorry I woke you, just trying to get comfy think the painkillers are wearing off"

"Shall I get your mom?" Grace asked

"Do you think you can, I didn't want to wake everyone"

"Yea no problem"

Grace slipped from her bed and tiptoed across the floor to Jack's mom, Jack heard a "Huh, What?" then his mom was next to him and Grace was back in bed.

"You ok baby?" his mom asked

"Yea mom sorry just think I need some more painkillers"

"Of course hang on two secs"

His mom moved back to her bed and soon returned with some tablets and some water.

"Here you go"

"Thanks, mom, you can go back to bed I'm ok now thanks"

"Are you sure honey? If you need anything else let me know"

"I will, I promise"

He lay back down and turned to face Grace, she smiled warmly, Jack smiled back and mouthed thanks.

He settled back into his pillow, closed his eyes, and tried to let his mind wander. Eventually, he drifted off to sleep.

In his sleep he dreamt of cities burning, planes falling from the skies, people running and screaming, the sky was red as though the whole world burned. A black shape in the distance appeared to move towards him, gaining speed as it got closer an ear piercing scream echoed off every building as the shape raised a huge black sword to strike him down.

"Nooooooo!" screamed Jack, he sat bolt upright in bed eyes wide open sweating profusely. He scanned around the room and saw everyone looking at him.

"You ok bud?" asked his dad

"Yea just a bad dream"

"How's the leg?" Kara asked

"Ok at the moment thanks"

"Breakfast is on, won't be long" his mom chirped up.

"Anything else on the radio?" Grace's dad asked

"No, just static at the minute" replied Jack's dad.

"I have checked the perimeter, I have seen rabbits and deer so food should not be a problem for a while" Viggo reported.

"Did you see anyone else out there?" Grace asked

Viggo shook his head.

Breakfast was served and they all sat there eating in silence.

"What should we do next?" Jack suddenly asked

"Next?" said his mom

"Yea about this that's happening, we have to do something," Jack said

"I think this event may be beyond us all" answered Grace's dad.

"I feel we should be doing something, I fell it deep inside. Do you?" he said looking at Grace, then Kara and Viggo.

They all nodded in agreement.

A crackling noise broke the silence as the radio burst into life, they all jumped. Jack's dad quickly grabbed it and turned up the volume.

"This is London, this is our final emergency broadcast. Europe has fallen, Africa and the Middle East have now also gone dark. Reports have come in that parts of South Africa are still under human control. The enemy is nonhuman, we have no exact reports on this. Most governments are now in hiding. New reports are coming in of the enemy now appearing in parts of North and South America, as yet we have no numbers or details. Australia is still unaffected as is Japan. The weapon being used by these creatures renders all technology useless, our warning stations on the South coast have gone quiet so we know it has now reached us.

Keep as safe as you can, find the most secure place you can to hide, and take enough food and water as possible. The British government has created three strongholds Edinburgh, York, and Chester. If you can safely get to these places then all our remaining armed forces have been sent there.

Be safe, be aware and God help us all"

The radio went dead.

"This weapon they are speaking of, it must be the spell that Thrall wanted to do," Kara said.

"The one that negates science and technology," Jack said

"That's how they were able to overcome our armed forces so easily," Grace's dad said

Jack suddenly felt that familiar charge of electricity, the hairs on the back of his neck stood up. He looked at Grace who was staring open mouthed at him. Little bolts of lightning danced across the room as though riding a wave and then vanished.

Jack looked at Viggo and Kara "Did you feel that?" they both nodded.

"Jack, your sword," Grace said pointing to his sword hanging in the scabbard by the bed.

It was glowing bright blue, he reached down and grabbed hold of the handle. Immediately the room buzzed with electricity, lightning bolts danced around the room, he saw Grace, Viggo and Kara all pull out their swords, he knew what was happening.

The noise got louder, the electricity danced and swirled around the room, he saw his parents and Grace's dad pressed against the wall open mouthed.

"Mom, Dad its ok, but get ready for a change"

The light grew brighter and brighter until there was a blinding flash.

As the light cleared and their eyes began to adjust to the gloom, they stood side by side the four Katari. The others stood pressed against the wall in a state of shock.

Jack realised he was standing and his leg was ok "Mom, Dad it's ok it's us"

"Jack!" said his mom and dad

"Gracie?" said Grace's dad

"It's ok dad, it's me just different" Grace replied

"And older," her dad said reluctantly stepping forward.

He moved towards here holding out his hand, Grace outstretched her arm and grasped his hand

"It's ok dad," she said pulling him into an embrace "Oh Gracie" he sighed

This gave a cue for Jack's parents to move to Jack, they both hugged him hard. It was difficult for Jack as they were now both so much shorter than him it seemed weird.

"I guess the age of magic has returned to your world," Viggo said at last.

After an hour or two of constant questions by the adults, some semblance of normality returned to the group. They had shown their parents their armour but as yet had not summoned their creatures, they thought they had had enough to digest for the time being.

"So that's it then, no more technology," Jack's Dad said rolling his phone over and over in his hands.

"I wonder how the rest of the world is faring?" Grace's dad said.

"We can't just sit here and wait for something to happen surely," Viggo said.

"At the minute I really don't know what to suggest, we have another Katari to find in this world somehow" Jack responded

"And that's going to be difficult as we've no seen anyone for days," Grace said

"Is it worth going over the books again, see if we've missed something, they have to have been kept secret for a reason" Kara suggested keenly.

"Good idea" Jack agreed

Viggo went and dragged the two chests over, they opened them both, the stones in the chest were glowing dimly.

"I wish we could decipher all this scroll, I'm sure they would help," Kara said frustratingly.

"I will have another look through the last book, see if I missed anything," Jack said reaching into the chest and taking out a volume.

He took it over to his bed, he withdrew his sword and lay it next to him. Grace came over and sat next to him.

They read through once again sometimes reading bits twice, but as they drew close to the end there was nothing new or important they had missed. Jack turned the last page and looked at Grace with a sigh.

"Don't worry" she said nudging him in the side smiling.

She nudged him a little harder than she intended and he fell to the side landing on his elbow, the book landed on top of his sword, immediately the blank page light up with blue writing.

"Wow look at this" Jack exclaimed

The others came over to see "It must be hidden text that can only be seen with the sword, whoever this Merlyn character was he certainly retained his magic" Viggo said.

"What's it say?" Kara asked

Jack began to read aloud

"1975 it is worse than I feared, this world is in great peril, there is little I can do as my power wanes. I will hide these tomes until they are needed, but my time of passing must be delayed, I must also go into hiding for I have a feeling this world will need me once more before the end.

I am now residing in Candesford this will be my final move for a while, I know what is coming but I know the Katari are also destined to arrive. I have foreseen this and much more. I have found a house that I have cast a spell on, it will remain empty until the right people arrive.

I cannot stay in this form until the time is right, I must change my form to be able to wait the years needed. Chase Green forest is one of the oldest in the land, it still holds on to the last remnants of magic in this world.

There is a place known locally as Castle Ring, it is an old place from ancient times, I think it is connected to my world somehow but the magic is still strong there. I will hide these tomes from spying eyes then I will go to Castle Ring and cast my spell, there I will wait until the time is right.

If you Katari are reading this seek me out there, just say the words Ainth Trawey Gederum I will be waiting."

"Holy crap!" Jack's dad said "I'm finding this so hard to take in"

"So is he saying we were meant to buy that house?" Jack's mom said

"I guess so" Jack agreed.

"So how far is this Castle Ring?" Viggo asked

"I'd say about an hour from here," Graces Dad said

"Well, it will be dark soon so I suggest we go at first light" Viggo suggested.

They all agreed, Jack's parents began to get the food ready for dinner, Grace's Dad was washing clothes, Viggo and Kara went to patrol the perimeter. Jack and Grace sat at the table with the map his dad had bought.

"So we are here" Jack marked the map with a pen "And this is Castle Ring here"

"It's directly north of here" Grace said tracing a line along the map with her finger.

"Anyone got a compass" Jack joked

"Yep, if it still works" Grace's Dad replied "It's an old fashioned one so it should do because I take it the poles are still magnetic," he said rummaging in his bag

"Ah hah, here it is, and yes seems to be working fine"

"Great so we can use that to travel north from here," Jack said.

"Are we all going to go?" Jack's mom asked nervously.

"I think it will be safer if you three stop here" Grace replied

Jack's mom looked very relieved to hear that. Jack and Grace's Dads both nodded their approval.

They all ate their meal together, cleared up, and went to bed.

Jack, Grace, Viggo, and Kara had had to make beds on the floor as they were now too big for the beds.

Jack lay down and closed his eyes, his mind was filled with a thousand thoughts about tomorrow, eventually, he began to drift away.

He opened his eyes and sat up with a start, he was sat on a hillside, all around him was a dense, thick mist, it rolled and swirled around him like the lightest of water. He reached out his hand and dragged it through the mist it swirled and wrapped around his fingers, flowing through them like grains of sand. He could see nothing apart from the small clearing of grass around him.

"Am I dreaming?" he thought.

He squinted as the mist in front seemed to start to swirl more frantically, as though it were taking shape. It was taking the shape of a figure and it was moving towards him, he instinctively went to draw his sword but it was nowhere to be found. He jumped to his feet and took a step backward as the figure came into view.

"Jack, we must speak" it was Selendrial

"How, how can you be here"

"I am and I am not, now your worlds magic has returned we can come and go as we please"

"Can't you do something? People are dying over here"

"There is very little I can do," she said sadly "I am here to give you instruction and to warn you"

"Warn of what?"

"I cannot say too much, I cannot influence what is about to happen. You must all prepare yourselves for a difficult road. You must overcome this if we are to succeed"

"Can't you say more?"

"I cannot, but when all seems lost you will know you are not alone"

"After the next few days things will never be the same again, the Hellions are now in your country in great numbers and they look for you and the others. There will be few survivors in your world, they were so unprepared. Some will survive and of those you are their last hope, they will come to you, they will not know why but they will. You must decide how to keep them safe, your powers will grow but you will need instruction on how they work and you will have that soon"

Selendrial started to slowly walk back into the mist

"Wait!" shouted Jack

"Yes? I have questions"

"I will grant you one answer for one question that is all so choose wisely"

Jack thought for a moment.

"Who is the final Katari?"

Selendrial smiled "I can give you but a name, he is called Artus"

She took a few steps back and disappeared into the mist.

The mist began to swirl around faster and faster slowly closing in on Jack, at first he felt a sense of panic, then calmness as the mist washed over him and he slept.

Sadness and Joy

Jack woke early the next morning, his parents were up already and sitting by the small gas heater they had, for some reason certain low tech devices still worked like the gas heater and gas stove. He sat up and swung his legs out of bed, his parents smiled at him, he knew they still found it difficult to understand the change that had happened to him and the others but they were slowly getting used to it.

He looked down at his legs, they were powerful looking the muscles clearly defined a stark contrast to his own legs which he felt were the weakest part of his body. He himself still found it difficult to comprehend the change and found it difficult to trust this new body. Always in the back of his mind was its going to let you down at some point.

"You ok son?" his Dad's voice cut through his thoughts as he came over and put an arm around him.

No matter what he'd been through in his life his parents were always there, always his rock when he needed them. He loved them so much and was so glad they were here now.

"I'm fine thanks Dad"

His Dad smiled and turned to walk back to his mom

"Love you Dad"

His Dad turned and smiled the biggest smile "Love you too Jack, since the first moment I held you in my arms"

The others were starting to wake now.

"Breakfast will be ten minutes," his Dad said as his parents rushed to prepare everything. He looked at the others looking at his parents and smiling and realised they had become everyone's parents.

"Morning" Grace said sleepily to Jack

"Morning, anyone have any dreams last night?" Jack asked

Everyone shook their heads.

"I dreamt of Selendrial, she said something bad is going to happen, she also said the Hellions are now in this country. She told me survivors will start coming to us for protection and we have to keep them safe, she also said someone will come who can instruct us in magic"

"Well that's particularly vague and unhelpful" Kara scoffed

"Anything else, that is maybe useful?"

"She said the final Katari's name is Artus"

"Artus? And he's supposed to be in our world? Not really a common name around here" Grace said

"There's not much to go on so we stick to our original plan and go to castle ring today and see what happens," Jack said

They all agreed.

"Breakfast!" his mom shouted

They sat around eating breakfast and discussing the options for the day.

"Are we all going to go?" Viggo asked.

"No point us three going we will only slow you down, plus it's probably safer for us here," Jack's dad said gesturing to his mom and Grace's Dad.

They both nodded in agreement.

"I will stay here just to be safe," Kara said

"No don't be silly, you don't know what's out there you all need to go to give you the best chance," Grace's Dad said.

"He's right we will be fine here, we can get this place sorted, make it feel a bit more homely" his mom agreed.

"Are you sure? I don't like leaving you here alone" Jack asked

"We will be fine son," his Dad said squeezing his hand.

After breakfast preparations were made for the journey, they didn't need many supplies as they didn't think they would be gone long.

They said their farewells and went outside. They summoned their creatures, Kara had not summoned hers before so they all watched with great anticipation as she did.

A huge eagle emerged from her sword, it had a golden saddle on its back. It stretched out its wings as if stretching from a long sleep.

"I will call you Aingal" Kara stated climbing onto his back.

Jack's mom, dad, and Grace's dad stood open mouthed at the creatures before them.

Grace hugged her dad and kissed him as she said goodbye and mounted Silvermane.

Jack walked to his parents. "Be careful, please" his mom said hugging him tight, "I'm so proud of you, I always have been, I love you so much"

"Love you to mom, I will be fine, we won't be gone long"

His dad grabbed him and pulled him close "Stay safe out there, love you son"

"Love you too dad"

Jack climbed onto Ragnar "Kara, you and Viggo fly ahead and check what's out there, Grace and I will go through the forest"

They turned to leave when Merlyn started barking.

Jack's dad went to him "It's ok boy they will be back soon"

But Merlyn would not stop, Jack looked at his dog, he locked eyes with him and a feeling came over him.

"I think he wants to come too"

"Don't be absurd he will slow us down" Viggo said

"I think we have to take him," Jack said again.

"Do you want to come to Merlyn?" Jack said.

Merlyn immediately stopped barking and trotted over to Ragnar and plonked himself next to the great lion. Ragnar looked down at the dog and sniffed him, Merlyn raised a paw and placed it on Ragnar's nose.

"Did he just smile?" Kara asked

"Who?" Grace said

"Ragnar, I'm sure he just smiled at your dog!"

Jack shook his head, this day was already starting out to be extremely strange already.

"We need to go now, make sure you lock up after us," Jack said

Kara and Viggo took off and vanished over the tops of the trees. Jack smiled at his parents and yanked Ragnar's reigns and the great lion took off followed by Grace and Silvermane. Merlyn ran beside Ragnar through the gate.

"Jack there's no way Merlyn will keep up," Grace said

Jack shrugged "We will cross that bridge when we come to it"

After about fifteen minutes of riding it was clear that Merlyn could keep up and didn't seem like he was tiring at all.

"How's he doing this?" Grace asked

"I have no idea" Jack replied

They had been riding for about half an hour when they broke out of the forest and into a clearing, Kara and Viggo were waiting for them.

Viggo went to speak then saw Merlyn sat next to Ragnar. "How is your dog still running?"

Jack shrugged "No idea, what's up?"

Viggo sat staring at Merlyn Throdin stretched out its neck towards Merlyn, again he raised a paw and placed it onto his head, Throdin seemed to nod and moved his head away.

"What is going on with your dog?" Viggo asked

"Look it doesn't matter at the minute, what's up?"

"There's a small camp ahead, about twenty people from what we can see" Kara answered

"What shall we do? If we go riding in they are more likely to try and attack us than think we are friendly" Grace said.

"We go around them," Jack said

"What! But we may be able to help them" Grace sounded shocked.

"We need to do what we came here for, we will visit the camp on the way back," Jack said

Viggo and Kara nodded.

"If that's what everyone thinks, fine!" Grace said.

You two fly ahead, we will follow you so we avoid the camp. Viggo and Kara took off followed by Jack, Grace, and Merlyn.

As they entered the forest again they could smell burning wood coming from the camp of survivors. It soon vanished and they knew they were clear of it, they could see Kara and Viggo occasionally as the foliage above parted or became less dense.

Not long after they could see them vigorously waving and pointing, gesturing forwards. Jack knew they had reached their destination.

Ragnar leaped through some bushes and out into a large open space, Jack knew this was Castle Ring although he'd never been here before he had seen pictures of it.

It was a large open space, a few stones jutted out from the earth at various angles and various sizes. The stones were sand coloured like the stones of the pyramids in Egypt. Historians had no idea how the stones were moved here or where they were from. It was supposed to have once been a castle of some sort but dating it had proven very difficult.

The most amazing thing was in the middle of the clearing were four large stone slabs, they were square and had been placed side by side to make a bigger square, each corner pointed to North, South, East, and West and was so accurate it had stumped scientists for years. The centre of the slabs where the corners met was a circular stone with carvings and markings on it.

Jack jumped down from Ragnar and walked to the centre followed by Grace and Merlyn. Viggo and Kara landed just a short distance away and they too came over.

Jack stopped staring at the circular stone at his feet, carved into the middle of the stone was the Tree of Anu.

"This just gets stranger and stranger," Grace said.

"So what now?" Viggo asked

"Guess we say the spell, see what happens" replied Jack.

They stood at the four sides of the stone slabs and Jack said "Ainth Trawey Gederum"

Nothing happened, he said it again "Ainth Trawey Gederum", still nothing happened.

"Are you saying it right?" Kara asked

"As far as I know" Jack responded.

"Well guess this was a waste of time," Viggo said.

Merlyn came trotting over and plonked himself in the middle of the stone circle, he looked at Jack then placed a paw on a line chiseled into the stone.

"Hang on" Grace exclaimed that's not a mark it looks like a slot, she drew her sword and slid it easily into the stone slab. Viggo and Kara did the same, Jack unsheathed his sword and held it above the slot.

"How come there are only four, Ben should be here also if he wasn't, I just mean how can it be possible"

He slid his sword in and straight away there was an audible click, the swords began to glow. Merlyn stayed where he was looking decidedly pleased with himself.

"Guess we try again" Jack sighed "Ainth Trawey Gederum".

This time the result was almost immediate, the swords grew brighter and brighter and bolt of blue energy shot from one sword to the other creating a box around Merlyn.

"Merlyn!" Jack shouted reaching out his hand he tried to grab him but he hit an invisible force field around it and his hand bounced off. The light began to grow as the stone circle became encompassed in a brilliant blue light. They all turned away shielding their eyes, eventually, the light began to fade, the energy in the air began to dissipate.

Jack turned back and Merlyn was gone, in his place stood an old man. He was about six feet tall, he wore a blue suit and held a silver cane. His white hair was pulled back into a ponytail and his white beard was neatly trimmed. He had piercing blue eyes, his eyes seemed to tell a story, a story of years lived and an underlying sadness. He smiled at Jack.

"Good day Jack, I am Emrys, last of the Hanori in this world, last of the great magic users, keeper of the knowledge, you can call me Merlyn"

Jack stood open mouthed unable to speak, he glanced at the others all of whom had the same expression he presumed was on his face also.

Merlyn pointed at the swords "Grab those you may need them" and he stepped off the stone circle. He stood and closed his eyes and inhaled deeply "Ah how I've missed those smells, everything is so different when you're a canine"

"You, your Merlyn my dog?" Jack managed to stutter out.

"Yes in a way, I was never really your dog, I came with the house but the spell on the house meant you thought you'd had me for a long time before you moved there"

"Are you the one who wrote in the books?" Grace asked.

"Ah yes, my memories will come back soon, things are a little foggy at the moment. I knew what was starting to happen in this world, Thralls growing influence and return to power. I knew of the Katari and I was told it would have to be me to teach them. However, my time was growing short as the magic grew weaker. My only option was to metamorphosise myself gaining that extra time I would need until the magic returned. Ah yes I can feel it coursing through the earth beneath my feet, I can feel it running through the air like water cascading down a mountainside"

"I erm, we have no idea what we are doing," Jack said to him.

"I know my friend, firstly I am sorry for your friend he was extremely courageous, it was written that one Katari may fall in the early days."

"We need to find someone called Artus," Viggo said.

Merlyn's head snapped around "Who? Artus? Hmm, a familiar name that seems just out of reach for me at the moment. I'm sure it will come back"

"And you're here to help us?" Grace asked

"Yes my dear, as much as I can, to train you in magic for you are destined to become the greatest magic users there has ever been. I just need to remember a few things first. I'm sure it will come back"

"Your sure it will or your hoping it will?" Viggo said

"Ah, now that is the question!" Merlyn replied.

"We found a camp of survivors not far from here, we are going to see if we can help then we need to get back to our parents," Jack said

"Of course, of course, I see you have various modes of transport," he said waving his hand towards their creatures.

"Hmmm now one for me, what shall it be I wonder"

He closed his eyes and began to mutter under his breath, he opened his eyes and they glowed with blue energy, the air around them came alive, he raised his cane into the sky, electricity danced all over it as he continued to mutter things under his breath. He lowered his cane and touched it to the floor, a small ball of light appeared growing larger and larger, the brightness growing as it grew in size. There was a loud crash of energy and the light was blinding causing them to turn away.

As they turned back Jack knew straight away what creature was before them, it was a griffin. Its body and back legs were of a lion, the tail seemed to resemble Throdin's tail, it's wings were the same as Silvermanes, it's front legs and head was that of a giant eagle, it was though the creature was made up of a piece of each of theirs.

"Ah Styx it has been a long time my friend," he said stroking the creature's head.

"Right lead the way, we had better be off" he urged.

They all climbed aboard their creatures, Viggo and Kara took to the skies followed just after by Merlyn.

"What the hell just happened," Jack said to Grace.

"I have no idea, and I'm not sure he does at the moment. C'mon before we lose them" Grace said pointing to the sky.

They set off at a quick pace and soon made it to the camp. They stopped just out of earshot to decide the best way of approaching.

"Grace and I will go in first try to speak to them, then we will call you in. Leave your creatures here, for the time being, we don't want to panic them" Jack instructed.

"Right let's go," Jack said setting off towards the camp.

As they got closer Jack shouted "Hello there"

They heard frantic rushing about in the camp, as they broke from the covering of the bushes they were confronted by about twelve men all brandishing various types of crude weapons mainly made from gardening tools.

"Who the hell are you?" One of the men said.

"I am Jack, this is Grace we don't mean you any harm"

"What the hell are you?" the man replied looking them up and down his eyes fixing eventually on the swords at their waists.

"We are friends and we can help, we can offer you protection," Grace said softly.

"How are you two supposed to protect us" the man snorted.

"Like this!" Jack drew his sword and his armour covered his body, Grace did the same, they stood there their armour glistening in the sunlight.

"We can help," Jack said re-sheathing his sword.

He held out his hand and approached the man who had been speaking "I'm Jack"

The man tensed as Jack approached but as he got closer his stance softened, he lowered his weapon and took Jack's hand "I'm Mark" the group immediately softened and crowded around them, a few women approached from the tents behind.

"Do you know what is going on?" Mark asked.

"Yes, in a way but you probably won't believe us. We have some friends just in the woods is it ok to call them in" Jack asked. Mark nodded.

Not long after Viggo, Grace, and Merlyn appeared.

"Ah my good people, you have done well to survive this long" Merlyn blurted out.

"Can you tell us what happened? The last we heard was the creatures who'd appeared in Europe had emerged from some caves in Wales. The army had held them off until everything stopped working. We are trying to make our way to Chester to one of the safe zones" Mark said rambling.

"The simple version is that a creature has attacked us from another realm, he's a creature of magic and has made all technology useless and made magic the driving force in the world now," Viggo said matter of factly.

"Yeah right," one of the men scoffed.

Jack whistled and Ragnar along with the others emerged from the trees. Some of the women screamed and they raised their weapons.

"It's ok, it's ok," Jack said walking up to Ragnar and stroking him.

"Magic, how can that be possible" Mark asked.

"That is a long story but if you come with us we have somewhere that is safe for the moment, it will be a bit crowded but it's better than being out in the open" Jack advised.

Mark nodded "I don't know why but I trust you, I feel it inside. Ok let's pack our stuff up, we are moving"

It took about half an hour to pack their stuff up, but eventually, they began to move through the forest. Jack led the way, Grace brought up the rear, the others flew ahead scouting the route back. Jack knew this would slow their return but he also knew he couldn't leave them in the forest.

They had been walking for about an hour and Jack knew they must be getting close.

All of a sudden Viggo came crashing down through the leaves above.

"Jack, Grace get to the tower now, somethings wrong"

Jack felt an uneasy feeling wash over him, Grace rushed past on Silvermane she was waiting for no one. Jack looked at Viggo "Go we will bring them in!" he shouted.

Jack urged Ragnar forward, with a huge roar he leapt forward crashing through the forest with great speed, he could see Grace just up ahead, she had drawn her sword and was covered in armour. Jack followed suit, he could see the tower in the distance, nothing looked out of place as they approached.

They raced around the side to the front, the gates were wide open. They both quickly glanced at each other and leaped down from their rides.

The ground around the gates had been torn up, they could see the chain had been broken.

"Mom, Dad!" Jack shouted.

There was just silence. They walked forward the second gate was also open, they got to the door, it was slightly ajar.

"Mom, Dad!" Jack shouted again

"Dad are you in there?" Grace shouted.

Jack slowly pushed open the metal door, he saw a dark stain on the floor and his heart sank. His feet wouldn't move. Grace was trying to force her way past so he had to step forward.

Inside was chaos, everything was strewn about the place, beds and chairs had been tossed aside.

"Mom, Dad, are you here," Jack said quieter now, he felt he didn't have the strength to speak.

They both walked into the room and looked about.

Jack spotted it first, a hand sticking out from underneath one of the beds, he rushed over and flipped the bed. He gasped and spun round to Grace just as she screamed. It was Grace's dad he had been attacked, he lay there his eyes wide open, long claw marks across his chest and arms.

"Nooooo!!" Grace screamed dropping to her knees. She dropped her sword, her armour vanished. She tenderly picked her father up cradling him in her lap, tears streaming down her face, uncontrollable sobs emanating from her hunched over body.

Jack wanted to console Grace, but he had to find his parents "Mom, Dad!" he said again.

Then he saw something in the corner of the room, he knew immediately what it was. Tears flowed instantly, he dropped his sword to the floor, the loud clattering disturbing the silence and the sobbing of Grace. His armour vanished as he walked to the corner, there sat his dad, cradling his mom in his lap. They were both covered in blood and lacerations, and it was clear they were both dead.

"Aaarrghhh!" screamed Jack, the noise was a primal roar of anger and pain. He dropped to his knees taking his parent's hands in his.

"I'm sorry, I'm so very sorry" He sat there and held his parent's lifeless bodies and sobbed.

Viggo and Kara burst in, the scene before them cut through them like a knife. Tears streamed downed Viggo's cheeks. Kara sobbed as she walked over and held Grace. "I'm so sorry," she said to Grace.

Merlyn entered the room "Oh my, oh dear, we need to make sure they aren't still about"

Viggo nodded, "I will go and scout around see if I can see anything"

As Viggo left the other survivors were just arriving

"What's happened?" Mark asked

"Our camp has been attacked"

"Anyone been hurt?"

Viggo just shook his head as he left the compound to find Throdin.

Merlyn came out of the building and saw the others hovering in the gateway.

"Come, come, we must get this place secure. There are people inside who will need help soon, just a few of you, not too many"

Mark nodded and gestured to two men and two women to follow him, the others moved into the main compound and began to unload their stuff.

Jack saw a group of the survivors enter the building and saw the shocked looks on their faces, he knew they had come here to be safe and after this, they would not feel safe at all. He got up gently resting his parents on the floor and walked over to Grace and Kara.

"Grace," he said drawing her attention to the new arrivals.

"We have to bury them, they deserve to be laid to rest" the lump in Jack's throat as he said the words almost made it impossible to speak, he was hoping Grace would not need too much convincing as he didn't have it in him at the moment. Thankfully Grace looked up, her eyes red and puffy with tears, a look of sorrow and helplessness that was almost too much to bear. Then she nodded and slowly got to her feet.

Jack walked over to Mark and the others "Would you be able to help us please?"

"Of course, anything, we are so sorry, we have all lost someone," Mark said sympathetically.

Jack walked out of the building towards Ragnar, he didn't look back, he didn't want that to be the last memory of his parents.

Ragnar sensed the sorrow in Jack and nuzzled him as he came close, Jack smiled and he stroked his great mane. "We have an important job to do my friend"

He mounted Ragnar and they slowly walked out of the compound and around the side to a small clearing about twenty feet from the perimeter fencing.

"This will do I think," Jack said looking around.

Ragnar seemed to know exactly what Jack wanted and began to dig. His huge paws and claws made quick work of the task. Jack helped as much as he could but in less than no time at all they had dug two holes. One for Grace's dad, the other for his parents, he wanted them to be together not in separate graves. The thought of the word grave immediately let loose all the emotions once again and Jack collapsed to his knees sobbing into Ragnar's mane. The great cat knew little of what to do so stood there comforting his friend as best he could.

Jack had no idea how long he had been away as he walked back through the gate into the compound. A few of the survivors were milling about outside stacking provisions. He walked inside, everyone else was inside, the place had been tidied up and cleaned. The bodies were wrapped and laid out on three tables at one side of the room, Grace was sat on a chair near the bodies staring lifelessly into space.

He walked over to her, she saw him come over and watched expressionlessly as he came to stand by her, he reached out his hand and placed it on her shoulder, it was as though this touch, this momentary pressure broke through her grief, she sprang to her feet and wrapped her arms around his neck. She squeezed so tight it was almost unbearable, eventually, her grip lessened and he wrapped his arms around her, feeling her sobs wracking through her body. He glanced over at the wrapped shapes laid out on the tables and cried with Grace.

The others in the room did not know what to do, eventually, Merlyn walked over to them.

"Their passing is but another corner on their long road, they will always be with you inside. Be thankful for your time spent, for their support, for their strength, and their love. It is time we laid them to rest"

The bodies were carried carefully to the two graves and laid gently inside. The sun was starting to fade, the sky glowed a deep orange bathing the clearing in a warm glow. No animals were heard, no birds singing, it was as though the forest was also paying its respects.

Merlyn stood at the head of the graves and spoke solemnly "Their lives were short on this earth, but it was not fruitless, it was not without purpose. Their lives were full of joy and happiness, even if tinged with some sadness. Three unassuming people who are parents to two of the most important people in history, can you ask for more when you are remembered as the custodians of salvation. They will not be here to finally see the darkness forced away, to see the shadows finally defeated. But know that without them there would be no hope, no salvation. Continue now my children on your journey, do not fear or be sad for those left behind, be joyful of the part you have played in saving two worlds"

With that Merlyn raised his hands a ball of blue light swirled and rolled in front of him, he raised his arms above his head and the ball shot off into the twilight sky, as it got higher and higher into the sky it suddenly split into three, one shot of into the sky with great speed. The other two stopped and hovered high up in the sky, everyone watched as the lights danced about.

"It is ok, you have done your job, the time is now," Merlyn said and looked at Jack.

Jack stared up into the sky "I love you" he said, the two lights burned brighter and shot off into the sky.

Merlyn used his powers to cover the bodies, each one was marked with a stone. Slowly they drifted back to the compound, leaving Merlyn with Jack and Grace.

"It is time to go. We have much to do my friends" Merlyn said ushering them along the path.

As they entered the building Merlyn said "I need the stones from the chest"

Kara and Viggo were waiting as they entered. "Why?" asked Kara.

"For security my dear, they are protection stones, if we place them around the perimeter it will mean we cannot be seen by prying eyes, but we will be able to see them" Merlyn explained.

"The chest is over here," Viggo said dragging the chest out.

"If you would like to accompany me we will get this done in no time" Merlyn stated.

As they left Grace and Jack plonked themselves down at the table, they were joined by Kara.

"I am so sorry," Kara said

Jack nodded and Grace smiled, they both felt exhausted but were in no rush to try and sleep.

After a few minutes of silence, Merlyn and Viggo returned and joined them at the table.

"Today is the day for mourning, tomorrow we must plan our victory," Merlyn said

"I cannot see a victory in our futures," Viggo said.

"Ah but you are destined, it has been written, but there is much to do and much more that could go wrong. We all need rest, today has been a drain on us all. Tomorrow I will explain what I know and we will begin again"

New Day

The next morning Jack opened his eyes, he did not rise from his bed but lay there glancing around the place they now called home. Home could it now be home, will he ever have a home again, he scanned the room looking for familiar sights, looking for his parents, looking for his mom smiling at him, a smile so full of love. He closed his eyes as the tears threatened to come again, his parent's faces were there smiling at him. How could he go on, he felt so empty inside, as though he was somehow on autopilot.

He opened his eyes again, everyone was up Grace and Merlyn were sat at the table deep in conversation, Kara and Viggo were preparing breakfast with the help of a couple of the new people who's names Jack had yet to learn.

Jack sat up, immediately Grace shot him a glance and smiled, he smiled back, it must have looked so false because he certainly didn't feel like smiling. He swung out of bed and walked over to the table and sat down.

"Good morning Jack? How are we this fine morn?" Merlyn asked

Jack managed another smile, talking was a different matter.

"When the others join us we will begin our plans for what to do next," Merlyn said.

They sat in silence for a while before Viggo, Kara, and Mark brought breakfast over and sat with them. No one spoke as they ate, as Merlyn finished his last mouthful he pushed his plate away saying "Gentlemen, ladies, we have much to discuss, but I feel I must give you some information first so we are all aware of what we must do. The first thing we have to do is find Artus, he and I crossed paths a long, long time ago, I have not seen him for many years now and have little idea of where he may be. However, I do know where we can get the information to find him. It is a couple of days ride west from here, it is a very old forest and I am hoping someone there can help us"

"Who is it?" Grace asked

"She is from our realm, when we came over the last few remaining Elhuri moved to this forest and cut themselves off from the rest of the world. The place is hidden by magic, but only now magic has returned am I able to find it again" Merlyn answered "Her name is Gana"

"What about my people?" Mark asked, "Will we be safe here?"

"Ah well that is a choice we must make, you can stay here, the stones will protect you, but it may be a long time before we return, if at all. Or you all come along with us and hope Gana and her people will take you in and shelter you. If you choose to come the journey will be longer than if we go ourselves"

"I will have to speak to the others and we will let you know" with that Mark got up from the table and went outside to where the others were.

"I want to know more about the Katari" Grace said

"Ah indeed. The legend of the Katari has always been with us, since before Thrall. It had little relevance for a long time, a group of warriors able to command magic like no other would come when our need was greatest. We did not know how many, their names anything. Most of us wondered why we would need such a prophecy when our world was so tranquil and calm.

When Thrall attacked the first time, we all wondered if they would arrive then as if this was the point in time the prophecy foretold, but nothing happened and it was left to us to banish Thrall and his Hellions.

I do not know about those that remained but those of us who were also taken with the great spell wondered how bad it has to be for the prophecy to come true. I guess now we know, the fate of both worlds is now in your hands"

"So we travel to see this Gana who we hope will tell us where this Artus is, then what?" Viggo asked

"Then my good sir, then we fight back"

"With the magic, we are all pretty much at a loss as to how that works, none of us have ever used it before" Kara stated.

"The magic will come, you will need some training but you will find it comes naturally, just open your minds to it," Merlyn said raising one hand "open your minds to a whole world of possibilities" He began to slowly rub his hands together as though creating a snowball. Lights began to dance about inside, tiny flickers of every colour slowly merging into a ball of light.

"Your mind is the only thing to hold you back, magic is infinite, magic is everywhere, it is the lifeblood of every living thing" the ball of light swirled in a multitude of colours as he held out his hand.

"Magic is ours to control, it is ours to use" the ball began to rise from his hand hovering over the table between them.

"Magic is beautiful, it can create, but also destroy, there must be a balance kept at all times. Too much destruction and it will destroy you"

He closed his hand quickly and the ball burst into showers of stars that twinkled down to the table and disappeared.

"You are all Katari, beings of magic, magic flows through you, do not try too hard to make things happen just feel for it, it is always there"

"But what are the Katari?" Grace asked

"The legends say that the Katari were the firstborn of each race, each represented by one powerful being. From these beings, all others came. For some reason no one knows why they disappeared, we don't know where they went but it was said that when our need was greatest they would return"

"When do we leave," Jack said expressionlessly

"I think it best if we leave in the morning, we will pack what we need to take today" Merlyn answered.

The door opened and Mark and two others came in, Mark stood at the head of the table.

"We have decided to come with you, we are already packing our things together"

"Ah excellent, we can take the stones with us and use them when we camp," Merlyn said gleefully.

He stood up banging his hands onto the table "Friends we must prepare ourselves as best we can, we move out at first light" he turned and walked outside.

The next morning everyone was frantically preparing for the journey, Jack was pleased as it gave him less time to dwell on his thoughts. He wanted to talk to Grace, to console her but his own emotions were so exposed he couldn't bring himself too and he felt very guilty. A couple of times he had caught Kara giving him the eyes to speak to Grace but he pretended he hadn't seen.

A couple of hours after sunrise and they were ready to leave, he had managed to fashion a sort of saddlebag to fit on Ragnar with provisions for himself in, they had all been responsible for their own food and drinks as they had no vehicles to carry things in.

Mark and his group had no form of transport and would be walking unless they stumbled across anything on the way.

He made his way outside to release Ragnar the morning sunlight hit him, already it was warm. Blue sky was everywhere, there was not a cloud in the sky. He closed his eyes listening to the birds singing, the warmth on his face everything for a split second was normal, for just a second he forgot everything, became oblivious to the hurt and pain as though the earth itself was trying to heal his pain.

"Let us make haste my boy" Merlyn's words cut through like a knife, shattering that one peaceful moment. Jack couldn't help but give him an angry look.

"Ah sorry," he said genuinely as he walked over to Styx loading his provisions onto his mount.

Jack felt Ragnar stirring and released him from the sword, he heard a few gasps from Mark's group who I guess we're still getting used to magic.

"Hello my friend," he said running his hand through Ragnar's mane.

"Hello Jack," a voice in his head said sadly.

"What? What was that?" Jack blurted out.

"Ah-ha at last my friend you hear my voice, it is I Ragnar" the voice responded

Jack stared at Ragnar open mouthed "I can hear you, in my head!"

Merlyn overheard and came over "Ah excellent, you and Ragnar are now one, you are joined so you can now hear his voice"

"What, you never said this before. So he's been trying to talk to me since the start"

"Yes of course, but only when you are truly connected can you hear. I guess I should have mentioned that" he said walking off back to Styx muttering to himself.

Viggo, Kara, and Grace came outside, "What's going on?" Viggo asked

"Well, apparently when we are truly connected with our" he waved his arm at Ragnar "animals, we can hear their voices"

"What!" exclaimed Grace

"So how do we do that then," said Kara.

"It will come to you all soon enough" Merlyn shouted over "Come on now, time for moving not for talking"

Viggo and Kara walked away to find room to release their mounts.

Grace touched Jack's arm "Are you ok?" she asked full of concern.

"I will be" he replied with a slight smile "I'm so sorry I haven't been there for you, I don't think I would have been much help"

"It's ok Jack," Grace said smiling, she stepped into him and wrapped her arms around him.

"I won't let you down again, I promise" Jack whispered into her ear.

Grace pulled away and smiled, her face lit up, her eyes shining bright "I..... I had better get ready" she stuttered and moved away. She looked back and smiled at Jack as she walked away. A warmth flowed through him that was not from the sun, as though his grief had been pierced for the first time.

"Well my friend, it is good to finally hear your voice," Jack said to Ragnar

"It is good to finally be heard" Ragnar responded, his voice was a deep growl in his head.

Jack looked about and could see everyone was ready so he leapt onto Ragnar's back.

"Ok everyone listen carefully, Kara and Viggo you fly just ahead and warn us of any dangers, I will take the lead then Mark and his people, Jack and Grace you cover our rear. We must all keep our eyes open and if you see anything strange point it out better to be safe than sorry" Merlyn instructed, then shook Styx's reigns and they all set off.

As Jack left the compound he looked back one last time "Bye mom, bye dad, I will love you always" he said in his head a tear rolling down his cheek. He glanced over at Grace, her eyes were filled with tears, he could do nothing but smile at her and hoped, for now, that was enough. He snapped his head forward and concentrated on the road ahead.

A couple of hours had passed and they had just been discussing to take a break soon when Kara flew down from the sky.

"There's a farm ahead, there looks like there may be some survivors there" Kara explained

"Then we go and see," Jack said

"It's not that simple there seems to be a small group of Hellions moving towards the farm from the south"

"Even better," Jack said determinedly.

"We cannot rush in my boy," Merlyn said. "Do you know how many?" he asked Kara.

"We think about fifty"

"Merlyn you and Grace stay here with Mark and his group. Kara you and Viggo keep an eye on things from the sky, and I will go and say hello to our friends" Jack said his voice full of anger.

"Ha I like this plan," Ragnar said in his head

"I'm coming too," said Grace

"No it's too" Jack was about to say until Grace said "If you say dangerous I'm going to hit you"

"Ok we have a plan, Jack and Grace will go say hello as Jack put it. Kara and Viggo will keep an eye out from the sky and I will watch the sheep" Merlyn said smiling.

"Erm, the what?" Mark said "we can fight too"

"Ah yes, I maybe should have done something about that before we left, please remind me when this problem is resolved" Merlyn answered.

Jack pulled his sword and concentrated, his armour covered his body within seconds, Grace did the same. Ragnar and Silvermane were also ready for battle.

"If you head that way through the trees you will come out behind them," Kara said pointing, then she took off into the sky.

"Are you ready?" Jack said to Grace. She nodded back.

Ragnar reared up and sprang forward followed by Grace.

Within moments they had reached the edge of the tree line, they stopped and there ahead of them was the group of Hellions, these were different to the wild savage beasts they had fought before, they were more like people, but clad in black armour. You could not see any faces but their eyes glowed red.

"Shall we?" Jack said

"Yes let's" Grace replied smiling.

"Yaaah" Jack cried. Ragnar leaped forward with a huge roar that echoed through the forest.

Silvermane reared up his front legs thrashing the air as it charged forward.

Within seconds they had covered the ground between them and crashed into the rear ranks of the Hellions. Jack swung his sword from side to side, each stroke a death blow to those in front of him, Ragnar was doing as much damage as Jack his claws slashing backward and forward.

Their impetus had taken them too far forward and within moments the enemy had closed in behind them, however, they fought like animals and the enemy had no chance. Jack swung his sword a blue arc of energy flew out dropping five of them instantly, his sword was a blur.

Grace attacked with vengeance in mind, her sword glowed as she cut through the enemy armour as though it was not there.

The battle lasted about three minutes after that all the enemy lay dead or dying.

Kara and Viggo had watched the battle unfold from the skies. "Oh my, that was no battle that was a slaughter," Viggo said as they flew down to join them.

As they landed Merlyn and the others were just breaking through from the treeline.

Merlyn and the others soon arrived at the battle scene.

"No problems then?" he said looking around.

Mark bent over and picked up an axe and shield, he swung the axe about left to right as if judging its weight.

"Good idea my boy, collect any weapons or armour you want"

"What about the bodies?" he said disdainfully.

"Ah yes". Merlyn raised his hands and swept them out over the battle scene, a blue sheet of light washed over the bodies, as the light touched them the bodies vanished leaving just the armour and weapons behind.

"Gather as much as you can carry and we will make our way to the farm" Merlyn instructed.

Jack was in somewhat of a daze as he watched them grabbing weapons and trying on different pieces of armour, eventually, they all had weapons and some sort of armour on. He still felt the rage of battle dying down inside him, he disconnected himself from his armour and it disappeared he saw Grace had already done the same.

He dismounted from Ragnar and walked over to the others.

"I think it best if I approach the farm with Mark and a couple of others you wait here and wait," Merlyn said, "we don't want to spook them".

They all nodded in agreement. Merlyn set off toward the farm with the others when they got within about a hundred metres they saw five people emerge from a barn all with bows drawn and arrows notched.

"We had better be ready just in case," said Viggo jumping onto Throdin. The others followed suit and moved up to the edge of the trees so they were still invisible to those at the farm.

Jack watched as Merlyn approached arms outstretched showing he was unarmed, there was some frantic gesturing from one of the farm occupants. Merlyn turned and pointed back to the rest of them then again turned to face the farm occupants.

After a few minutes, Jack watched them lower their bows, Mark and the others stepped forward showing the weapons and armour they had taken, and hands were shaken.

A collective sigh went around the group still in the woods, they didn't want to be fighting survivors.

"Perhaps it would be best if we walked down" Jack suggested.

"Yes maybe best" Grace agreed.

They all withdrew their mounts and walked out of the forest down towards the farm and the others. Jack watched the group from the farm as they walked down, Merlyn was constantly speaking as they drew closer, they looked nervous and very much on edge.

They eventually joined the group "Hello" Jack said nodding. "What the hell are you four?" the woman who seemed to be the leader said.

"That's a long story, but we mean you no harm and hopefully we can help," Grace said.

"What do you want?" another woman in the group asked.

"Just somewhere to rest for a while before we carry on our journey" Viggo answered.

They looked unsure and shot quick glances to one another. "How long do you want to stay?" the leader asked.

"Maybe an hour or two, if you good people will allow," Merlyn said.

The leader nodded "I'm Abigail, this is James, Andy, Beccy, and George", they all nodded at the group.

"I'm Jack, this is Grace, Kara, and Viggo" Jack replied with his own introductions.

"We have a bunkhouse over there if your people want to rest, there are beds and running water, we used to do team building from here, before, well before it happened," Abigail said pointing to a large green building to the side of the main farmhouse.

"If whoever is in charge wants to come to the house and swap info that would be great" Abigail asked.

"Excellent, Mark you take your people for a rest we will go and try and fill these good people in," Merlyn said.

Mark nodded and led his group of now weirdly looking soldiers to the bunkhouse. Jack and the others followed the group into the main house.

They entered the house through a large wooden door, straight away they were in a large kitchen. There was a large wooden table running the length of the room, surrounded by chairs. There was a door at the far end leading to the rest of the house. The kitchen was very large, one side was covered in vegetables of all description, a huge range cooker sat at the end next to the door, pots and pans hung from a rack next to the cooker.

"Please have a seat," Abigail said

"Are any of you hungry?" Andy asked leaning his bow against the wall.

"Only if you have some to spare my good man" Merlyn replied smiling.

They all sat around the table, Andy and Beccy fetched water for everyone then bought out bread, cheese, and ham for them to eat.

"This looks lovely thank you," Grace said

Abigail smiled "Have you been travelling long?"

"No, just for a few hours, we need to get somewhere as quickly as possible" Jack answered.

"Really? Why?" James asked.

"It is a long story," Kara said "Yes not sure how to make it any shorter either" Grace agreed.

"Perhaps I can try to explain" Merlyn offered.

Merlyn proceeded to tell them as much as he could and as quickly as he could. There were a few laughs at first, then a few "Yea rights" but eventually after a demonstration by Kara they sat there pretty much open mouthed and listened.

"I, I don't know what to say" Abigail blurted out after Merlyn had finished.

"How come you stayed at your farm?" Viggo asked

"Oh this isn't our farm," Andy said "We were stopping in the bunkhouse, we are an archery team, we were here on a retreat for training before nationals"

"Guess that was a waste of time," James said

"On the contrary, you may find those skills invaluable to you," Merlyn said.

"We were planning on a move to Chester that was the last thing we heard on the radio as a safe zone," Andy said.

"Have you seen anyone or anything else?" Jack asked

"No, not a soul," Andy said

Jack realised how lucky they were that they happened along, those things would have surely killed them all here. "How come those things were different?" Jack asked Merlyn.

"It would seem they are using the local populace to grow their army"

"They were humans?" Grace exclaimed.

"Once," Merlyn said with a sigh, "Unfortunately it seems there is no way back for the demonised ones"

"We must be thinking about moving on at some point," Merlyn said

"You can't just leave us here" exclaimed Abigail.

Jack remembered what Merlyn said that survivors would come to them, that they would be drawn to them.

"You can come with us," Jack said.

Everyone shot a glance at Jack, even Merlyn raised an eyebrow.

"Are you sure that's wise?" Viggo said.

"We cannot leave anyone behind or unprotected, they come with us," Jack said with authority.

"There are horses," George said "I've been looking after them and a wagon of some sort in the barn, it may need a bit of fixing up but it seems ok"

"This is great news, how many horses?"

"I think about thirty, it was a trekking centre also, part of the team building stuff" George replied

"Excellent lead the way my good man we shall go and investigate," Merlyn said jumping up from the table and burst out of the door followed closely by George.

They all followed them outside, they were just quick enough to see them vanish around the outside of the bunkhouse. Mark and a couple of others were outside.

"What's going on?" Mark asked.

"We think we may have horses for you all" Kara answered.

Mark and the others followed them, as they rounded the corner they could see a large barn and a huge stable block, the whinnying of horses could now be heard.

"Are there enough saddles?" Merlyn asked

"I'm not sure, I haven't looked its all in that building there," George said pointing to what looked like a large log cabin.

Just as Merlyn was about to disappear Jack said "I'm going to patrol the perimeter make sure we don't get any unwanted guests"

"I will come too," Grace said smiling.

Jack turned and walked away with Grace following behind him, Jack could feel Ragnar itching to get out so released him as he strode along. The great lion leaped out ahead of Jack and began to walk alongside Jack away from the farm.

"Jack" Grace shouted to him

Jack stopped and looked around "Don't be in such a rush!" she said

"I'm not I just want to make sure everyone is safe"

"So where are we going?"

"There's a hill just up there, we should be able to see quite a bit from up there"

"Ok lead the way" Grace said as she called Silvermane from her sword and jumped onto its back.

Jack jumped onto Ragnar's back.

"I like her" Ragnar said in his head.

Jack smiled, "What are you smiling about?" Grace asked pulling up next to him.

"Oh er nothing, c'mon let's go" Jack quickly urged Ragnar forward and they set off towards the hill.

They did not try to speak they just rode as fast as they could, the wind blowing in their faces, the warm summer sun beating down on them, the smell of grass, the sweet smell of the outdoors.

They finally reached the top of the hill and stopped, surveying the surrounding area.

"Oh god look," Grace said pointing away from the farm to the other side of the hill.

In the distance was a small town, or what was left of it. Most of the buildings were destroyed, the odd fire could be seen burning brightly, smoke drifted up in plumes from several places around the town.

That wasn't the worst, people were being herded into large pens by the same creatures they had fought earlier, there must have been about two hundred people and at least three times the number of enemy troops.

Jack felt a surge of anger rise inside him.

"There will be plenty of time for fighting," Ragnar's voice said inside his head.

"I don't think we can help them at the moment," Grace said noticing Jack's face.

"Jack! Jack! There's nothing we can do for them now" Grace reiterated.

"We can't just leave them," Jack said through clenched teeth.

"Let's go back see what the others say" Grace suggested turning Silvermane away and back towards the farm. Grace could see the tenseness in Jacks's body and knew she had to snap him out of it quickly.

"C'mon Jack, let's go," She said loudly.

This broke Jack's gaze and he turned his head "Ok let's go back"

He turned Ragnar around and they set off back to the farm. As they arrived they saw Viggo and Merlyn had attached some horses to an old wagon and were loading it up with supplies and weapons from their previous encounter.

Jack and Grace went straight to them.

"Ah here they are, good news the wagon seems in good order and there are enough horses for everyone so that should quicken our journey," Merlyn said excitedly.

"What's up?" Viggo asked noticing Jack's stern face.

"People are being herded into pens in a town over the hill by those things we encountered earlier," Grace said.

"How many people?" Viggo asked

"About two hundred and three times as many enemy troops" Grace answered.

"Hmmm, we cannot do anything about that at the moment," Merlyn said sorrowfully.

"What!" exclaimed Jack. "We can't just leave them, there are kids too"

"Jack" Grace began.

"Don't we can't just leave them or that makes us as bad as them" Jack said angrily.

"We can't draw attention to ourselves yet, the quieter we can be the more chance we have of making it to Gana in one piece" Merlyn explained.

"Viggo we have to do something, there were more wagons down there, we could easily use them to take them with us," Jack said turning to Viggo.

"Jack there aren't enough of us," Viggo said apologetically.

"Cowards, your all cowards" Jack shouted and stormed off.

Grace went to follow him, "Best to leave him I think, let him calm down," Merlyn said to her.

Jack was seething as he rounded the barn, Ragnar was stretched out on the floor relaxing in the sun. Jack moved straight over to him and he sprang up.

"I don't think this is a good idea," Ragnar said inside his head.

"Fine stay here then, no one else is bothered either"

"Don't be so quick to anger my friend, of course, I will help"

Jack leapt onto his back and raced away from the farm towards the hill.

Abigail was just leaving the farmhouse and saw him riding away over the field but thought nothing of it.

Jack reached the top of the hill and looked down at the village, their was a small woodland between the hill and the village giving enough cover that they would not see his approach.

"I don't like the numbers," Ragnar said "I think we have the advantage" and he gave a growling chuckle. Jack smiled, his face still expressionless and filled with anger, a rage burned inside him, to him that was his parents down there, he hadn't been there to protect them and he was not going to make the same mistake twice.

"Do we have a plan?" Ragnar asked.

Jack chuckled, "Yes we rescue the prisoners and don't die"

Jack drew his sword, the armour covered them both and he urged Ragnar forward. He felt a weird sensation inside himself, almost like an energy inside, the hairs on his body all stood up on end. He felt different and yet it felt familiar at the same time.

He urged Ragnar forward into a run, they were halfway down the hill, the trees were just ahead. His plan if you could call it a plan was to attack the enemy camp from the right away from the prisoners.

Ragnar gained speed and momentum as he crashed through the woodland, he could see movement ahead, they must have heard the commotion by now. The power inside him seemed to grow with every stride, he looked at his hands, blue bolts of lightning curled around his fingers getting brighter and brighter.

"Let's let them know we are here shall we," Jack said.

They burst out of the woodland, Ragnar letting out a huge roar that stunned the enemy troops. Within seconds they were crashing through the first few troops, Jack swinging his sword left and right, blue fire dancing from his blade.

He leapt from Ragnar's back into a group of soldiers grabbing his sword with both hands it grew into his broadsword. He landed ready to attack, he swung his sword in a great arc cutting through about five enemy troops, the blue fire emanating from his blade killing another twenty.

He could see the blue electricity dancing all over his body as he fought, he heard Ragnar behind him roaring as he fought protecting his back. He hacked and slashed, parrying blow after blow a never ending attack of enemy troops.

The mass of troops before him began to thin out, getting fewer and fewer "We are winning!" he shouted in his head. He blocked a blade aiming for his stomach, spinning round and severing the arm still holding the sword. His instincts had taken over and for once he was letting them. To his left they charged at him en masse, he pushed out his left hand as though he was saying stop, a burst of blue energy erupted from his hand blasting through the ranks of en-rushing screaming devils.

They began to turn and run, bodies were scattered all around him, a surge of elation took over as he watched them flee.

Then his heart sank, it was a ploy, the troops disappeared between the ranks of troops that now surrounded him and Ragnar on all sides, all in formation, all ready to attack.

Jack looked at Ragnar, "I'm sorry". Ragnar growled "It was a pleasure to fight by your side, my friend"

Black clouds began to roll in overhead blocking out the sun, a rumble of thunder in the distance as a storm approached. The thunder got louder and they still did not attack.

"C'mon then!" Jack shouted

Lightning cracked overhead a bolt lit up the sky arcing through the now black sky overhead.

Rain began to pour down onto the battlefield, still they stood there, it was then that Jack noticed somewhere looking up at the sky as if unsure as to what was happening.

"Maybe we still have a chance," thought Jack.

The thunder got louder and louder, a bolt of lightning arced down from the sky exploding amidst the troops to his left scattering them, another bolt smashed to the ground behind him. Still, they did not run, they just reformed their now dwindling ranks.

Jack guessed there were probably about half of the numbers left, another bolt of lightning crashed into the ranks in front of him leaving a hole in the formed ranks before him.

Suddenly the rain poured down, the rain was so intense you could hardly see, a huge clap of thunder shook the floor beneath him, making him stagger slightly.

A bolt of lightning so bright zig zagged down from the sky and hit the ground just in front of him, however, this one kept going, the brightness was so intense Jack squinted at it. Then Jack noticed a shadow form inside the light, it began to walk towards him.

Jack readied himself for the fight, he heard Ragnar roar behind him as the figure approached. The light making it too difficult to make out any features. Still, it came towards him, Jack noticed a sword in his hand. He felt a tension rise inside him, is this why they did not attack they were waiting for this. Suddenly the lightning bolt burst outwards in a blinding light. It knocked the first couple of ranks of troops off their feet, Jack managed to keep on his feet but for a split second became blinded by the light.

He felt the rain ease and he began to blink vigorously to try and regain his eyesight. When it did come back the figure was stood a few feet in front of him, all clad in armour, a sword in each hand.

"Are you ready to dance?" it said to him.

It can't be Jack thought, how can it be?

The figure turned and ran towards the enemy.

"Ben!!" Jack shouted charging forward.

A tiger suddenly leapt into the ranks of the enemy. They fought side by side destroying everything before them. Nothing could stand in their way, from a distance you would have thought they danced a choreographed dance, so in tune were their movements as though they were of one mind, one deadly mind. They brought only death to the enemy.

Jack saw in the sky a dragon and an eagle, the others were here, he saw Mark and the others charging down the hill into the rear of the enemy, dressed in a mismatch of armour. He saw Abigail and the others standing on the hillside firing arrow after arrow into the ranks of the enemy. A light flashed from further back and he saw Merlyn's Griffin rear up scattering black armour everywhere. The battle was joined, this was the first strike back.

The battle raged for what seemed to be an eternity until eventually, the enemy began to thin then run away. A cheer erupted from the pens over the left of him.

He searched the battlefield and finally laid eyes upon his friend, his friend he had watched die, his friend who seemed now very much alive. He couldn't move or speak he just stared as Ben walked around the field.

Eventually, he managed to snap his gaze away and noticed Grace walking towards him.

"What the hell were you thinking you absolute idiot!" she screamed, as she got close to him she repeated her words but followed it up by smacking him in the chest.

"You could have died Jack!"

"I know I'm sorry, but have you seen," he said nodding in a direction over Grace's shoulder.

"Seen what?" she said turning her head.

"It can't be" she whispered.

Ben was now walking towards them his helmet off and holding his hand up in greeting.

"Hello, I'm Ben," he said to them

"Er yes we know, don't you know who we are?" Jack asked.

"Do I know you?" Ben asked quizzically.

Merlyn came storming over "Jack you fool, whatever did you think you were doing?"

"I'm sorry I just wanted to help them," Jack said

"This could have gone so wrong and been so much worse than the casualties we have sustained"

"There are casualties?" Jack asked.

"Yes, eight of Mark's group have been killed, five are quite seriously injured"

"Oh no, I'm sorry, they should have stayed away" Jack mumbled.

"We are in this together my friend" as the last words died on his lips he noticed the other person stood there. "Ben?" he asked

"At your service sir," Ben replied.

"How is this possible" Grace asked overwhelmed.

Kara and Viggo came striding over.

"Jack you fool!" bellowed Viggo.

"I know, I know, I'm sorry but" Jack replied gesturing his head towards Ben.

"It can't be!" Kara exclaimed.

"Ben?" Viggo said questioningly.

"Yes, I seem to be at a loss as everyone knows me and I have not a clue who any of you are," Ben said.

"What do you remember?" Merlyn asked.

Ben looked puzzled for a moment "I remember a light, then a woman's voice saying Ben your friend is in need of you, next thing I'm here and I knew what to do then"

"You remember how to fight?" Kara asked.

"That's all I remember," Ben said.

At that moment Abigail came over to the group, "There's another one of you?" she said looking Ben up and down, "You've kept him quiet, we've opened the pens and let the people out, they are a bit hungry and thirsty but they seem ok. Question is what now?"

"We take them with us," Jack said.

"We what?" Viggo blurted out.

"We take them with us it's the only way they will be safe" Jack replied.

Merlyn nodded "Very well, but they must choose this path"

He walked over to the survivors and climbed onto the roof of a burnt out car. His voice boomed out over the field.

"Here me, listen well for you have a choice to make. You all have two options, option one you are now free and can go wherever you choose to go, option two you come with us"

"We need to head to Chester, that's the closest safe place" a man shouted.

"The decision is yours, I would suggest you scavenge the battlefield for weapons and armour that will be useful to you, we leave in one hour" Merlyn jumped down from the car and walked back over to the others.

He looked at Ben "We will try to figure out what's going on with you as we go, for now, we need to move before more arrive"

An hour past and their group were ready to move they had brought all the horses and the wagon from the farm, it was loaded with supplies are more weapons.

A woman from the rescued people came over "Hi I'm Sarah, I was a police officer here, some of us are going to come with you"

"How many?" asked Jack

"About fifty" she replied

"Fifty, that's not good enough you all need to come with us" Jack sounded exasperated.

Jack jumped onto Ragnar and rode over to the survivors "Listen to me, you need to come with us, we don't even know if there is anything left of Chester. These things conquered our planet in days, what makes you think they managed to hold them at these safe zones"

The man who spoke before stepped forward "We are going to Chester and that's that, we thank you for what you did but we will be safer there"

"You fools, you will all die! Don't you see that!" Jack shouted.

Some people in the crowd started to back away in fear.

"Jack, stop," Grace said placing a hand on his arm, "It's not helping, we have to save who we can"

Jack sighed and turned away from the crowd.

"Those coming with us, we leave in ten minutes" Merlyn shouted his voice booming out over the field.

They all gathered together waiting for the new additions to arrive, three of the injured had died, two had been placed in the wagon, Mark's group were now down to nine.

The group led by Sarah eventually came over, there was a mix of men and women and about five children. Jack smiled as they approached, trying to reassure them all they had made the right choice.

They had two wagons with them and a few horses, it still left about fifteen walking which wasn't ideal, they had salvaged weapons and armour from the battlefield so they had some protection now.

"We have about two days journey ahead," Merlyn said "keep your eyes peeled for anything strange or any provisions, do NOT be afraid to speak up, our lives may depend on it"

They set off in a column, Merlyn at the front, then Abigail and her group, behind them was Sarah and her group, then Viggo and Kara, Mark and his remaining few bought up the rear with Ben, Grace, and Jack in the rear. The pace was fairly slow due to the walking few, Jack had said it would be best if occasionally Viggo and Kara flew ahead to scout where they were going. He watched as they both took off from the column and vanished into the clouds.

Jack turned and looked at Ben, he looked exactly the same as before and he seemed the same if perhaps a little more distant, reflective even as though wrapped up in his thoughts.

"Are you ok Ben?" Jack asked.

"Yea"

"I still can't believe it," Grace said "We thought we'd" Jack shot Grace a look "We'd er that you'd gone for good"

"When did I leave?" Ben asked "I don't remember anything until the field in the middle of that battle"

"A while ago, we were very sad you left" Grace answered.

"Leo says he can't remember anything either," Ben said

"Leo?" Jack replied.

"Yea Leo" Ben said ruffling his hand through the fur on Leonidas' back.

"You can hear what he says?" Grace said

"Er, yea why?"

"Great that's just me now then," Grace said.

"Do you know what we are doing?" Jack asked trying to probe as much as he could.

"We are trying to rid the world of a plague of some sort, I take it those things were part of it?"

"Yea, I haven't had a chance to say before but thanks," Jack said smiling

"For what?" Ben asked

"For turning up when you did"

The next few hours went mostly in silence, the silence had spread throughout the column as they continued, mainly due to everyone being on high alert for any trouble.

The sun was starting to sink slowly in the sky when Merlyn called a halt. Viggo and Kara had landed in front of the column so Jack, Ben, and Grace rode up to see what was going on, they were joined by Abigail, Mark, and Sarah.

"Ah here you all are, Viggo please tell them what you just told me," Merlyn said

Viggo and Kara sat staring at Ben, who shifted in his seat, uncomfortable with their gaze.

"Erm Kara then," Merlyn said again

"Yes sorry, it's good to see you again Ben, really good" Kara replied "The road cuts through a forest, then opens up into fields again, the other side there's a large army marching through, easily a few hundred maybe more"

"I think it best we set up camp here for today, I will set the stones around the perimeter, that will give us some protection until morning," Merlyn said.

"If we move just over there a bit there's a stream and we will be far enough away from the road for the night" Viggo added.

They set up the camp and Merlyn placed the protection stones around it.

"How do they work?" Kara asked him

"They shift reality slightly, so even though we are here anyone who walks through here will not see or hear us" Merlyn replied.

"Can we light a fire?" Mark asked

"Yes of course" Merlyn answered.

They all sat about the camp mainly in silence, the odd word that was spoken cut through the silence like a knife and seemed so out of place. Eventually, people started to drift off to sleep, slowly they all settled down for the night.

Jack lay in his sleeping bag on the floor watching the sky above him, his thoughts drifted to his parents, he missed them every second of the day, how he wished for one more hug, one more I love you. He closed his eyes hoping sleep would block out his thoughts, but sleep was not there to rescue him this time.

He began to think about how much he had altered his parent's life, how his condition had become what every decision was made around, he knew they had wanted more children but had decided against it after Jack was born. He had spoken to his mom about when it first happened, he hadn't been walking long and just stumbled and fell to the floor, that was broken femur number one.

His mom had said that as if that wasn't bad enough the questions from the doctors and nurses all seemed to be towards whether they had done it and he was being abused in some way. The anger he felt when his parents first told him had burnt like a flame.

Holidays abroad were never a good idea as on a couple of occasions breaks had occurred whilst away, the running joke had been that he should have a sticker chart to mark off the hospitals he had attended.

His parents had never stopped him doing anything once he was old enough to understand the risks and at first, this hadn't stopped him either, he had thought about this a lot and he thought that he wasn't going to let it beat him, he wasn't just a kid with a condition. But as he got older he realised that the condition was part of him, he couldn't beat it or ignore it.

Winter was the worst, seeing everyone sliding about on the ice, making snowmen, and having snowball fights was always the worst, this was probably one of the biggest things to try and get over, something that bought so much pleasure to people filled him with a sense of dread, every footstep a tense, nervous step into the unknown, every step carefully placed, every piece of floor scanned for the glistening signs of ice. He learned to walk with his eyes fixed to the floor, looking for trip hazards, potholes anything that could cause a fall.

But, every fall, every break, every ambulance trip or hospital stay would not beat him, it would not bring him down, his parents were there always. Always there to hold his hand, for a hug if needed.

Now somehow he was normal, well above normal, he was able to do things he had always dreamed of, always wondered what it was like to do. It was exhilarating and yet still also petrifying that it would be taken off him again.

He had a memory of being a child in hospital, waiting for his parents to arrive then hearing the footsteps echoing down the corridor, he recognised the footsteps every time, he knew it was them. The doors to the ward opened and his parents came in all beaming smiles, he loved them so much and he missed them more than he thought could be possible.

Tears streamed down his cheeks as he lay thinking of his parents, trying to think of happy times, of Christmas's and birthdays, of laughter and fun. Eventually, sleep did come, it washed over him like the gentle lapping of the sea.

He dreamt he was sat upon Ragnar in full armour, next to him were Grace, Ben, Viggo and Kara, he could also make out another in golden armour but as hard as he tried to focus on them he could not, it was constantly just on the edge of his vision.

They were sat upon a hillside, to the left of them were the massed ranks of the Hellion Horde, there were thousands of them covering the ground like a carpet of ants.

Off to his left trumpets began to sound and drums began to bang out a beat, thunder rumbled in the distance, he could feel it through the earth beneath him. As the sound grew closer he could see another army approaching from the left, three columns of troops, on the, left a green and golden army marching in perfect unison towards the enemy. In the middle were ranks of troops carrying a variety of weapons, splitting the column in the centre was a section of archers, these were all dressed in mainly black armour that seemed to have been painted different colours. To the right was a section of cavalry, the horses walking in rows, their riders carrying lances and shields.

Jack watched as they drew closer to the enemy and stopped. What was happening, where had this other army come from, he knew of no army left especially not of this size.

Horns blasted from the left a low guttural sound that reverberated through the hills, the enemy began to bang their shields as a huge figure appeared from nowhere walking slowly through the ranks. Jack knew immediately who it was, it could be no one else but Thrall. Thrall turned to look at them sitting on the hillside. "I see you young Jack" a voice whispered inside his head "You have made yourself known to me, I am coming for you" With that, there was a loud roar as the Horde charged forward.

The cavalry charged from the right hitting the right flank of the horde, but they were getting overrun quickly. The rest of the Horde had reached the ranks of the rest of the army, the two sides crashed together with a noise akin to a loud explosion. Again the Horde seemed to be pushing them back.

"We have to go now!" Jack shouted to his friends, they all sat there in silence watching the carnage unfold. The sounds of battle and the cries of dying and wounded people filled the air.

"Let's go!" Jack shouted again and spurred Ragnar on, but even Ragnar would not move. Jack sat and watched as slowly the Horde overran the army stood to oppose it.

"Noooooo!" shouted Jack as dust from the battle momentarily obscured his view, the dust swirled round and round getting thicker and denser blocking out the sounds from below, he waved his arm in front of him trying to see. Slowly it began to clear to reveal he was now sat inside the tree opposite Selendrial.

"What's going on?" Jack asked

"you had to see where your actions were taking you," Selendrial said

"What do you mean?"

"Your anger was drawing you closer to Thrall before you are ready, since you attacked the town he now knows where you are"

"I couldn't leave people like that," he said almost apologetically

"I understand they needed help, but there was a better way. Be warned you will be pursued all the way to your destination now" she said sternly

"Thrall is coming for you all, he now knows where you are"

"Good let him come, I will kill him!" Jack said through gritted teeth

"Do not let your anger and your grief cloud your judgement, or you will put not just yourself at risk but also your friends"

Jack's posture softened slightly and he sank more into his chair.

"I should have been there, I should have saved them. I failed Ben and now" His voice trailed off filled with emotion.

"There time had come Jack, they are in a better place, you will see them again along the road, when your time comes," Selendrial said smiling, giving Jack some hope in his heart again.

"Ben is back, how is that possible, can't we die?"

"Yes you can all die when it is your time, it was not Ben's time, he still has much to do"

"He seems different, not the same Ben as before"

"No," Selendrial said sadly

"Unfortunately the magic that bought him back has made him more Katari than Ben now"

"Will he remember?"

"Yes he will remember but the memories will seem like someone else's to him, he will be detached from them"

"Listen to me Jack, the place you go to now will become your people's last hope. You must protect it, people, survivors will be drawn to it. It has remained hidden for thousands of years they will be wary of you but they will help you. You must stand together if we are to win the day"

"What is happening with Silari and Straven?"

"They are occupied here, Thrall has been preparing for a long time, he has grown a huge army here and they are preparing to meet him. Do not expect help from here anytime soon"

"Now return Jack, return and ready your friends for the road ahead for it will be a dangerous one"

Selendrial raised her hand and the light in the room suddenly became unbearably bright, he held his hand up to shield his eyes, blinking and squinting, trying to clear his vision.

He blinked his eyes frantically, slowly his vision cleared to reveal a starlit sky above him. He was back in the camp again, lying in his sleeping bag, the fires that had been lit were still burning but no one seemed awake.

"Are you ok my boy?" a voice spoke from behind him. Jack's head snapped round to see Merlyn sat on a log by one of the fires.

"I'm fine, thank you"

"Get some sleep, we can talk in the morning" Merlyn smiled broadly at him.

Jack smiled back and lay down, he closed his eyes and slept.

Sanctuary

Jack's eyes opened slowly, he tried to blink away the last vestiges of sleep as they tried to drag him back. He slowly sat up in bed watching the hustle and bustle of people preparing breakfast and packing things up. How their group had grown he thought as he watched unfamiliar faces hurry about.

He saw Grace sitting with Kara and he smiled as they looked over to him, they both smiled back and Grace beckoned him over.

He got up and walked over to them.

"Rough night?" Kara said frowning

"You could say that," Jack said smiling, "Where's Viggo, Ben, and Merlyn?"

"They went out for a scout around, they should be back soon," Grace said

"We need to talk when they are back," Jack said "I'm just going to go for a walk, I won't be long"

"Want some company?" Grace said

"Erm no thanks, I'm off to find the men's tree," he said with a smile.

"Oh I see, sorry," Grace said blushing slightly.

Jack walked away from the camp and into the woods. The sun was hanging low in the sky, it was a warm summer morning and the birds were singing in the trees. He walked into the woods just far enough that he wouldn't be seen from the camp and positioned himself by a tree.

His head snapped up, the air suddenly felt different, heavier somehow, and it had gone quiet, too quiet. No birds were singing just the gentle breeze rustling through the leaves on the branches overhead.

His hand dropped slowly to his side and a cold chill ran down his spine, he'd left his sword, he hadn't picked it up when he had gotten up. He closed his hand into a fist, trying to scan the forest with his eyes without making any sudden movements.

"I see you Katari" a voice whispered from behind him

Jack spun around, further back as the trees became denser he could see a figure, the figure was all in black it was difficult to make out as the outline seemed to shift almost blur as if shrouded in mist.

"You have no hope, you cannot save them like you could not save your parents Katari" The figure almost seemed to spit out the word Katari.

The rage began to build inside Jack, but he managed to hold it back, his fists squeezed tight, his knuckles white with rage.

"You are alone Katari," the figure said now beginning to move closer.

A black mist swirled around the figure occasionally showing an arm or a leg as it slowly walked towards him. There was a thud and a scraping sound broke the eerie silence, Jack made out an axe of some sort being dragged along by the figure. Jack knew he was defenseless, he also knew that running was no good. He crouched low waiting for the figure to make its move.

"Katari!" the voice made Jack's skin crawl.

Suddenly the figure rushed forward and Jack got his first real glimpse of it as the mist cleared. He was as tall as Jack and a lot broader, its armour was jet black and glistened as though coated in oil, the joints of the armour were a blood red. The helmet it wore looked like your worst nightmare and blood red eyes shone through the visor.

It let a blood curdling scream as it swung the axe at Jack, Jack was ready for it and leaped to the side, he heard the axe whistle through the air and land with a thud in the ground. Jack quickly regained his balance and crouched again waiting for the next blow, the creature spun around with an agility that took Jack by surprise, this time he swung the axe as Jack leaped away. This time however he stopped mid swing, he let the axe slide through his hands and hit out with the handle, the handle caught Jack in the side knocking him flying into a tree. He landed on the floor gasping for air from the blow to his side. The creature strode towards him axe raised, Jack tried to spin away but his head swam and he collapsed back down.

The creature was almost on top of him axe raised, Jack instinctively pushed out his hand, the air crackled with energy, and a bolt of blue energy shot from his hand hitting the creature squarely in the chest sending it flying through the trees, it landed in a heap several feet away.

Jack got to his feet, both hands blazed with blue energy, his eyes blazed blue with electricity. The creature got to its feet and stood there watching Jack. Jack noticed the black mist begin to appear again swirling around it.

"Your time is short Katari" whispered the figure as the mist enveloped it then began to dissipate, the figure was no longer there.

Jack felt the airlift and birds began to sing again. Jack relaxed his fists and the blue energy vanished, he stared at his hands looking at his palms, then the backs of his hands but they looked the same.

He stood there for a few seconds looking around, making sure he was alone, then he slowly made his way back to camp.

When he returned all the others were together obviously discussing their next move. Jack walked over to them.

"What happened to you?" Viggo said looking him up and down.

Jack quickly explained his altercation in the woods and how he had gotten away.

"I knew that last skirmish would have drawn attention to ourselves," Merlyn said thoughtfully

"It seems your powers are growing too"

"What do you think it was?" Grace asked

"I think it was Thrall," Jack said

"Thrall!" Viggo exclaimed, "Why would he risk coming here alone?"

"I think he had come to spy and thought he could take me out of the equation while he was here," Jack said.

"Sounds like he got more than he bargained for," Kara said smiling.

"That's not all, I spoke to Selendrial in my dreams last night," Jack said.

"Wow it's not even lunchtime yet," Grace said.

"We need to get to this Gana as quickly as we can, I think they also know where it is and the enemy is on its way there" Jack explained.

"We must make haste then," Merlyn said "If we make good time we may reach their borders before nightfall"

The group broke camp and got ready to move out, Merlyn retrieved the protection stones and they moved off. Kara and Viggo took to the skies, Merlyn and Ben were at the front of the column with Grace and Jack at the rear.

They rode in mostly silence for a few hours before the signal was made to rest. They pulled the wagons into a sort of triangle shape and started two fires inside the protection of the wagons. Most of the townspeople they had rescued lay about inside this area. Abigail and the rest of the archers were stationed on the wagons with Mark and the remainder of his people.

Jack was sat on Ragnar next to Ben and Leonidas, Merlyn was stood by the side of Silvermane talking to Grace. Viggo and Kara were still flying overhead.

A roaring sound from above drew everyone's attention, they looked up to see a ball of flame crash into the ground twenty feet away from the camp. Jack looked up to see Viggo and Kara swooping down, Viggo was frantically pointing towards the hill behind them.

Everyone had now seen Viggo gesturing and stood staring at the hillside in the distance.

Jack watched as the Horde washed over the hill like a black river.

"Oh no" someone shouted, some women screamed and children began to cry.

"Merlyn!" Jack shouted

Merlyn and Grace rushed over, so did Mark, Abigail, and Sarah.

"How far are we from Gana?" Jack asked

"I'm not sure, maybe an hour at the speed we were going" he replied

"We aren't going to make it," Grace said staring at the onrushing enemy

"I reckon we have about ten minutes before they are here," Jack said looking into the distance.

Viggo and Kara landed by the group.

"We need to hold them up and get the people to safety," Jack said.

"Merlyn, you know the way. Get all the children into one wagon, everyone else on horseback then ride as hard as you can" Jack said

"There aren't enough horses for everyone," Sarah said.

"We will stay and fight," Mark said

"So will we" agreed Abigail.

Jack looked at them and nodded. "Abigail you and the other archer's et up in the remaining wagons, Mark, you and your people protect Abigail and her friends. The rest of you, we need to fight and give them time to get to safety"

"I cannot leave you all here" Merlyn began

"Without you, all is lost, they will not know where to go" Jack stated.

"Any questions?" Jack said.

Everyone shook their heads, "Right then let's go!"

The camp became a frenzied but organised chaos, the children were loaded onto a wagon, the rest mounted the horses and Merlyn led them away at great speed.

Abigail, Mark, and the others occupied the wagons. Jack and Ben sat side by side in front of the wagons atop Ragnar and Leonidas, clad in full armour swords drawn. Grace, Viggo, and Kara were going to take to the skies and attack from above, hopefully causing chaos in the enemy ranks.

The Horde was almost upon them. "Ready!" Jack shouted and Viggo, Grace, and Kara took to the skies.

Jack turned to Ben and smiled "Time to dance" Ben said splitting his sword into two.

Ragnar and Leonidas let out deafening roars as they sprang forward into the onrushing Horde. Arrows whistled by them as they hit the front ranks of the enemy. Jack and Ben's swords blazed with blue energy, the fought like things possessed their weapons a blur as they cut the enemy down, Leonidas and Ragnar just as fearsome ripping and clawing their way through the enemy.

Viggo swooped down Throdin clearing a path through the enemy with his fiery breath, the heat hit Jack as Throdin flew close to him. Jack heard the sounds of fighting behind him and turned to see the wagons were being overrun, Grace and Kara swooped down crashing through the enemy ranks.

Jack realised they had pushed too far forward. "Ben!" he shouted, "Fall back!"

Ben nodded and they began to inch slowly back to the wagons.

They were grossly outnumbered but still, they fought, Jack watched as those on the wagons began to fall one by one, there was only Abigail and another archer left.

"Ragnar, get me to the wagons" Jack screamed in his head.

Ragnar roared and leapt the last ten feet to the wagons, Leonidas just behind him. As Ragnar and Leonidas were about to land Jack and Ben leaped from their backs and into the enemy attacking the wagons.

Jack placed both hands on his sword and it grew into a broad sword, he sent an arc of blue energy scything through the enemy. Ben landed his blades burning blue, the swirled and spun as he cut through the enemy. The enemy ranks began to thin as the onslaught continued and they began to fall back, slowly at first then they quickly ran away.

Viggo and Kara hassled the retreating enemy as they went.

Jack quickly surveyed the scene before him, there were just two survivors Abigail and James and he knew he had to get them away fast.

Kara and Viggo returned "I think they are regrouping" Viggo shouted.

They all looked around to see the enemy forming ranks again just on the hill behind them.

"Grace, you and Kara take Abigail and James away to the others. Viggo go with them, we will cover your retreat as much as we can, what we don't want is them catching up to Merlyn and the others" Jack said with authority.

Grace looked as though she was going to say something but just nodded, this was not the time to discuss decisions. They got Abigail and James on behind them just as a low drumming started and horns began to blow.

"Go!Go!Go!" Ben shouted.

Grace, Kara, and Viggo took of flying fast away from their two friends, within moments they had vanished over the trees.

"Ok Ben are you ready?" Jack said smiling at his friend

"Always," Ben said grinning.

They leaped onto Ragnar and Leonidas just as the Horde began to charge again.

Ben spun his swords around so he was holding both handles in one hand, they began to glow and change shape until he was holding a bow, there was no string just a line of blue crackling energy. He pulled back on the string and a blue energy arrow formed, he let it go and it soared into the sky, it landed like a bomb scattering the enemy and creating holes in the ranks. Bolt after bolt he let fly causing mayhem and destruction. Still, the enemy came on their numbers seemed to be growing not diminishing.

"They are getting too close now let's go!" Jack shouted over the screams of the enemy.

They turned and rode away Ben's bow reverting back into two swords "You have got to show me how to do that" Jack said smiling.

They rode through the woods, crashing through branches and bushes, leaping over ravines all the while the enemy pursued them, every time they looked back the blackness of the Horde could be seen behind them.

They broke through the trees onto a dual carriageway, one side was empty the other a column of military vehicles stretched into the distance, all had been abandoned. Ragnar leapt over the barrier and onto the other side of the road, he jumped onto the back of a lorry that had a tank strapped onto it and turned to see where the Horde was. Leonidas leapt up next to him and spun around so they could see.

"They're still coming!" Ben said pointing into the trees.

The Horde crashed through the trees and into the open, they saw Ben and Jack and they let out blood curdling screams.

"Time to go," Jack said turning Ragnar and they set off again back into the trees. Jack tried to see above him through the trees looking for Grace, Kara, or Viggo but the canopy of leaves was too thick, occasional beams of sunlight broke through as if the sun was firing at them.

The chase continued for what seemed like an eternity, Jack could feel Ragnar tiring, "We can't keep this up for much longer," he shouted to Ben "Or we will be too tired if we have to fight"

Ben nodded "What do you suggest? We can't try and hide because of the others"

"We need to find somewhere we can fight, for as long as we can," Jack said

"There!" Ben shouted pointing ahead "It looks like the woods finish"

They spurred their mounts onwards, the denseness of the trees was slowing the Horde down as they seemed to have opened up a lead on them.

They crashed out into an open space, a large rolling meadow stretched in all directions before them, it rose slightly in front of them meaning they could not see that far ahead.

"Let's get to the top of that hill," Jack said pointing.

They got to the top of the hill and stopped dead.

"Oh No!" Jack said desperately

Before them at the edge of the field right before the tree line was a large camp of survivors, there were tents and people everywhere. Jack could see the others at the edge of the camp, Viggo was flying towards them. He landed by the side of them.

"Have they given up?" Viggo said hopefully.

"I'm afraid not," Ben said

"How many people are there?" Jack asked

"A few hundred, I guess," Viggo said "There's a few soldiers but not many ready for a fight, Merlyn's trying to get them into the forest but they aren't going. He said he's going to try and set up the protection stones but he's not sure if the area is too big"

"So he will need time," Ben said.

Viggo nodded "Well this looks like a beautiful spot for a last stand"

The three of them turned as the Horde could be heard crashing through the woods, they broke free of the woods in front of them and stopped when they saw the three facing them.

Ragnar, Leonidas, and Throdin let out deafening roars, Throdin blasted a jet of fire into the air.

The Horde charged.

They reached the bottom of the hill in no time, Throdin stepped forward and blasted a wall of fire across the front ranks, the screaming frenzied creatures still rushed on, many in flames before they collapsed after a few steps.

Then they were on them and the battle was on. They kept close together fighting as one, not as three separate beings. As Ragnar ripped one in half, Leonidas grabbed the one about to stab at Ragnar.

Ben, Jack, and Viggo suddenly leapt from their mounts forward into the massed enemy ranks. They all sent forth a wave of blue energy as they jumped, the landed on the ground and a shockwave of energy flashed out from them knocking the enemy closest to them off their feet.

The sound of battle echoed across the field, the three Katari danced a deadly dance, cutting and slashing through the enemy force.

Jack swung his sword killing two, as he turned a blade thrust towards his back, Ben spun around taking the blade away with one sword and killing the creature with his other. Ben turned to see three creatures lunge at him all three were dispatched by Viggo's swinging axe, and so the dance went on.

Jack fought like he was possessed, as much as he was fighting to stay alive he was also doing everything he could to protect Ben and Viggo, he didn't want to lose anyone else.

The fighting was fierce and the enemy was closing in on them, the enemies numbers were just too great, Jack hoped they had given Merlyn enough time.

Thunder rolled in the distance as the battle raged, the thunder got louder, edging ever closer. It must be one hell of a storm Jack thought, I can feel the thunder in my feet.

"Is that an earthquake?" Ben shouted above the din.

It can't be an earthquake in England, can it? Jack thought as the thunder got closer and the ground shook.

Something flashed past him to the left and crashed into the enemy, then another and another. The Horde was falling away not concentrating on the three of them anymore, a new enemy had arrived.

Jack spun around, spread across the field were hundreds of horses, all in full emerald green armour, the riders carried teardrop shields and lances, they wore emerald green armour with golden helms and they charged at the enemy.

The noise as the two forces met was like a sonic boom, the cavalry crashed through the ranks of the Horde, riding down creature after creature, they had no hope. The Horde began to run back into the forest what was left of it, their force had been decimated. The cavalry gave chase to the edge of the forest and then they turned back. They rode passed the three of them back the way they had come, one rider pulled up in front of Jack and removed its helm.

It was an Elhuri, the features were identical.

"I am Gana, and you are trespassing in our lands," she said sternly

"Follow us, we have your friends and they are safe for the moment"

She placed her Helm back on her head and rode down the hill.

Ben shrugged and leapt onto Leonidas and followed her down the hill, Viggo not far behind. Jack climbed onto Ragnar. "Guess we've found who we were looking for," he said to Ragnar, "Looks that way" Ragnar replied with a growl.

When Jack arrived at the camp he could see Merlyn waving him over, he jumped from Ragnar and began to walk over. "Get some rest pal," Jack said to Ragnar as he walked away. As he joined the group he saw Merlyn seemed quite agitated.

"But you must!" he said desperately.

"We do not HAVE to do anything," a soldier next to Gana said with contempt.

An argument broke out that began to get very heated.

"Enough!" shouted Gana raising her hand, "This is getting us nowhere"

She turned to Jack "I watched you and your friends fight, very impressive, this old man wants us to open our borders to these people"

"Huh, old man indeed" Merlyn snorted.

"Perhaps you can explain to me who you are and why we should do this?" Gana said to Jack.

"I am Jack, this is Ben, Grace, Viggo, and Kara and we are Katari" Jack began

There was an audible gasp from the group around them, this set of a series of whispers through the remaining Elhuri troops.

"That is not possible," said the same man who argued with Merlyn.

"The old man is Merlyn, last of the Hanori in this world" Jack continued

"We are here because nowhere is safe, Thrall and his Horde have arrived and millions have died, will you refuse to except families, children who need help?" Jack continued

"We must now more than ever put aside petty squabbles and join together, this is the only way we have a chance of defeating the Horde"

There was a silence, everyone looked at Gana waiting for a reply.

"Our realm has been hidden for thousands of years, it is the last sanctuary of our people in this world, you ask much for us to now throw open our borders, we have never before gotten involved in the humans problems"

"Nothing like this has happened before, the events taking place now threaten all our survival. Thrall will not let you stay peacefully hidden once he has conquered this world. You have revealed yourselves to him, the Horde will return" Merlyn warned.

"I have much to think about and much to discuss with my advisors. For now, your people may enter the forest and make your camp there. You will not be permitted into the city unless invited, but you will be safe and hidden from the enemy"

She placed her helm back onto her head "I will leave a contingent of cavalry with you until everyone is safely inside, then we will speak again soon"

With that she turned and leapt onto her waiting horse, a horn sounded and they moved away disappearing into the forest.

"Right let's get everyone moved," Merlyn said.

Jack sat near the campfire with the others, Merlyn was off seeing if anyone needed help of any kind. They had not seen anyone since the cavalry had escorted the last of them into the forest. Jack looked around, this forest felt different from any he had ever been in, it felt alive and it felt ancient as though every tree was watching them. The trees were packed together but a few clear paths stretched through the dense forest, the trees were partly covered in a silver and green moss that seemed to glow slightly as it got darker. Around the trees bushes and flowers of all kinds grew, Jack found this confusing as hardly any sunlight was let in through the canopy of leaves overhead.

The air smelt sweet and clean, it was almost intoxicating as you inhaled. The smell of this forest was almost an assault on your sense of smell but left you feeling invigorated and calm.

"So what's next" Grace said breaking the silence.

"I guess nothing until these people decide what to do," Viggo said.

"We need their help, and they need to realise they need ours too," Ben said.

"How much time do you think we have before those things come back?" Kara asked.

Jack shrugged "Who knows that's why time is not on our side"

Kara suddenly stood up and pointed down one of the paths "What's that?"

An orange glow was coming into view along the path.

Merlyn arrived "Get ready, I think we have company"

The orange glow grew ever closer, spreading further through the trees the closer it got, eventually, footsteps could be heard growing louder as they approached. Four soldiers appeared in full armour with their familiar teardrop shields, two of them were carrying torches.

They approached the group and Merlyn stepped forward.

"I am Anlon head of the city guard, her highness has requested an audience with you"

"With all of us?" Merlyn enquired

"That is correct, please follow us," they did an about turn and marched off back the way they came, not waiting to see if they were following or not.

Merlyn shrugged "Guess we have an audience to attend to"

They all got up and followed the guards down the path.

Jack watched as the guards went out of sight around the bend, they all quickened their pace and soon caught up to them. The path was lit slightly by the glowing moss on the trees, the torches enabled them to see a lot more of what was around them. Jack could only see about three feet into the forest from either side, after that it was as black as night. Above

433

them, the branches of the trees entwined blocking out any moonlight from above. The path itself twisted and turned, occasionally another path broke away from the main one and vanished into the night.

Grace moved alongside Jack "Hi"

Jack turned and smiled "Hi, you ok?"

"Yea not had the chance to speak much just lately"

"I know, it's been a bit crazy"

"Well that's the understatement of the year," she said smiling

"Seriously how are you coping since, erm," she said sheepishly

"I'm ok, not easy and I miss them every second, I'm sure it's the same for you"

"Yea I miss him so much"

"I'm sorry, I'm er sorry I've not been there for you," Jack said looking at the ground.

"Hey, you've saved a lot of people, even if you have been a bit of an idiot."

Jack smiled and looked up into her eyes, both of them were finding it difficult to talk about their parent's deaths and they both were close to tears. Jack reached out and squeezed Grace's hand, her face suddenly lit up and the forced smile was replaced by a look of love. Jack smiled back, he thought he must have looked an idiot because his cheeks had started to ache from smiling too much.

"How do you think this is going to go?" Grace asked still smiling.

"Will we see soon enough I suppose" Jack replied conscious that he was still holding her hand.

They turned another bend in the road and it began to widen, also the trees seemed to be getting taller, not just taller but the trunks were getting thicker and thicker as they carried on. Jack had read about giant Redwood trees in America but these were even bigger.

As the road grew even wider they were met by more guards, these flanked the group as they continued. Jack was sure he could hear running water in the distance, eventually, the road proceeded to take a large curving bend, and as they came around the corner the sight before them took their breath away.

The road ended in a sort of large clearing, however all around the clearing was a great chasm, stretching out in front of them was a wooden bridge, this spanned over to an island in the middle. The bridge seemed to have grown there rather than been made, root like tendrils twisted from the earth in front of them, entwining together and spanning the gap before them.

The island in front rose from the ground, all along the front of the rock face water roared into the chasm below, it glistened in the eerie light of the glowing moss and the burning torches. The bridge was about fifty feet long and wide enough to easily get six or seven horses across side by side.

The bridge itself was stunning but the city that rose before them was even more breathtaking. The bridge led to an open gateway, two huge wooden doors stood open, guards were stationed at the entrance. Either side of the entrance were two huge trees, after a few seconds Jack realised these were being used as towers, you could see windows situated along them and several balconies situated along the trunk. The branches of the trees stretched over the rock wall that spanned the gap between the two and entwined together, their leaves were of a golden hue. Along the front wall of this city were another ten of these huge trees all intertwined with all of the spaces spanned by a rock face. It looked as though the city had been grown from the earth.

Rising above the trees from behind were two more trees hundreds of feet high and enormously thick they extended up like spires of a castle, windows illuminated by lights were visible around the trunk, their branches stretched out and grasped each other like two friends holding each other for support, the leaves were a copper colour and glistened in the twinkling light. In the centre of these trees was the biggest and tallest of all the trees here, it reminded Jack of Anu but on a smaller scale.

All the branches entwined with each other as though forming a barrier between themselves and whomever they did not want to enter. The leaves of the middle tower were silver and it was a breathtaking sight.

"Welcome to Helgidmur," Anlon said "Follow me"

They followed Anlon across the bridge in silence, no one spoke except to let out a couple of wows as the sheer size of the trees became more obvious.

They followed Anlon through the main gate, through a tunnel that looked like it had been chiseled from the earth itself, then out into the open the other side.

Inside was a huge open space and at first, glance looked uninhabited and overgrown with vegetation and vines, however on closer inspection it became apparent it was a living, breathing, thriving city.

Trees grew in all shapes and sizes but it was as though the trees had been grown for different purposes, nearly all had doors and windows in, some with interconnecting bridges, the trees stretched far into the sky but non as impressive as the three huge trees in the centre of the city.

Jack had never been into a city that smelt so fresh and vibrant, there were a lot of people moving around all Elhuri, some occasionally stopped to stare as they walked past. Weird creatures flew about through the tree branches, they looked like a cross between birds and tiny dragons.

Small creatures walked about through the bushes and everyone seemed oblivious to these weird and wonderful creatures.

"Helgidmur is the final sanctuary on this planet for anyone from the great spell, unfortunately non of the others heeded our warnings that is why only we remain," Anlon said.

They passed through an archway of blossom trees, the smell was overwhelming and intoxicating, the colours so vibrant like the most beautiful painting you had ever seen. At the end of the avenue they passed over another bridge, a crystal clear river ran below. Jack watched fish and other creatures swimming about in the clear water.

"It's so beautiful," Grace said

"Thank you my lady" Anlon replied.

At the other side of the bridge space opened up and the tree buildings were breathtaking, Jack couldn't comprehend what he was seeing, several trees had grown together to form a large building, but it wasn't a twisted mismatch of branches and leaves, they had created beautiful ornate buildings.

"On the left here is the assembly, where the laws and such like are passed, on the right is the court next to one of the barracks for the guards" Anlon continued

As they crossed the large open area it was like walking through a meadow from a fairy tale picture book, several paths were intersecting the area leading to various locations. People were sat around on the grass enjoying themselves, it was broken up by various carving of weird creatures he had never seen before and also some familiar ones.

"You have some talented artisans here," Merlyn said pointing to the carvings.

"Ah yes we do, but it is the trees that create the statues, they grow them how they want to" Anlon replied

Jack then looked closer and noticed that each carving was growing from the ground.

"How can this place have been hidden for so long?" Grace whispered to Jack, to which Jack shrugged.

They followed Anlon down an avenue of trees, however, they were housing as the doors and windows showed, Jack was dying just to go inside and look around one. Although the branches arched over the road it was not dark as some of the trees had that luminous moss on and there were lamps situated along the road. The road seemed the busiest since they had entered the city and Jack found out why when it came to an end.

As the avenue finished it opened into a circular space, inside this space were the three huge trees they had seen from the outside, they were so big it was hard to comprehend that they were trees.

"Here we are the centre of the city, the tree on the left is where we hold all our artifacts a sort of museum for learning, the tree on the right is the residence of all the important dignitaries of the city. The centre tree is the royal palace" Anlon explained as they approached.

"They are impressive," Viggo said, "But maybe a little susceptible to fire?"

"The algae that grow on the trees do not burn giving the trees the protection they need" Anlon answered "Please follow me"

Anlon led them through the doors of the royal tree and inside.

"Wow" Grace whispered as they entered.

The room opened up into a huge round room, the wooden floor was polished and gleamed brightly, carved into the floor was a sigil of a tree, the same as they had seen before, it was Anu. The room was decorated with sculptures of all different things, some emerging from the floor, some looking as though they had been hung on the walls.

A staircase swept up from the middle then split into two as it curved around and upwards, the staircase itself was so beautiful in design and intricately carved or grown.

"This way," said Anlon walking across the polished floor towards the staircase. At the top of the first staircase as it split into two was a huge round door, the door had two gold bars running down the length. In the centre of the door was a large golden disc, Anlon placed his hand on it and pressed.

There were a series of loud clicks, the door dropped back as though sinking into the wall and began to roll to the side.

"Please follow me," Anlon said stepping through the door.

They all followed Anlon inside, this room was not as large as the entrance room but was no less grand. A large round wooden table was situated in the middle, at the far end, Gana sat on her throne.

The whole room was shaped like a large dome with branches from the tree crisscrossing the walls. The walls of the dome were a light brown, the branches much darker, a silver fluid coursing through the branches, making each one shimmer and shine.

The floor showed the rings of the tree and looked as though it had been polished a million times.

"Please sit," said Anlon walking around the table to sit next to Gana.

They all sat around the table, as they sat Jack couldn't help but look at Merlyn.

"Yes this is where the idea came from," he said sighing.

Jack, Grace, and Ben all smiled, Viggo, and Kara looked confused.

"It has been many years since your last visit Merlyn, we thought you had perished along with the others," Gana said regally.

"Unfortunately I am very much still alive," he said with a chuckle.

442

Gana's expression did not change "Why do you come here and bring such trouble to our borders"

"In case you hadn't noticed trouble is everywhere" Merlyn replied. "You need to help, you cannot hide behind your borders any longer"

"We don't need to do anything!" Gana said sternly.

Anlon looked visibly shocked at the outburst.

"We have always helped those in need, your highness" Anlon said trying to calm the situation.

Gana gave him a frosty stare "If we open our borders, we put all our lives at risk, my people must be my priority"

"Your highness, people are dying out there, not ten, twenty, not even hundreds, but millions of people. We know you cannot help them all but you cannot stand by and watch families be slaughtered" Grace interrupted.

"Our magic is strong again, our army is strong but to risk it all, now after all this time, I just don't know," Gana said shaking her head.

"We have all lost family and friends, we have watched innocents be slaughtered or enslaved, do not fool yourself into thinking you are safe because eventually, they will come for you here. Stand with us and we are stronger together, do not foolishly think you can do this alone" Jack said with authority.

Anlon looked shocked at Jack's blunt tone.

"I see you are the leader of the Katari, you speak truthfully and with heart. If we agree to this we cannot take the world's refugees inside our walls" Gana said.

"Hopefully you won't have too" Merlyn replied.

"Do you have a plan?" Anlon asked.

"We need to find Artus" Kara replied.

"Artus!!" Gana scoffed "Why do you need to find that fool!"

"Erm, what do you mean?" Jack asked.

"You do mean Merlyn's protégé Artus don't you, the king of the outsiders," Anlon said

Merlyn nodded looking a bit uncomfortable.

"He is the last Katari" Kara said

"Oh, in that case, all is lost already," Gana said sighing.

"He can't be that bad surely," Grace said.

"He was a fine warrior and a just King, but," Gana said shrugging

444

"But what?" Viggo asked.

"He unified the factions of the outsiders for the first time, he kept Thrall at bay with his power but alas love was his downfall," Gana said.

"Yes, the fool threw it all away for love" Anlon agreed.

Jack looked at Grace and smiled, he looked up and Gana locked eyes with him, it was as though she was looking into the depths of his being. Jack blinked and looked away and Gana smiled knowingly.

"Do you not know where your protégé is?" Anlon said turning to Merlyn.

Merlyn shook his head "The last I saw of him he was heading hereafter, well after things went wrong"

"And you have not seen him since?" Anlon said smiling.

"This is no joking matter, I do not see the funny side of this" Viggo said sternly.

"Yes of course please forgive us," Anlon said.

"We must find Artus otherwise we have no idea how to stop this" Grace exclaimed.

"We have very little we can tell you, Artus left us to return his sword, he said it had bought him nothing but trouble and hoped someone else could use it. He did not however say where he was going" Gana said.

"Merlyn do you know where he might have gone?" Jack asked.

"To where he was given the sword is my bet" Merlyn replied.

"Which is?" Kara asked forcefully.

"Scotland or the Isle of Arran to be more precise" Merlyn sighed.

"Scotland!! That's miles away" Grace exclaimed.

"We may be able to use the portals now that magic has returned," Merlyn said.

"What portals?" Jack asked.

"When we first arrived here there was no way to get quickly from place to place so we established a series of portals around the world so that we could move about easily. These stopped working when science began to take over" Merlyn said.

"Do you still have your portal?" Merlyn enquired looking at Gana.

"Yes but it has not been used for hundreds of years"

"We will rest today and leave first thing," Jack said.

"Will you take in refugees your highness? I implore you please!" Jack begged.

"I will consult with my council and we will decide together. I will see to it you are given somewhere to rest and get refreshments, I will call for you when I have made my decision" with that Gana stood and left the room.

Anlon escorted them through a side door and up a spiral staircase to a small complex of rooms, one main lounge area with several bedrooms leading off it. There was a door leading out onto a balcony that overlooked the city.

"I will come for you once a decision has been made, I will get refreshments sent to you shortly" Anlon explained and then left.

"Well let's get comfy this may take a while," Merlyn said sinking into one of the large sofas in the room.

Jack opened the doors onto the balcony and stepped outside, they were a lot higher up than he thought they were, he had an unobscured view of the city below.

"Beautiful isn't it?" Grace said joining him on the balcony.

Jack nodded taking in the sight before him, it was like looking at a forest but one that had been trained to grow in a specific way.

"How are you Grace?"

"I'm ok Jack, mostly anyway" Grace smiled at him.

Jack put his arm around her and pulled her close.

"Hope I'm not interrupting," Ben said from behind.

They moved apart so quickly it looked as though they had been struck by lightning. Ben laughed loudly, a familiar Ben sound that made them smile.

"What about the people we left outside?" Ben asked.

Jack looked guilty as though he had almost forgotten them. "I er" Jack began.

"How about me and Kara go make sure they are ok," Ben said shooting a glance at Kara who smiled back.

Jack let out a loud laugh and quickly stopped when Ben spun around to stare at him "Something you wish to say, Jack?" Ben asked.

"Me? No, no, no. You do that sounds like a great idea" Jack agreed.

Ben and Kara left the room a guard escorted them back out of the city to the refugees.

Jack and Grace joined Merlyn and Viggo in the seating area, a large selection of food and drink had been delivered and they were currently sampling the food.

"None of my people made it here did they?" Viggo asked.

Merlyn looked sorrowful as he spoke "A few, mainly scouts or patrols that were not in Stonehaven when it fell"

"Were there any in this land?" Viggo asked.

"Yes some, they loved the mountains, this land has very few apart from a place called Scotland where we have to go. There used to be a small group living up there but I have no idea what happened to them"

"Would they have had a portal?" Jack asked

"Undoubtedly yes, I never went there myself but I was aware of it," Merlyn replied

"Did all the races settle here? In Britain I mean?" Grace asked.

"I know the Kandar had a settlement in Wales and my people the Hanori had a settlement in England around what you call Stone Henge but my people are long gone, I think because we were so in tuned with the essence of magic we found it harder to adapt when it began to disappear," Merlyn said sadly.

"Should we see if any of the Kandar or my people are still there?" Viggo asked hopefully.

"I very much doubt any still survive, the Illuminati saw to that" Merlyn said angrily

"Were you not a part of the Illuminati?" Jack asked.

"Once, when the magic began to fail a group of my people joined together to try and protect this world from Thrall, unfortunately, one by one they were turned by Thrall, those that couldn't were hunted down and executed"

"That's why you became a dog" Viggo stated

"Yes that's why I became a canine," Merlyn said angrily "Also my power was fading and I would not have been able to protect myself"

"I wonder if any of my people survived?" Viggo said

"We will try and find out," Jack said smiling, Viggo smiled back hopefully.

"We should look for the Dwafen and the Kandar if they are still alive they may be able to help us" Grace said.

"We do not have time for us to go on wild goose chases," Merlyn said

"Wild goose chases!" Viggo snapped.

"I'm sorry I did not mean any offence old chap, but we must prioritise our time" Merlyn smiled back.

"We may have no choice," Jack said, drawing quizzical looks from the others.

Their discussion was broken by a loud knock on the door, the door swung open and Anlon entered.

"Her highness and the council have made a decision will you please follow me"

They all got up and followed Anlon from the room and back to the room with the circular table. Gana was sat where she had sat before, now two other females were sitting with her.

"Please sit," Anlon said as they entered the room, he assumed his position he had been sat in previously.

"First may I introduce Brana the city steward and Rezka the leader of our scouts," Gana said as they sat.

"We have discussed your proposition and decided we will take in some refugees"

"Ah thank you" Jack began

"But!" Gana said raising her hand "We will allow only women, children, and the elderly into the city. All males will be given weapons and taught to fight, camps will be erected in the forest around the city. If the numbers grow too much we are fairly certain we can extend our borders and remain unseen"

"That is a fair proposal your highness" Jack agreed. "But I fear that Thrall is already aware of you now and time is short"

The door burst open behind them. It was Kara who came charging in.

"There's an army approaching from the South, it's the Horde and Thrall is leading them!" Kara shouted.

"It seems you are right Jack, time has run out quicker than you thought. Prepare the city, get those refugees inside the walls, arm those who can fight, we will need all the help we can get" Gana said sternly.

The Ride of the Elhuri

Jack needed to see what they were up against, so he rode out to meet Ben accompanied by Anlon and a small number of troops.

"I must gather as much information as possible" Anlon had said to them as they were leaving.

They passed the refugees coming through the forest towards the city as they rode out, they all looked very frightened, as they passed a section of soldiers they flagged them down.

A tall man in camouflage gear and a sword stepped forward "Hi I'm Captain Brown Staffordshire Regiment, I was wondering if we can be of service?"

"Captain the best thing you can do is make sure these people get to the city and look after them, the people in the city are going to need your help," Merlyn said.

The Captain saluted "Gods speed"

Merlyn smiled and nodded and they continued. They soon reached the borders of the Elhuri lands and found Ben waiting for them.

"Where are they?" Jack asked as he stopped beside him.

Ben pointed down the slope of the valley, there about 2 miles away was the approaching Horde.

"Oh my goodness" Grace gasped as they all looked upon the black shape slowly moving towards them, they were packed so tightly together it was hard to distinguish between individuals.

"How many is there?" Anlon said open mouthed

"It is difficult to say, but easily five thousand or so" Merlyn guessed.

"How large is your army?" Ben asked Anlon.

"Three thousand cavalry, about a thousand city guard"

"Well we cannot leave the city defenseless so it will have to be the cavalry only, we leave the city guard in place, in case the worse happens," Merlyn said.

"They would have to break the border defenses to get to the city first," said Anlon.

"That large creature at the front, that is Thrall and he is one of the most powerful magic users there has been, he will have no problem with your defenses I'm afraid" Merlyn warned.

"We need to meet them before they get too close," Jack said, "When will you be ready Anlon?"

 "Maybe an hour at most, we were on alert before you arrived"

"We will need to slow them down then and give you chance to be ready," Jack said staring into the valley

"Slow them down? How?" Anlon exclaimed.

"Leave that up to us, get back to the city, and as soon as you are ready, ride out," Jack said.

"Good luck," Anlon said turning his horse and he and his guards rode back to the city.

"So what's the plan?" Viggo said.

Jack laughed "I think it's a bit late for plans don't you?"

"So what are we going to do Jack?" Grace asked him.

Jack turned to her and smiled "We are going to introduce the Horde to the Katari"

"I like the sound of that my friend," Ben said.

"Jack that is foolishness, that won't buy them time it will just get us killed," Merlyn said.

"You're going to the city, they will need you there," Jack said looking at Merlyn.

"Don't be preposterous, you need me, my boy!"

"We are the Katari," Jack said gesturing to his friends "This is ours, for now, you must trust us, the city will need you more if we fail"

Merlyn was about to protest again when he saw the looks in the other's eyes, he bowed his head and spoke solemnly "Do not rush blindly into the lion's mouth, you are the Katari and the fate of two worlds and millions of souls lie in your hands" he then turned his mount and rode off towards the city.

"Just like old times again, just the five of us," Kara said smiling

"Well, shall we?" Jack said gesturing forward.

Ben made the first move on Leonidas, Kara followed him on Aingal, next was Jack on Ragnar, Grace on Silvermane, and finally Viggo on Throdin. They walked slowly out of the forest into the brilliant sunlight, each one of them raising their faces to the sun, eyes closed basking in its warmth.

The air was calm almost serene as they moved out into the field. Jack looked down the valley towards the Horde, he knew this must just be but a part of it but the number of creatures was staggering. It seemed they hadn't noticed them as yet as they continued up through the valley.

They had now formed a line in the centre of the field looking down on the blackness that was the Horde, they sat there watching and waiting as the blackness got closer and closer.

The sound of them approaching echoed across the field like distant thunder rolling in, drums pounded a beat and still, they approached.

Jack reached down to grab his sword, they all followed in unison, it was as though something had finally clicked, the last barrier had fallen. They could speak to each other without words, they were five parts of one unit.

They drew their swords, the sunlight caught the swords as they appeared, their armour began to encase them all creating a blinding flash that halted the Horde. They sat there in a line ready for battle, swords drawn and encased in armour, the sunlight gleamed off them as though everything good in the world was now shining from them.

The Horde had stopped and just stood there, watching and waiting, Thrall was at the front, he sat upon a creature that resembled a large black wolf with blood red eyes.

"Hopefully they will stay like that for another forty minutes or so," Ben said smiling.

Before anyone could answer a horn blast echoed around them, then another and another.

The front of the Horde broke forward, charging up the field towards them. A thundering, screaming onslaught of savagery and ferocity.

Jack looked to his left and then to his right, they all nodded as though an unspoken word had been passed between them.

The Horde came charging on, there was easily a thousand that had broken away from the main force and was heading towards them. The middle of the line seemed to drop back allowing the two sides to advance slightly ahead.

Jack nudged Ragnar who let out a roar, he was followed by the others, the noise was like a bomb going off and the Horde stuttered slightly in their advance, but only slightly.

Ragnar leaped forward followed by Leonidas and Silvermane, Throdin and Aingal leapt into the sky.

Viggo went left, Kara went right. Throdin blasted the first few ranks with his fiery breath, Kara and Aingal hit the right side scattering troops as Aingal's huge talons ripped through their ranks. Kara and Viggo had crafted bows from their swords and were firing energy bolts into the massed ranks.

This forced the Horde back into the middle, the sheer numbers then went against them as they started to collide into each other, then the others hit them from the front. It was like a train crashing into a wall, the noise was like an explosion, bodies were flung into the air as the three Katari rode into the Horde.

Their blades burned a brilliant blue, blasts of blue energy sent creatures and bits of creatures flying in all directions, the carnage of that first encounter caused the Horde to turn and fall back. Loud blasts on the horns signalled the withdrawal.

Jack and the others were now fighting hand to hand but the ones that did stay and fight were soon dispatched and they were finally able to regroup back on the hill line from where they had started.

Jack looked back down into the valley and saw the massacre they had created, hundreds lay dead or dying across the field.

"How many do you think we got?" Ben asked smiling.

"A few hundred easily," Kara said.

"Great that only leaves four thousand or so," Grace said.

"We aren't here to destroy them single handidly, we are just trying to give the Elhuri some time," Jack said to them.

"Jack look," Grace said gesturing towards the Horde.

Thrall was approaching them on his wolf.

"Wait here," Jack said to them.

"Jack no don't be so stupid!" Grace shouted to no avail.

Jack walked Ragnar forward, "Think you can take the wolf," he said in his head, "Not a problem" growled Ragnar and Jack smiled.

They met on the field halfway between the two, surrounded by Thralls dead and dying troops.

Thrall looked around "You will not be so lucky next time, I will give you one chance to leave this place" his voice made Jack's skin crawl, it was like a whisper in the darkest night tinged with ferocious anger and dread.

"We really can't do that I'm afraid" Jack replied.

"You will all die!" Thrall warned.

"If that is how it goes then so be it, but we will take as many with you as we can," Jack said defiantly.

Thrall turned to move back to his troops, Jack was about to turn back when Thrall said "You cannot save the Elhuri, the same as you could not save your parents"

"Don't do it" Ragnar shouted in his head.

At that point, the Horde rushed forward and so did the rest of the Katari.

Jack leapt from the back of Ragnar, grasping his sword with both hands he raised it above his head as he flew through the air, the sword grew into his longsword glowing bright blue. Thrall spun around deflecting the blow with his axe.

Jack landed and rolled to a crouching position as Thrall leapt from the back of the wolf, at that point, the wolf leaped at Jack, Ragnar crashed into the side of the wolf altering it's leapt sending them both rolling across the field snarling and slashing at each other.

"You fool!" Thrall said raising his axe.

Jack danced to the left as the axe whistled past him, he stabbed with his sword as Thrall too span away. Jack slashed across Thrall's body a blue arc of energy crashing into Thrall's black armour making him stagger back a couple of steps.

The wolf had managed to get on top of Ragnar and his jaws were snapping at his face, Ragnar roared and threw the wolf off, Ragnar turned over onto his feet and leapt, his claws ripping down the side of the wolf making it yelp out in pain.

Jack knew the Horde was nearly upon him, just as the thought entered his head he saw Ben, Grace, and the others charge past him and crash into the oncoming enemy.

Jack stabbed again, Thrall blocked and pushed his hand out towards Jack, a burst of red energy hit Jack in the chest sending him flying backward. His chest hurt, he was sure he'd broken a rib too but he got to his feet slowly.

461

He went to swing his sword in a large arc but feinted at the last minute, pulling his sword towards him he reversed the angle and cut into Thrall's left arm. Thrall roared in pain and launched a ferocious onslaught that Jack was having difficulty blocking.

He had a quick look up and saw his friends were being forced back by the sheer weight of numbers. He wanted to see how Ragnar was getting on but he couldn't afford to take his eyes off Thrall. He heard Ragnar roar and another yelp from the wolf so that encouraged him.

He sprang forward, as he did so he split his sword into two taking Thrall by surprise, Thrall blocked the first sword but the second pierced his side, another roar of pain from Thrall.

Thrall began to edge back towards his Horde, Jack launched a ferocious double bladed assault that Thrall tried to block, however, another blow pierced his armour making him cry out. Suddenly creatures began to jump over his friends and attack Jack, the surprise caught him off guard and he was knocked to the floor, he felt something collide with them and suddenly he was free and sprang to his feet.

He noticed Ragnar had leapt at the creatures knocking them from him, Thrall's wolf lay dead and

Thrall himself was now surrounded by his Horde. His friends were being overrun.

Then he felt the earth shaking beneath his feet, a slow rumbling in the distance. He felt it before he heard the noise, a deep thunder in the distance rolling down the valley towards them. He was surrounded by creatures and his blades danced as they carved their way through the attackers.

A black shape passed above his head and he chanced a lookup, he knew immediately it was Merlyn.

The creatures around him suddenly dropped off slightly and he looked up the slope of the valley towards the onrushing storm.

It was the Elhuri, charging down the field towards the Horde in perfect unison lances raised in the air, the horses thundered towards them, Jack leapt onto Ragnar's back and with the others rode towards the advancing Elhuri. Before they met they turned again towards the Horde and charged with them, Jack, Ben, and Grace charging with Viggo, Kara, and Merlyn flying over the ranks of the Elhuri.

They crashed into the unprepared Horde, and rode through them like they were a field of wheat, they were speared or trampled by horses, they were scorched by Throdin or ripped apart by the Talons of Aingal and Styx.

Jack looked for Thrall but he couldn't see him in all the confusion, still, they rode on through the Horde and down the valley, however, the impetus was slowing due to the sheer numbers of the enemy. Jack noticed some of the Elhuri were now falling, horses cartwheeling over and over as they fell. Screams of Elhuri and their horses, yet still swept onwards through the blackness that was the Horde.

Then three deep blasts on a horn pierced through the battle and the Horde began to run away, Elhuri horns sounded in response holding the Elhuri and stopping them from giving chase. They began to form ranks again in case of further attacks but it looked as though the enemy had had enough for now.

Jack signalled Viggo and he flew down to him.

"You are one crazy idiot," Viggo said to Jack smiling

"Any sign of Thrall?"

Viggo shook his head "I lost sight of him just after the Elhuri attacked, he was certainly wounded though"

Merlyn and Grace joined them "Are you ok?" she said hugging Jack

"I'm fine" he answered somewhat embarrassed.

"Well we have certainly given them a bloody nose today," Merlyn said smiling.

"I know we've won today but I have a feeling there will be some losses along the way," Jack said.

"Where have they got all these from?" Viggo said waving his arm around at the dead enemy.

Merlyn looked saddened "A lot will have been turned here"

"You mean most of these will have been human at some point," Grace said looking around at the huge numbers of dead.

"Unfortunately yes," Merlyn said.

They were joined by Ben, Kara, and Anlon.

"A great victory for the Katari and the Elhuri" Anlon said jovially.

"For now yes" Jack agreed.

"Gana wishes to see you all back at the city," Anlon said.

Grace looked concerned "We need to help here"

"My people will tend to the wounded and the dead it is important you speak to Gana as soon as possible" Anlon said seriously.

Merlyn clapped Jack on the shoulder "Very well, Jack you and the others return to the city, I will help out here as much as I can"

Jack nodded and walked over to Ragnar, he climbed aboard and the others did the same. Grace came along one side, Ben the other, Viggo, and Kara took to the skies.

"I can hear Silvermane," Grace said suddenly "It happened just before the battle, it's amazing but she never shuts up"

Jack smiled and turned to Ben "Are you ok?"

Ben nodded "It was a good battle, was it not?"

"Can battles be good?" asked Jack

"Of course," Ben said "Race you back!" with that he shot off back to the city.

Grace laughed "Sometimes he's still the same old Ben" she kicked Silvermane and sprang after him.

"Ok Ragnar we better catch them up"

Ragnar roared and leaped forward in pursuit.

Gana was waiting for them in the same room as before, they all entered and sat down. Food and drink had been laid out on the table and Ben was ravenously tucking in before they sat down.

Jack smiled remembering what Grace had said, sometimes he is the old Ben. The others looked at Jack smiling, saw he was looking at Ben and they knew why he was smiling, they began to laugh.

Ben stopped mid mouthful "Have I missed a joke?" this made them laugh louder, the laughter a release from the tensions of the last few days.

Gana looked on somewhat confused and waited for them all to gain control.

"We are sorry," Jack said apologetically.

Gana smiled "It is fine, you have done us a great service today, without your heroics all would surely have been lost. I have summoned you here to say we will take in refugees, as many as we can who are drawn here"

"That's amazing thank you" Grace exclaimed

Gana nodded "It is only right that we should help. Also, we wish to give you some information that we should have told you before. There are two more hidden cities in your world"

"There's what?" Jack almost shouted.

"It is a long story, but when we arrived we tried to establish the five realms in this world to help keep Thrall at bay. The Hanori thought it best to help the people who were here already and helped them with magic to build and invent, however they became more interested in science than magic and when the magic started to vanish the other realms went into hiding"

"You mean some of my people are here?" Viggo asked excitedly

"We do not know, we have not seen or heard from any of the other races for thousands of years. We do know that the Dwafen were based in the Andes mountain range and the Kandar in the Grand Canyon in the US"

"What about the Seraphs?" Kara asked softly.

"They were very few in number when they arrived here, they went with the Hanori, I'm afraid I know of very little else, perhaps Merlyn is the one to ask," Gana said sadly.

"You say you must find Artus, we do know where he is"

"You do?" Jack said in astonishment.

"Ah yes, we should have been more truthful before," Gana said guiltily "Artus was a great King and a good friend to us here, however, he threw everything away for his bride. Everything he and Merlyn had worked for came crumbling down, it was such a waste. After that we kept ourselves even more withdrawn from your world" Gana said softly.

"Artus is indeed on the Isle of Arran, he went to return his sword, he said it would be his final resting place. It is where he ruled from but there are no signs of what was there before Thrall saw to that, everything was buried. However there is a way in, there is an entrance if you look for the signs and deemed worthy. He will be waiting for you"

"Very well then, we will rest today and leave in the morning at first light," Jack said standing.

Anlon entered the room "Please if you would follow me some people would like to thank you"

Jack and the others followed Anlon, they reached two doors, there was a guard stood either side, they saluted as they approached. The guards opened the doors and stepped through, Jack and the others followed out onto a balcony overlooking the square. The square was filled with people and soldiers and a huge cheer went up as Jack and his friends stepped out onto the balcony.

Gana came out with them and smiled "Jack we would love it if you would say a few words"

He looked at his friends stood beside him, he looked down at the crowd as it fell silent, so many expectant faces looking up at him. He took a deep breath "It is time to stop running, it is time to stop hiding, it is time to take this fight to our enemy, it is time to take back our world and put an end to this evil. Together we stand united a bright beacon in this dark world, let our light shine to every corner of this world, let our light attract everyone alone or afraid, let our light force back the darkness for our time is coming, our time to banish this evil once and for all" with his final word he drew his sword followed by the others and they blazed a blinding blue light, a huge cheer went up from the crowd that echoed around the city.

The crowd began to chant "Katari, Katari, Katari"

Epilogue

Selendrial stepped out of a shadow into a long dark corridor, part of the wall had collapsed one side and cobwebs littered the place. A rat scurried by squeaking at being disturbed.

She walked down the corridor her footsteps echoing, seeming unnatural as though no sound had been heard here for a very long time. At the end of a corridor was a wooden door, the door was cracked and aged but still stood firm.

Selendrial pushed and eventually it slowly opened with a groan, the hinges creaked in protest at being opened after all this time. She stepped through into blackness, whatever was before her she could not see for no light infiltrated here.

She raised her hand and torches around the room burst into life, she heard bugs and rats scurry away from this intruding light. Before her was a room, a room that would have been magnificent in its day. Now have of it had caved in, furniture lay scattered and broken around the floor. In the middle of the room was a large round table split down the middle, this had caused the two sides to tilt upwards making a makeshift corridor to the only chair that was upright and in position.

There on this chair was a golden suit of armour, covered in dust and cobwebs. It was obvious it had been here for hundreds of years. One hand gripped the arm of the chair the other held out as those resting on something, however, whatever it was had long ago been removed.

Selendrial reached to her side and withdrew the final sword, she looked at it with its panther shaped hilt and shining blade.

She held it out before her in both hands and it began to glow, a dull blue at first, slowly getting stronger and stronger. The light grew and grew illuminating every corner of the room, small bolts of lightning began to zoom around the room each one eventually landing on the golden armour. With each contact of energy, a cobweb vanished, with each bolt the dust vanished until the armour was also glowing.

The light then became so bright it was like staring at the sun, there was a final blinding flash and the room returned to being illuminated by the torches.

Selendrial looked at the armour sat before her, the sword now perched beneath the outstretched hand.

"Artus, Artus it is time, you are needed once more" Selendrial spoke softly repeating over and over.

"Artus, Artus it is time, you are needed once more, Artus, Artus"

She watched the hand resting on the sword as she spoke, first a twitch, then a tremble. Then slowly the fingers of the gauntleted hand curled around the hilt of the sword.

The sword flashed brightly, Selendrial smiled and vanished.

Printed in Poland
by Amazon Fulfillment
Poland Sp. z o.o., Wrocław

63529953R00266